King Alexander's Treasure Map

ଔ

The Legacy of His 13 Days With

Thalestris Queen of the Amazons

ଔ

James Saint Cloud

King Alexander of Macedonia (King Iskander in the East).

Detail of a larger mosaic (shown on page 22) found in the ruins of
Pompei, created 100 B.C. and based on a painting from 315 B.C.
Now in the Archaeological Museum, Naples.

When King Alexander returned to Hyrcania [south of the Caspian Sea] there came to him the queen of the Amazons named Thalestris, who ruled all the country between the rivers Phasis and Thermodon [south of the Black Sea]. *Her beauty and strength were remarkable, and her bravery acclaimed by her countrywomen. She left the main force of her army on the frontier of Hyrcania and arrived with an escort of three hundred Amazons fully armed.*

The King marveled at them and at their dignity. He asked Thalestris why they had come. She replied that it was for the purpose of getting a child, as he had shown himself to be the greatest of all men in his achievements, and she being superior to all women in strength and courage, that the offspring of such parents must surely surpass all other mortals in excellence.

The King was delighted at this and granted her request, consorting with her for thirteen days, after which he honored her with gifts and she departed home.

— Diodorus Siculus. **Library of History**, 17.77, writing 1st century B.C.

ISBN-10: 0692321047
ISBN-13: 978-0692321041 (Let It Be Publishing)

Library of Congress Control Number: 2014921383
LET IT BE PUBLISHING, SAN RAFAEL, CALIFORNIA

Let It Be Publishing
4460 Redwood Highway, Suite 16-227
San Rafael, California 94903 USA

As *King Alexander's Treasure Map* goes to press it is encouraging to see Adrienne Mayor's excellent cover article *Alexander and His Amazon Lover* published in the January 2015 issue of the British magazine *History Today,* exploring the evidence for the authenticity of this famous meeting. (Available in the *History Today* archives on the web.)

The Amazons of the Doeantian plain were by no means gentle, well-conducted folk; they were brutal and aggressive, and their main concern in life was war. War, indeed, was in their blood, daughters of Ares as they were and of the Nymph Harmonia, who lay with the god in the depths of the Acmonian Wood and bore him girls who fell in love with fighting.

— **Apollonius of Rhodes.** *The Voyage of Argo.* 2nd century A.D.

ଏ

There are those who believe that once there was a nation called Amazonia populated entirely by women.... The Amazons were a race that devoted themselves entirely to developing their skills as warriors. On certain days of each year, however, they set aside their military pursuits and visited the surrounding settlements to choose mates. Once children were born, the sons were left with their fathers while the daughters returned with their mothers to Amazonia to be instructed in the arts of warfare, hunting, and riding. It is thought that at the height of its power Amazonia extended over all Asia Minor and Ionia (an ancient region on the west coast of what is now Turkey, including nearby islands in the Aegean), as well as the greater part of Italy.

— **Marianna Mayer,** *Women Warriors.* 1999.

Reconstruction of the interior of the Temple of Apollo at Bassae (Phigeleia) in Greece. Around the top is a frieze of Amazons fighting Greeks (Amazonomachy). From Wikipedia.

Table of Chapters

c. 2000	Jason's voyage on the *Argo* into the Black Sea (others estimate 1400 B.C.)
c. 1280	Heracles and/or Theseus journey to the Amazons, abduct Antiope.
c. 1250	The Amazons attack Athens
c. 1200	Queen Penthesilea arrives at Troy to fight against the Greeks
c. 1000	David is king in Jerusalem, then his son Solomon
570	Nebuchadnezzar is king in Babylon; Daniel is Prime Minister
490-480	Persians attack Greece. Battles of Marathon, Thermopylae, Salamis.
360	Strax is born in the far north (modern-day Scandinavia).
356	Alexander is born in Macedonia.
337	King Philip's advance force crosses the Hellespont into Turkey.
335	Strax sails from Scandinavia. Battle of Cyzicus. Alexander becomes king.
333	Alexander crosses into Asia. Fights King Darius in Battle of Issus. Unfastens the Gordian knot.
332	Alexander takes Tyre. Enters Egypt, is declared Pharaoh. Journeys to Oasis at Siwah.
331	Alexander takes Persepolis. King Darius dies.
330	Alexander and Thalestris meet by the Caspian
329	Alexander proceeds to India; Svea is born.
323	Alexander dies in Babylon. Strax, Mara, and Svea leave Thymiscyra.

Alexander's route begins in Pella, Macedonia, and ends in Babylon.

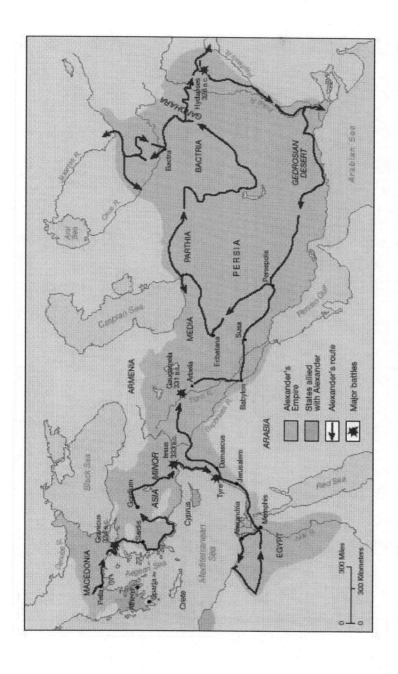

A reconstruction of the Apadana at the Persian capital Persepolis, a huge atrium that held large audiences. Persepolis held the Persian treasury, surrendered entire to Alexander as King Darius fled. (By Happolati. From Wikipedia)

Chapter One

King Iskander's Gold

Turkey, 18th century

Sharif Visits the Emir

The Emir's favorite cousin Sharif arrived to visit him. "This is for you," Sharif placed a heavy red silk sack in the Emir's plump ring-encrusted hands.

"A little gold elephant! Heavy! Where does it come from?"

"India most likely, the land where such beasts roam. Surrendered by some king there to pay a tax to the Persians, I'd guess, and gathered to the Persian treasury at Persepolis."

"The piled up plunder of three thousand years, Sharif! The treasury of Persia Iskander found intact when King Darius fled."

"Four thousand years of plunder if a day!"

"And this was found . . .?"

"In my garden plot at home."

"No!"

"Yes! I live along that route, the one Iskander took as he left Persepolis, on to Afghanistan and then to India, with the King of Persia's treasure hoard in tow."

"How fine!"

"Iskander's soldiers were loaded down with Persian gold he'd given them."

"Loaded down indeed! Dreadful plight!" The Emir's chuckle shook his entire frame.

"And what would you have done, cousin, getting tired of lugging your hefty bag of metal up-hill and down?"

"I'd find a place to bury it!"

"Oh yes. Buried quite privately at night near some landmark you'd hopefully discern again."

"And retrieve it on return." The Emir's eyes went wide. "And they never did! Never did come back that way!"

"All deposited in small heavy hidden piles. Still there in peoples' garden plots! It's nearly an avocation now, charting the route Iskander's army took."

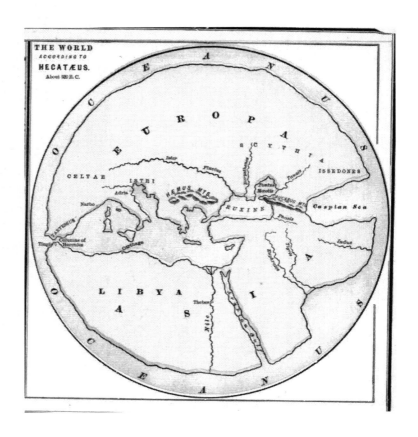

In Alexander's view of the world all the lands of Earth are an island afloat on 'Ocean' that encircles them

The Mysteries

Sharif and the Emir continued their visit in the palace garden's shade where date palms sprawled above and a hummingbird preened on a red bottlebrush tree.

"Amazing creatures," Sharif sighed, "I've never seen one stand around so long, much less preen like that."

"Mysterious bird, yes." The Emir stroked the brushy ends of his snowy beard with a bejeweled hand. "And Sharif, as to mysteries . . . Consider that young King of Macedon, victor over Persia in only five years' time. What was it Iskander wanted so, that he should make his leap across our world? Was it gold, all he found at the Persian treasury at Persepolis, intact and ajar awaiting him?"

"Iskander wasn't covetous of gold, my Prince. He gave it to his men. Then urged them to abandon it, lest it weigh the army down."

"What then, Sharif? What did he desire?"

"Fame of course, that hard-to-bridle mare. Second, to take vengeance on Persia for the attacks on Greece, part of Iskander's father Philip's dream that he inherited. And my opinion on that is this: Had the Persian kings been content with that wide world they owned stretching from Egypt to India and left Greece alone, not invaded Athens and burned her temples down --- they'd be ruling Persia still!"

"Ah."

"Third, Iskander's obsession, though it may sound trivial to us, was to go as far to the east as possible, to stand on the eastern-most shore of the 'world-encircling-sea.'"

"The what?"

"Iskander believed water surrounded all the lands of the world. 'Ocean' was the simple name for it. The Gates of Heracles were the boundary to the west and India in the east, all of it encircled by water. The Greeks and Italians were not allowed to know the truth of what the Atlantic and Pacific hold, kept in the dark by the sea-ruling Phoenicians and

Carthaginians who for centuries had been sailing far and wide, literally everywhere."

"A secret they kept well!"

"And of course that fourth goal Iskander had: initiation into the Mysteries."

"Which included what?"

"From what I've discerned it varied place to place. Strategies of human possibility and shards of truth locked tight in the control of the priesthoods and their initiates."

"What truth was that?"

"The truth it's intended we for us all to know, not meant to depend on priesthoods for it. Meant to be told on a mother's knee, the truth of who we are and why we're here. And why it's not well known, nor easy to think through."

"Though no one's mother does?"

"Indeed. So that the priesthoods' initiation maintains the power of the mysterious."

ଚ୦

Happy is he among men on earth who has seen these mysteries; but he who is uninitiate and who has no part in them, never has the lot of like good things once he is dead, down in the darkness and gloom.

— **Hesiod.** *The Homeric Hymns.* 8th century B.C.

Those who are acquainted with the mysteries insure to themselves pleasing hopes against the hour of death.

--- **Plato.** 427--347 B.C. Socrates speaking.

Heracles went to Eumolpus at Eleusis, wishing to be initiated. . . . But not being able to see the mysteries because he had not been cleansed of the slaughter of the centaurs, he was cleansed by Eumolpus and initiated afterward.

--- **Apollodorus of Athens.** *The Library.* Born 180 B.C.

Spirit Wings

"I was over at Gordium last month, Sharif, where Iskander severed the famous knot. How did the legend go? Whoever untied the knot would rule all Asia, yes?"

"Or else conquer it. As Iskander nearly did I guess. Though as for ruling it: That same victory the sea enjoys, to flood the sand and fall away again."

"Just so! A pair of wings he tried to ride too far with a greater weight than they could hold. Though he did conquer King Darius when he was barely twenty-five. Then went on to India. And why? India, Sharif! So rash a thing to do."

"Someone must have convinced him to," Sharif grinned, for he owned an opinion few seemed to have taken pain to reason out.

"Who might that have been?"

"Perhaps a royal visitor the King had. One in touch with the mysteries. What the priesthoods had no inclination to provide to Iskander yet, so he'd acquire his spirit wings."

The Emir stroked his stubbly beard. "Spirit wings?"

"Of wings there may be many offered, my Prince, though not all designed for the same sort of flight. 'Spirit.' A term so tossed about. And what is that?"

"What indeed!"

"Consider dimensions. We have length," Sharif drew a line along the table top. "Add width. That's two, and we can make a square along the ground. Add height and we have cubes and boxes and tables such as this one by which we sit. And there we are as well, curiosities of those three dimensions' possibility."

"And Spirit is a fourth?"

"Let's say that's so. Though it may be the tenth, with many in between! How would it relate to us? As I attempt to imagine it I drop back a step, as though I am a set of lines that tries to understand the table's cube. If we set a cube across the lines I am, it will only appear as another line to me. Lines are what I know and that is what I'll see."

"Not the height?"

"No. Though I may sense it in some way, that higher dimension reaching down to me. Does it invite me to know its possibility? Desire me to? And suppose I do somehow, what then? Suppose the table invites me to grow one dimension more, to come live as a table among them here."

"That's what the priesthoods knew? What they kept for us? How the dimension of sprit may be accessed?"

"Suppose it's so: Information held hidden by the priesthoods from ancient times as though in store for everyone. Why not be releasing it? Power! Why would they give that power up? Anyone who made certain discoveries about the inner life was promptly initiated and their lips sealed. And the populace was provided trans-dimensional mythologies instead of what the Spirit holds."

"As for instance?"

"What if there's a survival strategy the body devises during infancy, one that's a disaster and meant to be replaced? One we're not informed about. What if being told about it when we're young would save a lot of mental grief and misspent energy? What if we're meant to know, so to replace it with some alternate more kind? One not so body-centered, one with Spirit at center of intention's stage instead."

"And if not told? One can think it through?"

"That happens I suppose. Though it requires getting down past thinking where it's quiet enough, down past the noise where Spirit's quieter voice awaits an audience. The silence the priests concealed from view lest our Spirit wings take shape. One, two, three, the eggs are cracked and feathers grown for flight!

"The portal to silence in the inner life: This discovery leads on to the rest, for the spark we are to be fed by Spirit's fire, strong to push the darkness back. So to discern the reason Spirit clothes itself in flesh, its own intentions to perform."

"How deep does the silence need to be?" asked the Emir.

Sharif smiled to consider it, such a fine game he might make of it: The weight silence has, the tones of light and volume of veils and the depth at which thinking is eclipsed and sensation blooms, one world flowing toward the next. Stratagems to pass the Thinker's nets that lie in wait. The skill of being effortless. Though why play games that only pride will win?

"You'll know, my Prince, once you sort out the two voices in the mind and begin to be at cause inside, no longer pushed around by thinking's noise. Will know you are not simply a body as the mind insists. Such a little jump to take, but once your feet are off the floor you soar and what's small in you begins to fall away. Mysterious to hear it spoken of, though a situation simple in reality. The mystery's dispelled by the actual experience."

"And Iskander knew about these mysteries?"

"Oh, what he'd construed of them perhaps. The inner life was only one more battlefield to him, a world in need of conquering. He revered the 'initiates': Plato, Pythagoras, Heracles, Solon, Aeschylus. Wondering what they knew that he did not. Wondering, what is it possible for humankind to be?

"Does the Creator wait in each of us, ready to be related to? Iskander's gods were living outside of him. And worse than that, he believed he was a god himself. Had reason to believe it based on his family history, Achilles on his mother's side and among his father's ancestors, Heracles! That's why Egypt was his first goal, his most important port of call. Once in Egypt he made a hurried visit to the Oasis of Siwah, there to have assurance of his personal godhood. The priests of Ammon-Ra were there. He had reason to believe that's who his true father was.

"Iskander left Macedonia and crossed the Aegean Sea then battled his way south --- a first battle with King Darius then an unintended siege of Tyre that simply wasted time --- then finally on to Egypt where they crowned him Pharaoh on arrival, hailed for liberating Egypt from two hundred years of hated Persian rule. Then the goal in sight: He made a hazardous nearly fatal march across the sands to the Oasis at Siwah to visit the priests, desiring them to initiate him into the mysteries and verify his godhood as son of Amnon-Ra."

"And they did?"

"As to his godhood, Iskander was reassured by what he heard. Though as to the mysteries he was sent away with little more than instructions for preparations they insisted he should make. Those stingy priests! Insisting he go on waiting for initiation's chance! Impatience is too frail a word for what Iskander felt. He grieved, obsessed with it."

"Like a child that's not allowed a toy!"

"Though he may have been provided insight later on. Shown how we seem to have two voices in our heads, as though two selves, with the incessant voice of the lower drowning out the quieter higher one. Shown how that noise can be dispelled once the mysterious origin of the lower self has been discerned by . . ."

"Wait, wait. Provided this insight — by whom?"

"That royal visitor Iskander had. A warrior queen."

Wide view of the mosaic of Alexander in battle with King Darius of Persia found in the ruins of Pompei. Now at the Museo Archelogico Nazionale, Naples. (See a detail of this mosaic on page 2.)

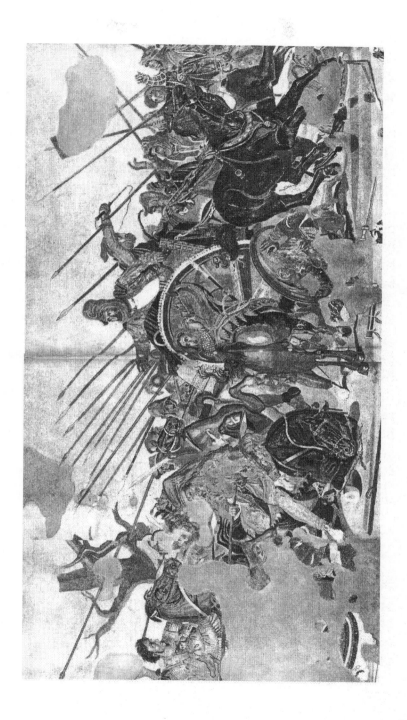

The Emir and the Sultan
The palace of the Sultan

The Emir made a visit to his friend the Sultan. "There's ancient gold to be found, I'm sure of it!" The Emir bounced about the room and waved his arms.

"You'll need to slow down if I'm to hear."

The Sultan had noble thousand year-old eyes and pointed silver slippers barely glimpsed beneath encircling robes. Turbaned in purple and lean as the Emir was squat he owned the confidence of those educated at the feet of scholars whose lives are vaunted legacies.

"It's King Iskander's gold! Taken from the treasury of King Darius."

"The gold from Persepolis?" The Sultan selected a pistachio from a bowl of amethyst. "Iskander gave that to his army or else sent it west."

"But not all of it! There was an incident!" The Emir's jeweled fingers flared as he bounced near. "Something Sharif said let me discover it. It's what I've come to inform you of!"

"All right, but speak more soft," the Sultan winced, "I'm listening. Though if you've come to discuss the myriad nocturnally hidden treasures buried by his men, so well spread out . . ."

"No, no. A much larger hoard!"

"Go on." The Sultan set the emptied halves of pistachio shell onto a growing pile of them.

"It comes round to this: What if Iskander had a child, one no one knows about? Would he have delivered royal gifts to the child? To the mother if the child's as yet unborn? Of course he would! Might there not be gold where that child lived, gold that remains there still?"

"A child of Iskander's? His Persian wife Roxanne had a son . . ."

"No, no! Another child, thoroughly unknown."

"What makes you think there's one?" The bottomless eyes of the Sultan flared.

"Sharif mentioned a meeting Iskander had with 'a warrior queen.' Just that; he said no more. As you know I hate a mystery! So I went to work to piece it out. Consulted my books to discover who it was he meant and where she might have lived. And yes, it's there! Greek historians report the meeting of the King and 'warrior' queen . . ."

"What exactly did you find?"

"This:

When King Iskander returned to Hyrcania [south of the Caspian Sea] there came to him the queen of the Amazons named Thalestris, who ruled all the country between the rivers Phasis and Thermodon [south of the Black Sea]. Her beauty and strength were remarkable and her bravery acclaimed by her countrywomen. She left the main force of her army on the frontier of Hyrcania and arrived with an escort of three hundred Amazons fully armed.

The King marveled at them and at their dignity. He asked Thalestris why they had come. She replied that it was for the purpose of getting a child, as he had shown himself to be the greatest of all men in his achievements, and she being superior to all women in strength and courage, that the offspring of such parents must surely surpass all other mortals in excellence.

The King was delighted at this and granted her request, consorting with her for thirteen days, after which he honored her with gifts and she departed home.
— Diodorus Siculus. **Library of History**, 17.77, writing 1st century B.C..

"What do the Greeks say happened when they met?"

"There's nothing to be found," the Emir shrugged. "No details at all."

"No mention of a child?"

"None. Though it occurred to me, certainly a possibility! Thirteen days! Might something not have come of it?"

"Hmm. These women warriors on the Black Sea's southern shore, I have some knowledge of them."

"Oh?"

"Homer mentions the Amazons, that they were 'subdued' by the Greek hero Bellerophon. So curious . . ."

"How so? What happened then?"

"Homer says no more than that. There's one more mystery for you to baffle at since you like them so!"

First Bellerophon was sent away with orders to kill the Chimera. He killed the Chimera. Next he fought the Solymoi, the fiercest battle he thought he had ever seen. Third he conquered the Amazons, who meet in battle with men. As he returned, the king with treachery set another trap for him.
— **Homer, *The Iliad,*** Book 6. 9th century B.C.

"When did Bellerophon do that?"

"Before the war at Troy. The Amazons fought on the side of Troy you know.

Thus they performed the burial of Hector. Then came the Amazon, the daughter of great-souled Ares, the slayer of men. — **Arctinus of Miletus. The Aethiopis.** 750 B.C.

"Fierce enough fighters that the Greeks made boast of fighting them.

We must make clear to you whence it comes about that we, rather than the Arcadians, have a right from our fathers to be the first among brave men . . . We have also a good deed to our credit in fighting the Amazons, who came from the river Thermodon and invaded the land of Attica [Athens]. And in the Trojan troubles we were as good as any.
— The Athenians speaking. **Herodotus. The History,** Book 9. Lived 484 to 425 B.C..

"It was after the Bellerophon incident but before the War at Troy that the Amazons attacked Athens with their allies the Scythians. This was in response to Heracles' invading them, and to Theseus who made off with their Princess Antiope. An 'abduction' as the Amazons decreed."

"Attacking Athens? Truly so?"

"Long before the Persians did. It was nearly rubble when the women left. Confirmed by Strabo in his rhetorical way.

But as regards the Amazons, the same stories are told now as in early times, though they are marvelous and beyond belief. For instance, who could believe that an army of women, or a city, or a tribe, could ever be organized without men, and not only be organized, but even make inroads upon the territory of other people, and not only overpower the peoples near them to the extent of advancing as far as what is now Ionia, but even send an expedition across the sea as far as Attica [Athens]? . . . Nevertheless, even at the present time these very stories are told about the Amazons, and they intensify our belief in the ancient accounts . . . — **Strabo. Geography, 11.5**. 63 B.C.–21 A.D.

Amazons fighting Greeks. From the Mausoleum of
Halicarnassus.

*The Parthenon in Athens: Sculptures on the metopes under the
cornice show Amazons fighting Greeks during the Amazons'
invasion of Athens prior to the Trojan War.*

"That attack on Athens is depicted in a lot of Greek art," the Sultan informed the Emir. "Friezes in the Parthenon, the Mausoleum of Halicarnassus, and the Temple of Apollo at Bassae / Phigaleia provide witness to the history. And the ancient travel guide Pausanias gives minute detail.

On entering the city [Athens] there is a monument to Antiope the Amazon. This Antiope, Pindar says, was carried off by Peirithous and Theseus, but Hegias of Troezen gives the following account of her: Heracles was besieging Themiscyra on the Thermodon, but could not take it; but Antiope, falling in love with Theseus, who was aiding Heracles in his campaign, surrendered the stronghold. Such is the account of Hegias. But the Athenians assert that when the Amazons came, Antiope was shot by Molpadia, while Molpadia was killed by Theseus. To Molpadia also there is a monument among the Athenians.
— Pausanias. **Description of Greece,** Book I, Attica. 1st century B.C.

A Plan
The Emir and the Sultan

"As for the report by Diodorus you brought along with you, that's not unknown to me. And now you mention it . . ."

"Yes?"

"It may have merit, this idea of gold by the Black Sea. I'll look into it." The Sultan stirred the remaining pistachios with his fingertip. "If it's there, how would it be found?"

"Leave that to me." The Emir could hardly contain his joy. "You'll 'look into it' how?"

"I'll begin with Sharif. Since he's the one that's caused all this."

"What if he waves it off, no matter what he's said to me? Says the Amazons are only myth."

"He won't. There's a proof I know he likely knows as well."

"What's that?"

"A quote from Arrian, Iskander's most-revered biographer. It substantiates that meeting by the Caspian, once you set your mind to work with it. Even provides the true reason Thalestris went to him! Such a tiny bit of reasoning to set it clear. So obvious when you know geography."

"Explain!"

"She may have had a child; though that's not why she went."

"Though in Diodorus' report she states . . ."

"What else was she supposed to say? Ha! Quite clever of her saying that. Though hardly the reason for her journey there. Think! What other reason might you discern?"

"Well . . ."

"Consider. What decision was Iskander busy making when he'd just defeated Darius, resting there by the Caspian Sea? Do you know the history."

"The decision to proceed on east to India as he desired, or to return home to Macedonia."

"That's it. Iskander's dream led him on farther east to India. But his soldiers were eager to go home. It's then the Queen comes to visit him. Easy enough to know why. What is the route Iskander's army would have taken home, west from the Caspian Sea to their homeland Macedonia?"

"Well . . ."

"They'd have plowed right through the southern coast of the Black Sea, the homeland of the Amazons! She went to bend the course his storm would take. On to India and away from them! She determined the course of history. And so few know!"

"Ah."

"And not because he 'just might decide' to go home. It was more than that. A definite danger those women faced."

"What?"

"What tips you off to it is the passage from Iskander's biographer Arrian, as I said, reporting one other monarch's visit to Iskander there by the Caspian: the Amazons' neighbor and enemy King Pharasmanes. Desiring that Iskander join him as his ally to invade the Amazons!

The King of the Chorasmians, Pharasmanes, arriving with 1,500 mounted men, told Alexander that his land shared borders with the Colchians and also the Amazon women, and that if Alexander would invade to take those lands as far as the Black Sea, then Pharasmanes would gladly serve as guide for him and provide his army all supplies for the campaign. -- **Arrian. The Life of Alexander the Great.** 2nd century A.D.

"She *had* to go to him! To provide a counterbalance to that meddling! To save her home from an invasion force."

"So we set a plan!" The Emir was jubilant. "To find the gift of gold Iskander surely would have given for the child . . ."

"We may agree she went to him, though as for the existence of a child," the Sultan shrugged.

"How shall we discern?"

"Sharif. I'll open a portal to whatever information he may hold. His uncle works with old manuscripts; who knows what he's been shown. Whatever pride resides in Sharif I'll prick, for him to open up whatever source he has. Then be unable to set it closed again."

Sharif and the Sultan
The palace of the Sultan

The Sultan invited Sharif to dine with him.

"I am concerned for the Emir," the Sultan frowned.

"Oh?"

"It seems he is intent on making an expedition — to search for Iskander's gold."

"Iskander's gold? Where? A lot of it was sent back west, to propped-up rulers Iskander didn't really trust. Some he took on east with him, deposited along the way. Some got as far as Afghanistan to be left in the castle he built for his Persian wife Roxanne, a ruin folks still keep finding treasure in. Some of the gold he gave his men. As for himself, it wasn't something Iskander really prized."

"Do you know how much gold Iskander acquired, Sharif? The entire Persian treasury from Persepolis! All of it waiting there when Darius fled."

"Well . . ."

"Hoary with age, dug from the edge of time; from ancient Assyria, Akkadia, Sumeria, Babylonia, finely worked and delicately rare. Gold taken in wars or paid in annual tribute to conquering kings by empires humbled to their knees, let survive as long as the gold came flowing in. Kingdoms toppled later anyway to pry from their fists whatever might remain. From Asia, Egypt, Phoenicia, India, all flowing into Persia's coffers to be heaped in great high piles, the newest always poured on top, the oldest on the bottom being crushed.

"The gold weighed Iskander down; his army became a treasure-caravan! And some of it went somewhere else, the Emir has decided, rather than west or east or to the men."

"Where?"

"You don't know? It's you he got the idea from!"

"He did? I don't remember . . ."

"Did you mention a visitor Iskander had, a 'warrior queen'?"

"Oh."

"Well, now he's decided just who that was! He's done research and thought it through: It's Thalestris, Queen of the Amazon warriors by the Black Sea. That's who it was you meant that day, yes, with your by-the-way comment to him?"

Sharif sat back into his chair. "Though I don't see how the idea of finding gold would follow necessarily . . ."

"The Emir took your bit of bait and has hooked a whale. If Queen Thalestris spent thirteen days with Iskander, what might have come of it?"

"Ah."

"Yes, ah. And what might she have returned home with, as a royal gift for the child she'd have?"

Sharif let silence settle in.

"Well?"

"I know the information's source, writings of the ancient Greeks the Emir has likely found, and though not a meeting altogether implausible . . ."

The Sultan's eyes went stout. "Do you intend to deny the meeting's authenticity? That Iskander and Thalestris never met? Surely you've read Arrian."

"Does it seem to me, you may put in with him?"

"I've considered it."

"And?"

"I'm wondering if I should."

Sharif grinned.

"What if we were partners in this, Sharif, you and I! Would we head off to the Black Sea, snooping under rocks like snails with the Emir?"

"Roiling the water like an eel!" Laughing.

"Interrogating moles!" Laughing just as loud.

"Go on along with him then! Such a fine tourist area, the Black Sea's southern shore, so safe these days. No more Amazons lurking behind trees guarding their golden hoards. All of them have moved on along, it's clear, to who knows where."

"I simply need some reason to have faith in it."

"Why is it I discern you're about to expend a lot of money on this enterprise?"

"Sharif, my friend so wise! My interest is not so much for the treasure's worth as in the thrill of finding it. Holding something so very ancient in my hands."

"Oh dear. You truly intend to sign on with him."

"Noble Sharif! Provide me your advice! For your pains, if I decide to go, accept my gift of the tenth part of whatever gold I may acquire. And if I decide not to go after hearing what you say, then ten per cent of what I save, that I'd have spent!"

"For your friendship alone I'd tell you what I know."

"My thanks. Let all that suffice, gifts and friendship, both. So go ahead! Interest me in this affair. Cause me to beseech the Emir by his plump gnarled toes to let me come along, allowing me to finance all necessities, commissar and hosteler and chef and general when danger comes. Make me lose sleep for dreams of it, Sharif!"

"What shall you require to be convinced? Well enough to have you take up pick and spade and tent and go with the Emir."

"That the visit likely happened I am content, based on Arrian's remarks. As to the child, what am I to think? What am I to believe about the gift of gold?"

"My opinion, my Prince? Meeting, child, golden gift, all indeed took place. An opinion borne out by the story I've been told. One I might share with you."

Living Apart From Men

The Sultan took up his cup, stared at the crimson juice of the pomegranate seed. "First as to my curiosity, Sharif: Why did the Amazons live apart from men?"

"It may be there was a legacy they kept, for all the Earth when it was time, the reason they trained for war and maintained their strength and kept themselves apart from men. As for the reputation they earned for killing any men that wandered to their lands, I have my own ideas about all that."

"Oh?"

"It's likely they were maintaining peace. That the entire area south of the Black Sea was an area of relative safety and sanity because of them, for centuries if not millennia, and most of the 'men that wandered there' were marauding bands intent on pillage and plunder who got what they deserved. The Amazons mated with men in the surrounding villages; kept the girls and gave back the boys. And kept themselves strong to keep the peace; though to the world they showed another face, as recorded in the story of the Argonauts."

The Amazons, of the Doeantian plain were by no means gentle, well-conducted folk; they were brutal and aggressive, and their main concern in life was war. War, indeed, was in their blood, daughters of Ares as they were and of the Nymph Harmonia, who lay with the god in the depths of the Acmonian Wood and bore him girls who fell in love with fighting. — Apollonius of Rhodes. **The Voyage of Argo.** 2nd century A.D.

The Mausoleum of Halicarnassus, one of the seven wonders of the ancient world, held brilliant reliefs of an Amazonomachy (battle between Greeks and Amazons) by the famous sculptors Scopas, Bryaxis, Timotheus, and Leochares.

Greeks fighting Amazons. British Museum. Part of the frieze
from the Mausoleum of Halicarnassus. 350 B.C.
From Wikipedia.

Sharif's Uncle

"So then, this story you're about to tell . . ."

"From an old manuscript."

"How are you aware of it?"

"My uncle."

"The one who translates old languages?"

"That's the one. Uncle came by for a visit a while ago, during which I read the translation of an old manuscript he had been employed to make. Uncle is very good with ancient tongues and was asked to perform the work by the governor of the port city of Sidon in Phoenicia.

"The manuscript dated from Iskander's days, Uncle said, and was essentially a chronicle about the visit to that King by the Amazon women, my interest in whom he knew was keen. Uncle had simply made himself a second copy as he went along."

"Were there no translators of ancient Phoenician on the Phoenician coast? Why bring your uncle in?"

"There were delicate matters included, perhaps, my uncle thought at first, so that a foreigner's attention might be more appropriate. And it may have been, though there was also a Greek dialect involved that few scholars know."

"What details can you provide?"

"The first thing Uncle did was to read the manuscript through. As he did he realized the danger he was in if he complied in full; though by omitting a few details he might remain secure. He left them out of the governor's copy, though included them in the one he made to keep. As I tell the story you'll likely know what they were."

"What danger? Why?"

"Those omitted details let him make a discovery: The location of Iskander's treasure map."

"Oh my. And he . . ."

"Found the map? Oh yes. Uncle spent an evening making an exact copy for himself of that as well, in the old Greek."

"Iskander's own hand!"

"Uncle had no reason to think otherwise. And as he expected Iskander to employ all manner of diverse symbols and codes, the copy Uncle made was as a mirror in exactitude."

"Which he showed to you?"

"Some copied segments, yes. The original he keeps safe from the vicissitudes of traveling."

"Did the ruler know he'd found the treasure map?"

"No. Uncle returned the map to its place of rest. Accepted his pay for transcribing the primary text and left for home."

"Where is your uncle now?"

"Traveling to the east of here. Everywhere he goes he has instant friends. As though some similar sort of smile they share."

"Did your uncle indicate any success as he inquired of the map, where its treasures lay?"

"Oh yes. Went in search of the sites on it, and there they were."

"And?" The Sultan's eagerness was spilling out.

"And you and I may involve ourselves! Unless of course you choose to go with the Emir . . ."

"Sharif! An ill-timed jest."

"My story then! It shall provide a context for true opportunity. To hold old objects in your hands as you desire, and this better use as well: for that wealth to assist the wider charity that is its proper use. Nor would knowledge of those locations prove of any value without Uncle's invitation to be joining him, as I'll make clear.

"As to Iskander's little map, Uncle shared this one detail: 'There are two hands at work on it,' Uncle said, 'One I take to be Iskanders's scrawl; and the second is inked into margins alongside. Iskander's Greek is 'Golden Age' precise, the sort he used in letters he wrote to his mentor Aristotle. It's not at all like the second person's Greek in the margins of the map, which must be someone taking notes as the map's explained to him.'"

"Or her?"

"As you may discern."

How Shall We Judge?

"How shall we judge the truth of stories we hear, Sharif, such as the one your uncle found?"

"What truth it holds must be discerned in that bright mirror deep in us, truth's own looking glass held up to know herself. A mirror not unlike the smile on the faces of those my uncle meets as he enters some new town and some new street, truth knowing herself as she observes her glass. Such smiles as the poor possess: Born of the seed that having nothing plants."

"Our hearts then, yes. And you have a story for us now, for our hearts to hear?"

"Into the labyrinth we go! It's with Pharasmanes I begin since that's a point round which veracity turns. One reason she went to him as it seems you have discerned."

"Yes."

"Here is our scene: Iskander is victorious after his five year campaign against King Darius and is encamped with his army south of the Caspian Sea to rest, deciding where he'll go next, home to Macedonia or on to India.

"It's there by the Caspian the mountain tribesmen steal Iskander's horse Bucephalos, on which he rode each battle he was in. Soon after that is the visit from Pharasmanes. And then the Amazons. So with those reports let us begin."

॰౩

*Believing himself sent from Heaven as the moderator and
arbiter of all nations he labored thus that he might bring all
regions, far and near, under the same dominion . . . The very
plan and design of Alexander's expedition commends the man
as a philosopher, in his purpose not to win himself luxury and
extravagant living, but to win for all men concord and peace
and community of interest . . . He believed that he came as a
heaven-sent Harmonizer and as a Reconciler for the whole
world; those whom he could not persuade to unite with him he
conquered by force of arms. . . . He bade them all consider as
their fatherland the whole inhabited earth. —* **Plutarch.**

Chapter Two

Iskander Encamped by the Caspian Sea

Watchers by the Fire

Themiscyra, on the southern coast of the Black Sea. 330 B.C..

Five women sit by the fire with their eyes closed. As a bird flies high so do their spirits rise and soar as one above the Black Sea's southern shore, then take wing on eastward to the Caspian.

The fire sputters but they do not heed its sparks, observing all in events far off. One listening ear, one eye's bright work they share, observing King Iskander's soldiers in their tents asleep. All the Macedonian army at rest, victorious over Persia's King Darius in five years' time. Rest their due indeed.

That eye the women share comes lower now, seeks him out from all the rest, that young King of Macedon whose tents and men and horses these all are. Persia's newest Lord, as foretold at Gordium he'd be when he loosed the knot with the blade's sharp edge.

They watch as rugged tribesmen arrive from the hills, men searching for a horse, one special one among the rest. Finding Bucephalos, Iskander's companion in so many battles, horse and rider that fight as one.

And taking it.

The five women see it all. They watch as dawn comes strong and the King awakes.

A Stolen Horse

Iskander's camp, south of the Caspian Sea.

Sounds of an army waking — armor, wagons, horses, shouts — overwhelm the voices Iskander strains to hear in his half-sleep. Dark hands tug at dreaming's threads unraveling all the tapestry they wove. Phantoms disembodied turn to go.

Iskander wills the disappearing visions back. "What is this twine you leave me holding, tied to apparitions of the air? Letting me believe I play some part in it before you tear it all to shreds and laugh."

He goes out into the morning air, encountering captains standing grumbled in debate, silent as their king appears. Through the tent's thin opening they troop inside with their bad news.

"My horse? My horse is gone?"

"Mountain tribesmen, in camp to trade their fish and venison last night. It was a ruse. They must have seen you on Bucephalos, they knew what they were looking for. They overpowered the guards and took the horse away." The officers are pale as moons, bracing for the storm that comes.

"Bucephalos! My father gave that horse to me!"

"It's gold they want. They seem to know some Greek. Here is their note."

Iskander seizes the written scrap. "Horse for gold. One man's weight. At sea shore, near the three big rocks." He flings it down. "Are these people serious? Are they so intent to die? Have I conquered all of Persia only to have these tribesmen steal Bucephalos? Have I not army enough to guard a horse? Did I sense a multitude encamped nearby?" Eyes fling fire; an arm sweeps angry through the unresisting air. "Am I awake? Is this some dream I'm in?"

His officers stare at the ground.

"Contact the tribes nearby — all of them! Get a message to whoever did this thing, no harm will come if the horse returns. Or I hold them each and severally responsible!" Iskander paces as he speaks.

"Give every pathway an invasion force. Cut their forest down tree by tree to root them up. Take axes out to fell the woods in great wide swaths, for them to hear the thunder as they fall. Don't stop until the horse comes back. We wage war on these people and their mountain forest until then. I shall have Bucephalos back or make a desert of this place! Have they not heard of Tyre, that island fortress strong that tried to hide from me behind the sea? Tell them how I built a road out through the waves to take Tyre down. How the water was a barrier too frail. Tell them, a forest will be easier than oceans are!"

Iskander falls into a chair. Buries his head inside his hands. "A whole army. One horse. Must I stand guard over my horse? Must I guard it for myself?"

A Visit from King Pharasmanes

A day with heart emptied for lack of Bucephalos. But full of visitors, foul-faced foreboding men to match Iskander's mood. Feasting late into the night, the hospitality of kings, carving alliances where strategies construe to overlap.

"India has been my destination," Iskander tells Pharasmanes, "To stand on the eastern shore of the world-encircling sea, to know it all is mine, as far as it is possible to go."

"World-encircling sea?"

"The Ocean surrounding all the lands of Earth," Iskander curves a circle through the air.

Pharasmanes quarries up his cliff-hewn brow, deep-caved with eyes. "I have never heard of this."

"No?" The angel with the sandy hair pours yet another cup of wine, pondering so much darkness hovering near. Explaining to the bat what the blackness holds! Scattering flour on the table's top to draw.

"These circles are small seas we know: This the Middle Sea, with Phoenicia at its eastern side and to the west the Gates of Heracles. Beyond those Gates, only Ocean, on and on, and nothing more. To the east of Troy the Black Sea; then east of that the Caspian, south of which we sit now and drink."

"I live between the Black Sea and the Caspian," a heavily ringed finger smudges down. "Here."

"And to the west is Macedonia where I come from. And enclosing everything is Ocean," Iskander sweeps a circle wide.

"Around them all?"

"To the west the circle-sea is the Atlantic, flowing south around Africa to Arabia, then curling east to India. But here is a mystery, the north," sweeping a hand along the drawing's upper rim. "Who can tell where Ocean stretches there? Only the North Wind is spoken of, whose home that is."

The angel regards the darkness, hoping for some light from it. "Tell me, Pharasmanes, does the Caspian Sea flow into any larger water in the north?"

"No. The Caspian is everywhere enclosed by land. Save for short rivers, like thin tails."

"Ah." Iskander claps the flour from his hands. "I was hoping I might build a fleet to go up that way. Then around to India by ship. How far above the Caspian is the great Ocean that I seek?"

"North of the Caspian? It is a vast tundra. Full of ice. And Scythians. On their small horses, with their bows. I know of no great Ocean there."

"Hmm."

"I see your plan, though."

"Oh?"

"You will take the encircling Ocean, if such there is, to make it yours. Join the many lands inside your fist. All of them one because of you, pulled tight into a sack. Then run commerce to them all, and feed your dreams on them."

"Exactly so. And feed them with my dreams as well."

"Well then, the area where I live between the Black Sea and the Caspian is a crucial one for you, the center of your vast expanding realm. And all is not well there."

"Why not?"

"To the east of me are the mischievous Colchians, unruly barbarians I do my best to keep controlled."

"Colchis? Where Jason went? Where the golden fleece came from?"

"I have not heard of Jason or his fleece. Though there is certainly gold enough littering the streams after winter's storms, enough to fill a fleece or two left on the rocks. Come have some if that is what you want! And to the west of me are the Amazons."

"The women warriors?"

"Female savages. Who kill all men encountered on their lands. Flowing out across the countryside in search of blood, to simply see it flow. They attack my people every summer when their battle-thirst grows hot. Taking slaves with whom to mate. Will you leave them to their whims? So much that is hostile at your back, as you go on to India?"

"Well . . ."

"That whole area can be quickly attained for you. Do it now while you are close by! Then, when you must move against the Scythians north of the Black Sea one day we shall have those horsemen from two sides: You from the north, launching your fleet on the encircling sea, and me down here, pinching them!" Flour leaps from the table as

Pharasmanes' big hand slaps down. "But I shall need help. I cannot conquer the Amazons on my own. Though I can provide provisions, enough for man and horse. And guide your way."

Iskander studies his circles' residue. "Is it true, they remove a breast to improve their marksmanship?"

"Ha, no! That is the mischief done by your Greek tongue, 'A-mazos,' without a breast. They are the warriors of the Moon, the 'Uma-Zoon.'"

"My kinsmen fought them, you know. Heracles met their queen Hippolyta. Took her famous belt. Achilles at Troy fought another one, Penthesilea was her name."

"Your fame shall outshine theirs! They each killed their few. You shall conquer their whole race!"

"Only Bellerophon has done that."

"Who?"

"Someone Homer told about, who 'subdued' them once."

"Homer?"

"You could govern the Black Sea area for me afterwards?"

"Of course."

Those That Overhear

The Watchers' shared ear has heard. The eyes blink open. Returning to the spitting fire by the Black Sea.

"A stolen horse," says one.

"Pharasmanes," says the next, "with invasion plans."

"I saw the same," nod the rest.

Chapter Three

Queen Thalestris

The Threat

Themiscyra, home of the Amazons south of the Black Sea.
330 B.C.

When she was small Thalestris played in the silver
streams, billowing great storms up from the bottom mud
with sticks to see small creatures scurry from their
dislodged worlds. Now she is tall. Now it is her world the
jagged sticks reach down to overturn.

The storm growls in from the Black Sea baring its
bright claws, a rumble long and low toward the high rock
where Thalestris stands. She bares her breasts to dance
with it, shouting to the lightning as it falls. "Whose voice is
this that shakes the dream of sea? Whose bright hands,
that tear the sky in two? Whose tears that come to meet
my own? See, how strong we are to keep what we've been
shown. But now this next wave of it, the shadows' tide to
overwhelm the world! Who shall keep the legacy, all we are
set to guard if we shall fall?"

Council of the Amazons

The Amazon Council is convened. Queen Thalestris moves to the front of the great half-circle hall.

"Iskander set out from Macedonia five years ago; swept south of us, he and his storm, and we were spared. All Persia now is his. Where shall he lead his army next? That decision he is busy making now, camped east of us by the Caspian Sea. Will he continue farther east to India? Or turn back toward Macedonia as his tired soldiers so desire him to? If he goes home that homeward march shall surely bring him here."

A murmur flows through the council room.

"Iskander's goal is India, to stand on the shore of the sea, to go as far as he thinks one can. But those watching him now bring me news," a gesture to the five Watchers standing near, "He may not go to India. He may come here instead."

The great room seethes.

"Our meddling neighbor turns Iskander against us, saying we are Iskander's enemies. Our neighbor Pharasmanes!"

A roar.

"You recall our battle with Pharasmanes six years ago when he marched into our lands, thinking he might take some slaves. He's not forgiven us for defeating him. Now he seeks Iskander's partnership to work revenge. 'Subdue these female savages,' Pharasmanes tells him, 'that raid the countryside to take whatever they may see to want, stealing the daughters from homes, looting and burning and hating men. Too long their madness goes unchecked! Protect these lands that now are yours. What riches you shall take! Gold, jewels, relics of a thousand years, all these Amazons have stored like serpents in their caves!'"

The Council hisses in response.

"Pharasmanes could harvest much from Iskander's storm: all this area, to govern it! Shall he succeed in his design? We will encounter Macedonia's full force, already lords of Greece, Phoenicia, Egypt, Babylon, Persepolis, so much of Persia's realm. Shall we turn away the storm the armies of a million men have not? Iskander built a path out through the waves to take down high-walled Tyre, that Phoenician queen secure on her island in the sea. Planted a road where ocean was! And what of us? What shall deter him when he comes? Are we prepared to fight? To flee? To live in the frozen north among the Scythians? Consider! What are we to do? Shall we bend Iskander's course away from us somehow? Or do nothing, only that; wait and hope all will be well?"

Whispers clutter the great hall.

"I offer a plan to you. Pharasmanes' words require a counterbalance to their force. Iskander must not be allowed to make this decision on his own. India must remain his goal. I will go to him."

Voice against voice breaks the brittle silence up.

"Would they truly come this way?"

"Would we not fight them if they do?"

"He must be convinced to go to India!"

"Let her go to him!"

Thalestris waits for quiet. "Iskander will decide to do what brings him battle, blood, and fame, and further pronouncement of divinity, to know he's a god as his descendants were. You have watched his trail of fire and tears these last five years: Egypt welcomed him with a Pharaoh's crown and the titles of godhood that attend on it. But Persia's Magi would not, they declined to proclaim him as their god; so Iskander burned Persepolis to the ground, their holy city richly built. He does what he decides. He must be hurried farther east to do it there."

Only silence now where murmurs were.

"How difficult it is to take the world inside a fist! Such a slippery foundation on which Iskander stands, sweeping across Asia to secure himself by grasping it. Such a lonely dance. Conquest, fame, the only way he knows to make life's shadow into something bright.

"Iskander holds himself so very closed, waging wars inside himself. Battles so violent, as all who kill a parent face. Oh yes, though he perhaps only acquiesced to it. His mother Olympias accomplished it by an assassin's hand. King Philip is gone, whose love Iskander wished so much to have and never did; who gave Iskander his first horse, the one that he still rides!

"It was his mother's plan, it's true. Philip's other wives, those four or five he took, didn't trouble Olympias so very much. But Philip made a big mistake; implied Iskander was not his true son perhaps, just as the whisperers had said, and he would sire another son to sit astride the throne of Macedon. That spelled Philip's doom. Queen Olympias took action then.

Now Iskander enjoys no peace; the Furies pursue him to avenge. Who shall guide him through the labyrinth in him to subdue the monster there? To be a light to him, as woman is designed to be. Shall I?

"I will go to him, and the safety of Themiscyra shall be my prize. I shall say we hold the southern shore of the Black Sea in trust for him. Shall he attack what is already his? No. What challenge would there be in that?

"What a shame if it shall tip the scales, Pharasmanes' desire — to bring Iskander west. And there is reason enough he would! His ancestors Achilles and Heracles each met Amazons in battle long ago. Iskander's curiosity is great. Shall he not also welcome us as visitors, reach out for us when he hears of our approach?

"Do you bid me stay or go? Do you bid me bend the storm upon its path, to keep us free from madmen who desire to rule the world?"

What Shall You Say?

That night Thalestris has many visitors. "What shall you say to Iskander when you meet?" they ask.

"When I am sitting by his side, the lights low and the soft red drink poured out? 'Oh Great King, it is said your body bears the scar of every weapon known. Tell me the story of each one, how you have danced with the god of war! Pharaoh of Egypt and Persia's conqueror, a comet passing through our sky thinly disguised in the garb of kings! Are you indeed so strong? Come, find us two swords! I have never fought with gods nor often kings before, to see their blood leap from my blade. Nor have you fought with anyone like me.'

"When he has told me all his wounds, received yet new ones at my hand and we have loved, I will ask to hear his pilgrimage, to know the journeys of his heart. How wonderful to have come so far, so much of the world beneath his feet!

"And now?' I'll ask. 'On to the Indus? The Ganges? To hidden Arabia? To encircle Africa and subdue the Ethiop?'

"Then I'll lead him on a voyage into himself, where the whirlwind holds him in its spell. Join him in his storms to guide him toward safe harbor in himself, a refuge in such fog he cannot find it now. He pursues mysteries and the lore of immortality, assurance he is a god, thus to escape the storms that overflow his dreams. I shall show him what a man may be.

"He has integrity of sorts; he demonstrated that by the way he treated the family of King Darius, that he took prisoner.

"I'll bring Iskander spiraling inside toward Creator's fire, for him to feel Creator reaching out to the spark he is. Thus in himself he shall do battle and with me, ever more fierce, ever more deep; pierced far enough for me to feel new life against the point. Then I shall return to Themiscyra to have a child."

&

But as Alexander was going to supper [after the second battle with King Darius], *word was brought him that Darius's mother and wife and two unmarried daughters, being taken among the rest of the prisoners, upon the sight of Darius' chariot and bow were all in mourning and sorrow, imagining him to be dead.*

After a little pause, more lively affected with their affliction than with his own success, he sent Leonnatus to them, to let them know Darius was not dead, and that they need not fear any harm from Alexander, who made war upon him only for dominion; they should themselves be provided with everything they had been used to receive from Darius. This kind message could not but be very welcome to the captive ladies, especially being made good by actions no less humane and generous. . . . He diminished nothing of their equipage, or of the attentions and respect formerly paid them, and allowed larger pensions for their maintenance than they had before. But the noblest and most royal part of their usage was, that he treated these illustrious prisoners according to their virtue and character, not suffering them to hear, or receive, or so much as to apprehend anything that was unbecoming. So that they seemed rather lodged in some temple, or some holy virgin chambers, where they enjoyed their privacy sacred and uninterrupted, than in the camp of an enemy.

--- **Plutarch**. 46-120 A.D.

The Lioness that Hunts for Kings

Journey to the Caspian, 330 B.C.

The trees are alive with the horses of the Amazons.
Three hundred women ride with me, my strong right hand
reaching out toward the Caspian Sea where Iskander's army
is encamped, the man who lives to conquer all the Earth.
As we ride we sing...

I am woman.
Have you forgotten, how we entered the labyrinth together
so long ago? "Partners," you said, "One flesh."
I am your journey mate, I offer you my open hand's caress.
But you tear your heart away, you take me in your fist.
I plead with you through tears
for you to know what we may be:
"Death need not hold us here! So wide a journey that awaits!"
But you would rather blame than break the curse.
More consumed with sparks sown to the wind
than with the spiraled fire we may become.
I am woman. I keep the ancient promise that was made.
I reach out to you but you wave me off.
The monster bellows, coiling through the maze toward us.
You grapple in the darkness, frantic at a great locked door
that bars the way, while I must stand behind you
where you've thrust me from your side.
Standing in shadows no less grim than yours and no less
urgent for release, with but one difference, this:
I hold the key.

When we are close enough we let ourselves be seen,
wondered at, reported to the King. "Envoys approach us
from the east," a captain brings me word.

"Receive them," I nod. "We shall learn what sort of god this Macedonian is."

Iskander's little band of messengers rides toward us a-flower with bronze and plumes among the summer trees so full of sun. We watch. Anticipate each breath they take as they draw close. One looks apprehensively about. One complains the day is warm and there is no breeze. Another removes his helmet to wipe his face. He hears a noise and turns his head . . .

Storm! We are the wind where only calm had been and the men are straw in the wildly turning air. A hundred bows aim a hundred arrows at their hearts.

"Are you indeed the legendary Amazons?" the envoys ask when they are brought to me. "Do you come as friends or foe?"

"Either! Tell Iskander I come with questions of my own if he shall choose to meet."

"Iskander will meet with you, yes, and we are come to tell you that. Make camp near here; we will return to lead you in some days from now. He will say he goes to hunt for lion and receive you privately."

We smile. Of course. An encounter with a lioness. A lioness that hunts for kings.

౭౦

Believing himself sent from Heaven as the moderator and arbiter of all nations he labored thus that he might bring all regions, far and near, under the same dominion . . . The very plan and design of Alexander's expedition commends the man as a philosopher, in his purpose not to win himself luxury and extravagant living, but to win for all men concord and peace and community of interest . . . He believed that he came as a heaven-sent Harmonizer and as a Reconciler for the whole world; those whom he could not persuade to unite with him he conquered by force of arms. . . . He bade them all consider as their fatherland the whole inhabited earth. — **Plutarch.**

Bright Yellow Bees

Some days later. Iskander's hunting camp.

Iskander ventures out in quest of lion as arranged, setting up his hunting party's spacious tents. The friends he brings with him are sworn to secrecy — and thirsty for good wine. Too much to drink and too late to bed, Iskander stumbles drunken onto dreaming's battlefields, as dangerous as any where arrows fly. Two hours, three. A bright orange wasp lands by his dreaming face. Startled he wakes, jerks back his head, hands flailing at the air.

The tent's high lamps give light enough to look. Nothing in the air. Covers thrust aside. Nothing again. Nothing on the floor. "Bugs! Why must I have such dreams?"

Iskander reaches for his water flask, walks to the tent's small opening and throws back the flap hoping to find the dawn outside. Nothing. Dark outlines of trees and a strange dark wind, cool against his skin. He drinks. Crosses the carpeted floor back to the bed.

"Dragon-headed bees! Why me? Only in battle am I free of them. So. Where shall I go next to fight? The Black Sea? Everyone is clamoring to go home to Macedonia and the Black Sea's on the way. To fight with Amazons! Pharasmanes says he'll provide supplies. Why not?

"Or on to India, to stand on the eastern edge of Ocean, to know I've gone as far as one can go. And to find the mountain where the gods are gathering, to join them there. Shall they not invite me in, to drink with them at eternity's spring? Am I not one of them, son of Zeus-Ammon? Is it not confirmed?

"Or ought I go back to Egypt for that unfinished business, initiation to the Mysteries? To feel the spirit loosed from the body's sheath at last, ascending on dreaming's wings — while I am yet awake! To travel on the wind wherever I desire as I give the spirit rein to go. I shall demand it this time, yes! Regardless what warnings the priests devise to bend aside my path, to thrust me back from that sweet taste of immortality I seek. Such a lengthy preparation they've proposed before I take my flight upon the wind. Six months. But why? That is for ordinary men, not me.

"'What will you encounter when you've left the body lying here?' they ask. 'Do you know the battle in the spirit realms? Can you calm the inner winds?'

"Ha! Why should they treat me so? Have I not liberated Egypt from two hundred years of Persian rule? Am I not their Pharaoh now?"

Iskander lies on the bed again, watching lamp-shadows dance on the tent's high roof.

"Should I have asked them what I did? My question that ruffled all their feathers so: 'Has justice been brought to all my father's murderers?' I said, 'Have they all been found?' How startled the priests were, how upset!

"What did I expect for them to tell me, anyway? Justice. Did I hope for some new definition of the word? Think they would acquit and cleanse, wash it all away somehow, my terror at what my mother and I did? My awkward confession! Certainly they saw into my heart.

"And then their strange response, saying I had blasphemed: 'How indiscrete to say such a thing, O King! Your father cannot die, your father is very much alive. The god Ammon-Ra lives! As for the man Philip, if that is who you speak about, then yes. All his murderers are found.'

"Found. Of course they are. I have found them all. 'It's the only way,' my mother said. And perhaps it was. At least now I know who my father really is. Unless . . . That is what these priests would want for me to think. So they can rule the world alongside of me, contriving some political-religious labyrinth to take control of it. King Philip . . . Ammon-Ra. How am I to know who sired me?"

Iskander pulls the covers up around his chin. Closes his eyes. Opens them again. Inside him is an angry sea and a strange dark wind where waves reach out for him.

And there are bees.

Was This a Big Mistake?

Day invades too suddenly. With reluctance Iskander sets the dreams aside, replete with omens and mysteries too soon forgot, flames too soon replaced by conjecture's thinning smoke.

"This woman I've come out here to meet — was this a big mistake? My messengers returned shaken, wide-eyed, lightning-tossed. What kind of savage will she be, this matriarchal queen — fierce, feathered, cantankerous, loud? This Amazon . . . Does she dance breathless-wild beneath the moon, coiled in writhing snakes as my mother did? Does she take potions to boil her blood? I doubt she has much interest in immortality or the storms that come in dreams — what could a savage know of battles in the mind? Are there lion indeed out here in these hills to hunt? Then it won't be a total waste of time."

Iskander reaches for his copy of the *Iliad* beside his bed to join the heros on their battlefield a while. Sets the knife aside that he keeps hidden there. "Where is that part about the Amazons? King Priam speaking. Ah yes, here:

Years ago, I visited Phrygia full of vineyards, saw the Phrygian men with their swarming horses there— multitudes—the armies of Otreus, Mygdon like a god, encamped that time along the Sangarius River banks. And I took my stand among them, comrade-in-arms, the day the Amazons struck, a match for men in war.

"What was that about? Sangarius River: Didn't I cross that east of Troy near Gordium where I loosed the tangled knot? Phrygia. Isn't that where I fought Darius the first time? Yes, a fine long battlefield, vineyards drinking deep and red where I escaped from sleep and dreams awhile to begin my conquest of the world."

Iskander takes a draw from his water flask.

"Amazons. Women who fight. I wonder, what it is to meet them on the battlefield? Why were they attacking Mygdon and Otreus that day? Yes, I have questions when she arrives; that's why I've let her come. Timely enough. Then I shall consider Pharasmanes' request to conquer the Black Sea area where they live, to subdue this nation of female savages with him. Heracles fought them. Achilles too. Who knows? It could bring me more fame than conquering Persia did."

The *Iliad* is set aside.

"Where is Homer now, that he might write of me?"

ಎ

Aristotle was Alexander's most famous and important tutor. The famous philosopher trained Alexander in rhetoric and literature, and stimulated his interest in science, medicine, and philosophy. His gift to Alexander, a copy of the Iliad, was purportedly among the young king's most prized possessions and was kept under his pillow, along with a dagger.

— **Wikipedia.com**, the free web encyclopedia

ಎ

Riding In

Thalestris gives account.

We make our camp and wait several days. Then Iskander's envoys ride toward us a second time through the trees so streaked with sun and the shadows they know are watching them. They top a hill, suddenly to see our full force on horse, three hundred Amazons in motion for their eyes.

"I am Queen Thalestris," I greet the messengers, "These will come with me."

We set off down the hill toward Iskander's camp, the Macedonian captain with me side by side discussing weather and weaponry, then news of Macedonia, Egypt, Babylon, and Greece. My sources keep me well informed; he is amazed at all I know.

Those who ride near me keep their arrows always notched upon their bows. "Are they very good with those?" the Macedonian captain asks. I motion to a woman with my hand. Instantly the bow is bent and the fastest bird plucked from the sky.

"Impressive. Thalestris, I cannot help noticing . . ."

"We have all our breasts?"

"Well, yes."

"What a strange thing to think we do! As you see, even so we shoot well enough."

I consider telling him we were stringing our bows while Greece was nothing more than sea and rock.

"What are the many red ribbons on the boots and bows and in the warriors' hair?" he asks.

"It is a marking of the company assigned to my protection night and day. They have proven their courage in battle, or in competitions and tournaments at home with blood poured out. Therefore red is the color they wear."

"Tournaments?"

"It was a stratagem in the treaty of an enemy some years ago designed to keep us weak, a decree that we should compete among ourselves at home which we had never done before. But it has only served to keep us strong."

"How I wish I could be there to behold such spectacles!"

"Ha! Themiscyra? You would not be pleased. You would be sacrificed! Do you not know the legends, Orestes and the rest, the fate of all men shipwrecked on our shore or found wandering through our lands?"

"Sacrificed? All men then?"

"All. Unless he is to be a treaty's guarantor."

"Guarantor? Of the enemy's decree for tournaments and blood?" The captain has been listening at least. He presses me to unbind this mystery for him but I turn the talk again to happenings in the world. We speak like old friends a while catching up on the strange behavior of the many relatives. Though his curiosity remains. "All male visitors?"

"All."

"I was hoping, one day . . ."

"Captain, your nobility is appealing and you are charming to have conversation with. How welcome your embrace would be to many of those you see riding here, even to entertain that brief battle of desire that seems to content men so, such quickly disappearing sparks! Perhaps it might be possible one day when we venture out, as we do now. But we do not welcome men within our lands."

My veiled invitation ought encourage him if he shall think the logic out, though it seems that he does not.

"Why so harsh?"

"We? Harsh? Tell me . . . The women in Macedonia. Do they own property?"

"No. Not generally."

"Do they claim equality to their husbands? Do they control their own lives? Their own bodies? Those children who spring from them?"

"Well, no. Their husbands do."

"Shall the husband decide if she is to stay or go, to live or die?"

"I suppose so. More or less."

"Are we so harsh then? No more than you! Thus from ancient times we dispatch all men who wander to our lands lest loving them we let them take our property and equality and children for themselves, to bind us from hunting and riding and confining us indoors. To send us finally away upon a whim to dangle on the wind with a sad complaint. No. It is easier to be with men on our own terms, and to be strong."

"And that one man among you now, he survived somehow?"

"Though he had no intention of surviving us. His great heart was torn; he was hoping he would die."

The Captain sulks.

"And in Macedonia, what happens there?"

"In Macedonia Iskander's mother Olympias maintains firm control while he is away. And the General Antipater is there at the homeland-army's head."

"Are you enjoying this area by the Caspian?" I sweep a hand, "It is beautiful here, the green mountains with their streams."

"And the mountain tribes are mischievous. Just before you came some tribesmen made off with Iskander's horse Bucephalos."

"Terrible! What did Iskander do?"

"He was furious. He put a message out for them, that if the horse were not brought back he would have every one of the trees surrounding them cut down, one by one, to hunt them out."

"And?"

"They returned the horse immediately. Perhaps they knew he would do to their forest what he did to the sea at Tyre — carve a pathway out to them."

"A pathway through the sea — yes, I've heard about that time at Tyre. Sidon opened its doors to him, for him to worship the gods there and go out again. But Tyre would not."

"Ha! They threw our ambassadors from their walls and laughed. Iskander's hand was forced, though he wished quickly to go on to Egypt, only that."

So eager for godhood, yes. "And Iskander's father Philip now is dead?"

"Yes. Six years. We don't speak of it."

"Ah. So much you've conquered. Will you go home to Macedonia soon?"

"I hope so! We all do. We came to punish Persia and we have achieved that. But Iskander sees only what is not yet his. So much still to take. Why should he go home now? 'Macedonia is too small a world,' he says, and speaks of India. Tell me, is there truly a great sea the other side of India where Iskander thinks it is? How far is it actually? How many mountains bar the path? The mountains are harder for us than the battles are. The conquest of India seems a terrible idea. If only we could go home now."

"Or you might go on to conquer Africa, or Arabia. Or settle in Persia for a while." I award him a smile.

"That wouldn't be so bad. It's pleasant here. And the Persian women like us well enough. They are very beautiful." He looks me in the eye. His eyes are pleas. "But not as beautiful as you."

Arrival

My three hundred ride behind me into camp past
Iskander's bronze-clad men. I dismount to stand in front of
the King in my wine-red robe.

Iskander has wild sandy hair and huge blue eyes
where irises are black waters wide as seas. My whole being
swims in them. The sun that comes to search his depths.

"Who are you? Why are you here?" he asks.

"I am Thalestris, Queen of the Amazons. Here to
know if it is true what has been said to me."

"What is it you have heard?"

"There is one to come, it's said, who rules the storms
and hurls the seeds of light within the lightning flash. Who
forms solidity from the thunder's crash and throws the
worlds into their dance upon the avalanche of sky, then
holds them in their places with his breath. 'No one has held
so much of the Earth as Iskander has,' the people say. So I
am come to see you for myself, to learn if you may be the
promised one to come."

"How shall you know I have these qualities the
stories tell you of? By my own words? Words men speak
prove often frail. How shall you know I am this one for
whom you search?"

"He commands the five wild things that inhabit him.
The inner gates are his to pass among, nor can their
guardians bar his way. He rules the world to set it free."

"Whether I am he or no shall be for you to tell.
Come accept what hospitality I may offer you. And say
what you shall have from me to keep to repay this journey
you make to visit me."

I take the offered seat, one of the royal hunting
chairs. He provides me almonds and cakes of sesame.

"What do I ask of you, Iskander? To fight with me!
With heart and mind and claw; to loose the mind as
warriors do the blood. For me to know your strength as

your blade of thought drives deep. Then if the seeds of light are yours to sow that you touch the inner part of me, to fill me with this brightness you possess."

"What I am I gladly share with you. Though I am born of those who have not spoken of these seeds of light, nor of the promised one to come, nor the five wild things within that may be ruled. How shall you know I hold the power of the storm?"

"When the light you own has pierced the darkness with its jagged edge, and loosed the sea from the winds' tight fist."

"The sea . . . It is a dream I've had."

"Mysteries and dreams serve to chart our course, Great King, though they seem obscure. The little me we think we are, and what is that? No more than a face the moon has glimpsed a moment through the clouds and lost again. 'Come! Fly, out through the gate,' sighs the moon, and what you thought you were lets go, left far below as the moon sails by. 'Self,' and what is that? A gate to fling aside as one goes past. Of no more substance than a door no longer closed.

"'Me': It is too small a word for what we are! A smallness we insist upon. See how small a point we claim to be, looking out at all the rest. How little we remember of that greater dream in which the true self lives. Forgotten the bright thunderous stream on which we flow, the lightning we truly are. We imagine we are a spark."

"Thalestris, you ask to fight . . . Already I feel the struggle in myself at seeing you. Tell me, did the Amazons truly invade Athens once when Theseus was king? Is it true your women warriors fought at Troy? Did Achilles meet in battle with your queen Penthesilea there? Did he truly love her as she died? Did Bellerophon ride to conquer you in ancient days as Homer says?"

"Even so, Great King. And I shall tell you all that history."

Chapter Four

Strax the Chronicler

Sharif and the Sultan

Refreshments arrived for Sharif and the Sultan. Cherries and mulberries and cream with sprigs of mint and sugar crystals made from the sap of coconut palms.

"This man she mentions that the Captain is so curious about, he was living in Themiscyra?"

"Yes. A man named Strax. The old manuscript is his journaling --- all Thalestris reported to him on her return."

"But why him? What's he doing there? An enabler of their tournaments, you said?"

"It's well you ask. And now may be a good time to explain."

Susa

360 B.C. in what is now called Scandinavia.

Susa's hair streamed red and wild, eyes bright and glad and blue as lakes. She built her one-room house of stones and logs and moss with a glimpse of sea through the north pine woods. Here she lived at peace with everything, content with her two friends the wind and fire when all the world was veiled in mist or cloaked in snow.

She had the interest of two boys from the village by the shore, she enjoyed them both. Then she became with child. The two young men asked who the father was, hoping one of them might claim her as his wife. "Whose child do you bear?"

"I don't know," was her response.

Still they pressed her to choose one of them. "Which one of us is father of the child?"

"How am I to know?" is all she said.

They turned away then and determined they would fight for her. The survivor would be the one to marry her, was the plan they had. They removed their clothes and fought the old way, with one knife in the distance to grapple toward. They wrestled and hit and scratched and tore, and when they reached the blade the fight was fiercer yet. Both of them died.

Susa wept at it. Not for herself, not for them, but because of the control they insisted on — taking her in their fists when she had held them in her open hand. Because there was so much darkness now where she had shared her light with them.

The people in the village dug a single grave for the two boys. What would they do with Susa now? "Let her be buried with them there for her part in it!" the men said and took her by the arm to tie her hands. But the women insisted, "Let her go, to have her child in peace!"

At last there was a compromise, that Susa be put to sea, in a boat with no rudder, neither sail nor oar. The waves would decide her fate, the sea and wind would determine what became of her. So it was Susa found herself adrift with some water and a little food and a blanket to provide her warmth and shade.

After three days, when all the waves had taken turns to look at her and the stars all grew more numerous each night, the horizon that had fled appeared again out of the languid air and wind and tide brought Susa's boat to shore. The people nearby took Susa in, soon marveling at the wisdom and the strength she had. It was the wind that called her name they said, that made her spirit what it was. One day when their king was dead they asked her to rule over them.

Susa said she would agree, but only with their willingness to set woman free, no longer to separate her from her journey with the Earth. To no man would she belong, except as belongs the fertile land to the embracing wind, to fit so well and serve each other as they touch, learning to love as they partner ever closer in the dance of Earth. And henceforth, Susa said, there would be no kings! If there were no daughter to fill the throne when the queen would die, or niece or cousin or aunt nearby, then for a while a man would do; but only until a female entered the family and grew old enough, when he would step aside. To this they all agreed and made solemn pact.

So Susa ruled, and well. Harmony spread in and around that northern realm and they grew strong. And I am Strax the son she bore, for whom she was thrust out upon the salt and windy sea. Named for her calling, "Strax! Strax!" (Soon! Soon!), as I was born. And I shall rule our land of ice and snow someday until a daughter be achieved.

Whispers

Strax

My mother Susa has little patience with arrogance, so able to discern the shadows in the mind of man, lust for gold or power or pride. So sympathetic to the pleas of woman's heart that cries out for the summer to stay longer bright, to build her nest and tend her brood. And why should Susa feel surprise when the shadows let their whispered wondering out?

"What if there is war?" the whispering spoke. "Will her leadership be strong? Will she shrink from the battlefield, remembering her grief, those men that fought to win her for themselves that day?"

Susa swept the shadows all away. She knew her strength. Knew she would go to battle if it should require her leadership.

"But no," the whispers said, "It is not your readiness to die we question! But your willingness to send away all those you love, far from your heart, against what storms may come. Matriarchy is excellent in time of peace. But the world grows sharp, we must protect ourselves. Are you prepared for it?"

It only served to make her curious. Are there other women who have ruled? Other matriarchies such as ours? Are they so hesitant for battle, truly so? What do those women do when evil comes? And what is this evil's origin, that sharpens so the sweet soft stone of Earth?

ᎺᎧ

You shall understand (that which perhaps you will scarce think credible) that about three thousand years ago, or somewhat more, the navigation of the world (especially of remote voyages) was greater than at this day.
— **Sir Francis Bacon, *The New Atlantis*.** 17th century A.D.

ᎺᎧ

Ships

When I was young I watched the ships set sail — some south or east and some for the land far to the west, the Western Land we call it now, though others call it Vine Land for its wild grapes. Watching, wishing I could go with them. Stories the white-haired sailors told me fed my dreams.

"The Western Land is reached easily enough," they said to me, "with only brief stretches out of sight of land. Our grandfathers were sailing there, and also theirs. The great auks still lived then, birds that would float upon the sea and did not fly. As ships went ever farther in quest for them as they were hunted out the trail of auks led west to a new land filled with mountains and waterways. A land of mysterious forests like our own."

"When can I go there with you?"

"When you have skills enough to help, the sword and battle ax; and you could learn the healing arts perhaps that interest you so much."

"Who else is there?"

"The natives of the land. At first we were alone with them, trading our knives and the clothes we wore for gold. Then the Phoenicians began coming up from the southern regions where they'd been, intending to mine the copper ore. They were taking it back those days long ago for a king named Solomon, for a temple being built. We see them sometimes even now though it is rare, for the land is far across, and the rivers wide."

I could only listen then, though soon enough I also crossed the Western Sea. There I learned of other matriarchies in the stories of the Greeks, scrolls given me by Carthaginians I met. All my mother desired so much to know.

Far to the West

Northern Seaboard of North America. Strax is 22.

Our ship glides along the river in the Western Land. Trees along the shore are veiled in mist. Around a sudden bend the Carthaginian ship comes into view, drawn up onto the shore. Seldom do we come this close to them and if we do they simply stare at us as we go by. But today is different. They hail us frantically from the water's edge, full of energy to have us stop.

"Ignore them. Row on!" my comrades all insist, but I say we shall stop. And I am captain now.

"And if you're taken prisoner?"

"Come for me at dusk if I haven't called to you."

We drop anchor where the water shallows and I wade out to them. An avalanche of strange Carthaginian words comes down at me and wild gesturing toward a woman tight-faced with pain. They point to her stomach. Yes, I have seen this before, the organ that bloats, causing death if not attended to.

I explain to them with hands and sounds as best I can that something grows bigger and may rupture, and she could die. Yes, they know of this, but are obviously not prepared for it. They seem eager I myself do what I can for her, entreating me with their impossible rumbling words and their midnight eyes. And I do my best, though I know the risk failure may bring, with much cutting and sewing up and it ends well though many such do not. Her husband Urfi pours out gifts on me and we feast together late into the night, each of us listening to what we cannot understand and making grins.

Now I have many friends among their clans. And we are legendary to them, so that they watch for our appearance from the fog on seething oars. We blow our long horns for them as we pass by and they insist we stop to feast with them. Learning Carthaginian and Greek was the hardest part of what I had to do. The easiest was beating them at the wagers they insisted that I make with them.

Wager

One contest involves my battle ax.

The sweat is breaking out on Urfi's brow and the dark eyes are squints to see if I can hit the distant mark. Thrr-waack! My battle ax sings true into the small-drawn circle on the tree. I rush to claim my prizes, the ancient map and an omer of the sun's red tears so fire-hot to the taste, grown far to the south of here.

His Carthaginian boat-mates laugh as Urfi wails, hands on his head. Not that he has lost so much, there are other copies of the map and many more of the red tears they let dry to sprinkle on their food — but at surprise that I have thrown so true. He wails because he has not won what I wagered him, what he wants so much to have, my battle ax.

"Remarkable what you can do with it, Strax!" Urfi groans.

"This throwing the ax," I tell them, "is a game that can be played for even higher stakes. In our northern land the men get drunk and throw the ax to sever the braids of girls pinned up against the wall above their heads." I make gestures above my head to explain what I have no words for yet in their language I begin to learn.

"Higher stakes? What do they win?"

"A kiss. And the woman claims the right to go along with us to war. My mother disapproves of it. She rules there now."

"A matriarchy? Progressive." Urfi grins.

"We think so. Are there others you know of?"

"Well, there is the most famous one of all, the Amazons, a female-only clan south of the Black Sea. The Greeks tell stories about them. But their roots go deeper far than that."

"Is it written down?"

"The Greeks make mention of them here and there. And some longer passages. Warriors, fierce! Herodotus mentions them and Homer too. Those men they find in their own lands they kill. Is that the sort of matriarchy your mother has?"

I ignore the taunt and the laughter that follows it. "Can you find those Greek writings, to give to me when next we meet?"

"Of course. I will wager you again for them! That you cannot hit that mark a second time from five steps farther back."

I take five big paces back. "Here then? For how many stories?"

"All the ones I know about and can discover that mention them. And if you miss the little circle, the ax is mine."

I heft the ax, judge the distance out. Sssh-whup! The ax flies true again.

Urfi rolls his eyes and cups his ears, and howls. His friends all cheer. "Now I must get copies made," he moans. "And then, of course, you will want to have the old Greek words explained that you do not know. That will be an enterprise!"

"Do you want for me to go back five steps more and wager you again, for the education you propose? What if I simply make a gift to you of three of these axes: One for the stories, one for the help with words I do not know, and another for the tears of the sun and the map I now possess."

"Wonderful! Next summer then?"

"Next year at this very time, here by this very stream, three battle axes you shall have."

"As good as yours?"

"Every bit as fine. And you shall have found my stories yes? Now can you tell me . . . Why do the Amazons live apart from men?"

"Because men are beasts!"

The women standing near all howl with glee. I thin my eyes at him.

"And . . . It may be they have a legacy to keep, for all the Earth."

"What legacy is that?"

"Who can say? Whatever it is . . ."

"Yes?"

"They are strong to safeguard it."

Vigilance

The seasons made their dance, unclothed themselves a while and put on green again; then with writings acquired from my new friends I learn the ancient Greek. Drama, dialogues, histories, and Homer's epic poetry so strewn with wounds, a great war fought at Troy a thousand years ago.

"I may like to visit Greece one day," I muse out loud.

"Just be careful what you tell the Greeks about the journeys to the west we make," Urfi says, "They're not to know! Only a few years ago a man named Pytheas slipped past our fleet somehow, out the Gates into the Atlas Sea. He went up north toward you, around the islands with the great white cliffs, even went ashore to explore. Walked about too long, for when he continued north the ice grew thick before he'd gone as far as he had wished. Now he has returned and his fellow Greeks refuse to believe the stories he tells of where he's been. They laugh at him! The northernmost land he saw he has named 'Thule.'

"While they laugh we increase our vigilance. He should never have gotten out the Gates we keep so tightly closed to them, Greeks, Italians, all, lest they discover the Western Land. We tell them of a great abyss into which their ships shall fall."

"I could have gotten some help with my Greek from them."

"As permanent guests we hope."

"Are you so intent they shall not learn of it, the Western Land?"

"We are, and strictly so. As should you also be!"

"How long ago were people going there?"

"More years than counting has, back to those who made the map you won from me, showing Europe, Africa, the Deep-South Land and much of the Western Land in great detail. The map was a gift to our Phoenician race in a time far past remembering, when we were colonists from a land now sunk beneath the sea. And one thing is clear enough: Whoever drew it, drew it from the air."

ॐ

*The Turkish Reis and his uncle, Captain Kemal, captured rare and fascinating maps from a Spanish sailor during a naval battle in 1501. The sailor claimed he was one of Columbus' men, and that Columbus had used the maps to find America. He said Columbus had copied them **from a translation of a book dating back to Alexander the Great** . . . Admiral Reis copied and included the surprisingly accurate maps in his cartograhic compilation of 210 such well-drawn maps, the* Bahriye *or Book of the Seas. Two of these copies, dated 1513 and 1528, are presently in the National Museum of Turkey.*
    --- **Bruce Rux. *Architects of the Underground*. 2001.** (Emphasis added)

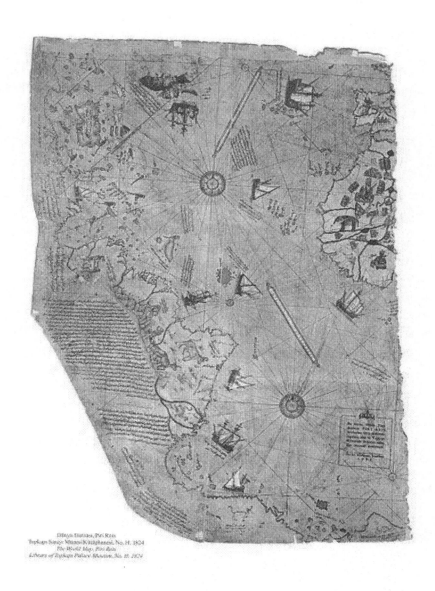

Segment of the Piri Reis map. From Wikipedia.

The Belt of Hippolyta

"So Urfi, only Phoenicians possess the map now?"

"Oddly enough, the Greeks have one made of leather, even older than our own that was stolen from the Amazon women. The 'Belt of Hippolyta' as it is called, that the half-god Heracles took from them in his ninth task. Not a belt at all but a treasured scroll, if they but knew. They've no idea what lies there traced on it with the language Sumer had, and with languages older yet from the sunken realm. Oh, the Amazon women could tell them what it means! Shall those warriors arrive one day to kindly explain it all to them? Ha! Its secrets shall remain. And the secret of the western sea."

༄

The ninth labour he [Eurystheus] *enjoined on him* [Hercules, AKA Heracles] *was to bring the belt of Hippolyte. She was queen of the Amazons, who dwelt about the river Thermodon, a people great in war; for they cultivated the manly virtues, and if ever they gave birth to children through intercourse with the other sex, they reared the females . . . Now Hippolyte had the belt of Ares in token of her superiority to all the rest. Hercules was sent to fetch this belt because Admete, daughter of Eurystheus, desired to get it. So taking with him a band of volunteer comrades in a single ship he set sail . . . Having put in at the harbour of Themiscyra, he received a visit from Hippolyte, who inquired why he was come, and promised to give him the belt. But Hera in the likeness of an Amazon went up and down the multitude saying that the strangers who had arrived were carrying off the queen. So the Amazons in arms charged on horseback down on the ship. But when Hercules saw them in arms, he suspected treachery, and killing Hippolyte stripped her of her belt. And after fighting the rest he sailed away .*

--- **Apollodorus of Athens**. Born 180 B.C. From the Loeb Collection. Translated by Sir James G. Frazer, 1921

Chapter Five

The Mystery of Bellerophon

First Bellerophon was sent away with orders to kill the Chimera. He killed the Chimera. Next he fought the Solymoi, the fiercest battle he thought he had ever seen. Third he conquered the Amazons, who meet in battle with men. As he returned, the king with treachery set another trap for him.
— **Homer, *The Iliad*,** Book 6. 9th century B.C.

Strax. The coast of North America.

I enjoy the midday meal beneath the trees with Urfi and his family. "One thing Homer said presents a mystery," I say to them.

"What is that?"

"Homer says the man Bellerophon subdued the Amazons; though Homer says no more than that, only that he went there and returned. What happened then? Who was this man Bellerophon?"

"That was before the war at Troy, even before the invasion by Heracles to take their belt. Bellerophon was a greet hero in the legends of the Greeks; but you'll find nothing more written about his journey to the Amazons. Though there are stories you'll hear told . . ."

"Let me tell him, Urfi," Urfi's wife speaks up, the woman whose life I saved when first we met.

"Yes, let Tanith tell you. She knows that story best."

"Few men ever come as near to the Amazons as Bellerophon did so long ago," Tanith said. "How those warrior women wondered at him til they knew his heart, realized he was in the grasp of some design, some power that was using him. He had no idea of the true reason for the nearly futile tasks being set for him, all designed for him to die."

"What tasks were those?" I asked.

"That much of the story's clearly told by the Greek writers. Briefly this:

"Bellerophon was from Corinth in Greece, of royal blood. He left home after he had killed someone; some say it was an evil king, others say his brother in an accident. Full of grief or fear he sought asylum in the palace of King Proteus nearby who gladly welcomed him.

"Anteia, the wife of Proteus, was filled with desire for their visitor; she approached him several times, wanting him to be close with her. Though Bellerophon did not respond as she desired, he did not think it correct thus to betray his host.

"Anteia, scorned, told Proteus lies, saying their guest had tried to force himself on her. As Homer tells her words, 'Ah, Proteus, may you die if you do not destroy Bellerophon, who tried to embrace me against my will!' But what was Proteus to do? This was his guest, a situation sacred in those days."

"What did her husband do finally?"

"He sent Bellerophon to visit someone else, passing the problem on — to Anteia's father, as it turns out — Iobates the King of Lycia, east of Greece across the Aegean Sea. Along with Bellerophon was sent a sealed letter that explained the incident, with instructions that the bearer should be killed. This set a great drama into play.

—

"Bellerophon crossed the Aegean Sea and Anteia's father welcomed him with feasting nine days. Then Bellerophon suddenly remembered the letter and delivered it with apologies for his forgetfulness. Iobates read of his daughter's anger and of her request.

"But Bellerophon was also now a guest to him! What could be done to comply with this demand his daughter made? King Iobates decided to conceive a task, designed certainly to be a fatal one: For Bellerophon to slay the Chimera, a beast nearby in Lycia with the head of a lion, the body of a goat, and a serpent's tail."

"Such a strange monster. Was it truly that?"

"Well, no. An enemy clan had come too close; that is what the Chimera was, made to sound like that in the tales they tell, a clan King Iobates had some reason to destroy. The Chimera's goat-body was the pastoral aspect the people had. The serpent's tail speaks of their origin, related to the Sumerian god Enki. The lion's head shows they are adept at war. They were menacing the shipping lanes in the western Echinades, like spiders' webs. Three Greek heroes — Perseus, Bellerophon, and Heracles — were one by one sent out against these invaders and their kin, to whom the Greeks have given monsters' names: Gorgons, Medusa, and so on. Bellerophon was provided the flying horse Pegasus by Athena, according to the stories of the Greeks."

"A horse that flew? Truly so?"

"The horse's wings may speak of the sails of ships. With the help of Pegasus Bellerophon and the soldiers that were provided him found and killed the Chimera and returned. Iobates winced to see him back so soon and sent him out again, this time to subdue the Solymians north of Lycia in a battle Homer refers to as 'fierce.' Again he returned unscathed! King Iobates was amazed. He would need to find another way, something even more desperately dangerous, if such a thing indeed there were. What could he find?"

"The Amazons!"

"Yes. The king sent Bellerophon north to find that warrior clan with strict orders they be subdued. There could be no doubt, this must surely seal his visitor's doom, the female warriors who live *in Phrygia of the beautiful vines* and do not welcome men."

"Ah."

"And you already know what Homer says happened then on this third quest: that he *subdued* the Amazons and returned. That is all the Greeks have said of it."

"Such a table set for us, and now no meat!"

"Yes, it must be sad to know no more. Bellerophon never told the Greeks what happened there. Not even Homer dared to guess. Though that story is one the Amazons told our clanswomen long ago on a visit there; and I shall tell it to you now.

"An ancient tree stood in a meadow near Themiscyra, the homeland of the Amazons by the Black Sea. Thirty arrows were embedded in the old tree's gnarled trunk, shot from a bow so long ago, feathers flown and shafts swallowed as the bark grew round. Called the 'Bellerophon Tree,' named for that man who lived among them for a filling and an emptying of the moon. And yes, he conquered them."

Bellerophon Rides North to the Black Sea

Before the Trojan War.

Bellerophon came alone, riding from the south on a great black horse. What were his thoughts? Did he know he rode to certain death? Did he wonder why King Iobates had given him so little thanks for his battles with the Chimera and the Solymoi? Could he have guessed at Anteia's lie — how she took revenge on him for what he had refused to share with her? How all his battles were at her whim, at her demand, to have him dead.

Our warriors watched him day by day, following him unseen as he neared the Black Sea. As for the horse, it did not fly. But the man had a noble spirit and a fine black plume upon his helm, resolute as he rode on. A hundred bows held arrows at the ready all along the hills on either side as Bellerophon continued through the valleys toward us on his northward ride.

Then one day when he had journeyed close enough word was given to encircle him, to find his mission out. Where only the forest and the wind had been warriors on horse filled all the sudden space and the great black horse spun round, a leaf in eddies of a winter stream. "Who are you?" the Captain of the women called to him, "Why are you here?"

"I am Bellerophon, sent by King Iobates of Lycia to conquer the Amazons. Can you lead me to them?"

The Captain put back her head and laughed. Laughter that spread like a summer storm til all the valley and the woods were filled with it. Then all grew quiet, as when the wind and rain have passed. "You have found us," the Captain said, "How will you conquer us?"

"I shall submit to whatever challenges you propose, until you are subdued."

"Come with us, Bellerophon. Others shall hear what you have said." Then all went riding into Themiscyra. There he told the Council all the story of his task. There was something other-worldly about it all, they thought; he is so innocent, but also troubled with a deep despair.

"We will prepare to meet your challenge," they said to him. "For now, you must be content to feast with us to keep your strength intact, for win or lose this must be a matter of honor for all of us. On the morrow you will be offered a demonstration of the Amazons' battle skills."

This reasoning pleased Bellerophon well enough, so the venison and boar were soon set roasting on the fire, the bread upon the hearth and the bright wine poured out. Many stories he told of his recent exploits for Iobates. The Solemoi and the Chimera-pirates in the south were no friends of the Amazons. Gently he pried aside the armor of their thoughts. Little by little he took captive all their hearts.

The next day Bellerophon watched the Amazons display their skills. The women rode on horse and shot their arrows into targets placed among the trees. Then even faster spurred their mounts and brought down birds upon the wing. Displayed prowess with the throwing knife and javelin. Bellerophon stood amazed at all he saw.

That evening at the feast the officers told him the decision they had made. "We shall prepare three trials for you, Bellerophon. If you shall satisfy two out of three of them you win. Then you'll set three trials for us in turn. These are the three we now propose:

"First, since you come with sword you shall meet one of our champions in a contest with swords, the Captain Aristomache, until some first blood from one of you is shed.

"The second challenge shall be with weapons that we own, the arrow and the bow. Have you knowledge of the bow? We shall train you in its usage every day; and each day you shall compete with it in a way we shall devise to make this competition fair for you.

"Meanwhile in the third trial you shall employ your skill upon the battlefield of thought with riddles we present. Once you discern any four from among those mental puzzles we daily give to you, that trial's victory shall be yours.

"When you have won any two of these — the sword, the bow, the riddles — you are proclaimed victorious and you yourself may determine the next battles to be fought. The javelin perhaps or battle ax; or trials of endurance, swiftness, flexibility; or riddles of your own, until we have won four of them ourselves. Two out of three victories and it's our turn again to name the games.

"If you are wounded at any time and bleed, you must be content to leave us when your hurts are healed and you are whole, so to go south again. Tomorrow the swords shall meet. Are you agreed?"

Bellerophon was agreeable. He asked to meet the swordswoman Aristomache, with whom he was to fight. When she came forward his spirit leaped in him. Never had he seen a woman so exceptional, beautiful and strong. She sat beside him at the evening meal. He feasted on her face and words.

"How shall I fight with you, Aristomache? You hold now both our hearts!"

"You must, Bellerophon. Your sword must draw my blood or my sword yours. If I have displeased you, you may thrust it through my heart and take your own heart back again. If I am to die it will be well, but only if you've held me through the night."

The morning came. When he awoke her head was on his chest.

There were many women seated on the surrounding bowl of laurel-forest hills that day to watch the contest of the swords. The two champions circled making thrusts to test, all their flesh exposed to reveal whose sword would be the first to touch. Aristomache pressed her attacks with strength and skill. Bellerophon defended himself with difficulty, though with little spirit for much more than that.

"Is this how Greeks fight now," those watching wondered, "so hesitant, so feeble in their thrusts?" So calculated, so reserved his sword's journey was in any light attacks he made.

When Aristomache seemed to tire Bellerophon let his point flash out to brush her skin. The crowd roared to its feet to see! Not so deep a taste as swords are known to take but drink enough. She let go her blade and went down to her knees looking up at him. Bellerophon flung down his sword and knelt to lift her up again. She put her hand upon his chest. "You have won the match," she said.

There was no feasting for Bellerophon that day. He was with Aristomache watching her wound bound up, his face all shadows. Her smile and then her laughter brought him from despair, renewed him to the brightness once again. He stayed the night with her and all the next day too.

"Your beauty and your mind are nature's finest work," he said, resting her head on his thigh as the stars streamed aloft from the evening fire, "How I regret the pain I've caused to you."

"Sensation is pure, Bellerophon. I celebrate it on each moment's wings, renewed. Pleasant and fierce, all feelings find me open to receive. Sensations are the body's fruit, I harvest them for energy. The battle is my wine-press; one I mix no thought within lest transforming what is pure with fear I turn it into pain. Awareness is my goal; power and ever greater openness are my rewards; sensation is my means."

"Truly so?" He frowned.

"What circles hold you fast, defining you? Will you clutch their contents tightly as you fall from them, as a flood flows fierce to tear you loose?

"When I go into battle I hold the moment with an open hand. I release the fist, whatever circles may be holding me, and become the open hand. Even this body's circle that I inhabit for a while. Ever more deeply into the unknown I fly, ever farther yet, welcoming battle's intensity and opportunity for wounds, so to harvest power as I do. Seeking out the fiercest fight."

"Placing your beauty at such risk? My spirit grieves as I consider it! That you would so easily release this circle I love so."

"You have won the contest of the swords. Your training with the bow will begin today, Bellerophon, studying with those who are most skilled in it. Every day you must face one arrow's flight, and also send out yours, but at a distance you will not attain to without training many days. If you manage to hit the Amazon archer, the contest is immediately yours. And to make it fair, the archer must not aim at you, but at a tree near which you stand. If the tree is missed the victory is yours.

"The challenge of the wits and mind shall also begin as every day a riddle is provided you. Answer any four of them, at any time, and you will have been victor twice — the riddles and the swords. Two out of three! The archery shall end, irrelevant. Then you yourself shall choose whatever trials you will."

"And if I am wounded later on, what shall happen then? I must depart?"

"You shall go, yes. But what is it you've been told? You'll go when you are 'whole' again. Your skin, your mind, your light! How shall you accomplish it? Who is to say the time that takes a man to do? Indeed, what man ever has?"

"My departure then . . . May be put off?"

"Indefinitely perhaps, as you may decide. Who else shall know what your wholeness is?"

"How excellent! To be with you is all that I desire. Tell me, Aristomache, against whom do I draw the bow? Who will send her arrows toward the tree?"

"It shall be myself, Bellerophon. Did you not know? The wounded Amazon goes to her feet to fight again, to seek a second wound — it is our way! Have no fear, soon you shall master archery; your arrow shall certainly find me where I stand so far away. Have no concern for me; there are herbs we brew to let us quickly heal, and more than that, more curious ways than plants to mend those deep-most organs sorely pierced, unless the arrow somehow finds the heart. A legacy of healing was given us in the far time."

He put his head into his hands. "How could I possibly draw the bow to target you? What if the shaft should find your heart?"

"Bellerophon! You must become skilled enough to send the arrow here or here in me, more low. For it is unlikely I shall ever miss the tree. Surely though it need not be prolonged, for you shall win the test of mental skill and all this first challenge shall be done: Swords plus riddles shall be two of three! Then choose what kinder weapons you may know as other opponents take my place. Wrestling perhaps; games of logic, fantasy, or chance; mysterious Greek lore or what you will. Such a long while we may be pleased to fight with you. You shall conquer us. You'll see!"

"Oh Aristomache, already you have conquered me. My mind is heavy with distress that I should bring you any further harm."

"Be brave, Bellerophon. See, already you are winning the mental war in this victory of selflessness."

As the days passed by Bellerophon considered the many riddles given him but answered only three, never the necessary fourth. Even his own life was a riddle to him, not yet reasoned out.

The Amazons asked him, "What goes on four legs in the morning, on two at noon, and on three at night?" This was the riddle the Sphinx employed according to the story Bellerophon already knew, and all who could not answer it when the Sphinx had asked had died. "It is a man," he correctly said, even as Oedipus had.

A second riddle he thought out thoroughly was this: "At night they come without being called; and by day they are lost without being stolen." He received no help from Aristomache! It took him part of a day and a night and a dawn, keeping a vigil with the dew, searching the sky to pry the answer out. "The stars," he said at last. And sought Aristomache's wide arms with a wide smile, to sleep.

And the third he perceived was this: "I wander fields and roads all day; under the bed at night I am not alone; I await the morning to receive a bone. What am I?" He guessed a dog at first but not correctly so. Then thought and thought, staring down at the floor from the bed as he pondered it, as he had the stars before, until suddenly he saw clearly what the answer was. The shoes.

What riddles did he not untie? Each morning Bellerophon heard a new riddle and rethought those many old, spending whole afternoons with his head inside his hands.

"I never was, yet shall always be; no one ever saw me, and yet I am the hope of all who live upon the Earth. Who am I?"

"There is a green house; inside the green house there is a white house; inside the white house there is a red house; inside the red house there are lots of babies. Whose babies are these?"

"A horse is tied to a length of rope of three arms' length, and there is a pile of hay the distance of five arms' length away. Yet the horse is able to eat the hay. How is this possible?"

"There is a white house with no window and no door. There is a lot of gold within. What is it?"

Aristomache showed the *Belt of Ares* to Bellerophon, a great leather scroll that fastens around the body with a strap. Thus, a *belt*. Written inside and outside with the ancient writing of Sippur and Eridu, resembling the tracks of birds. "Part of the legacy we keep."

"Why was it given to you? What does it hold?" Bellerophon took it in his hands.

What explanation could she give? It would be only another riddle that he already had too many of. Even so she shared some of it with him. *Access to wings, so long denied to you, for which your spirit yearns. To soar beyond the time-bound brittle bubble of the sky. Ways to knit again the tattered tapestry of flesh that tears so easily.*

"And this part inside is the ancient map," she held it to the light, "Here is the Middle Sea, here the Euxine."

"And all this?"

"Other lands, other seas. All drawn from high above, up in the air. More of that soon!" she rolled it up again.

"When you have won two of three battles and have conquered us, Bellerophon, you may rest a while as I shall tell you stories the scroll holds. Then when you tire of hearing it, the ancient history and the legacy we keep for all the world you shall design your next contests with us."

"It is our own private battles, Aristomache, here in your arms that I know I came here for. Woman's desire, yours, is it indeed so different from my own?"

"Bellerophon, a man's desire is a pebble thrown into the air that rises swiftly and falls so soon again. But woman's desire is the bird upon the wing that rises slowly and then soars. Man's desire is a rush of boulders cascading from a hillside in a spiral turning ever tighter toward

unraveling. His passion is the thunder as the great stones
roll, the crash of water and the waves hurled high and wild.
But woman's experience at first is a far more subtle one,
closely attuned to Earth that shakes her head, that
movement that sends the boulders down.

"A flame touching a golden autumn's leaf, so ready to
catch fire and then so brief, that is man's desire. But woman
is this log that takes a while to catch, and all the seasons of
the day contain her light: First the dawn, as man's desire
reaches out to hers, first red of day the darkness drinks.
Then bright yellow long past noon, ravenous with light.
And the orange of ashy sunset's hue, lingering pink and
violet across the sky's last blue. This is woman's long desire
and progress of the fire, a robe of darkness flung away and
she with it, that man wonders at and cannot comprehend.

"What 'beauty' is this I seem to own that sets in
motion your desire to touch, Bellerophon? How glad I am
for it, this celebration of openness you invite me to! The
promise of a journey to the other side of mountains where
I've never been, where I myself become the quaking of the
earth and the rushing boulders streaming through my body
with their avalanche of stars, such a flood of brightness that
takes me by surprise, again, again, waves of pleasure in
which I drown nor wish to save myself, dancing with this
thunder that you are, that I become with you."

"How can I make this pleasure last, Aristomache,
that seems so brief? How do I slow hot flames consuming
me, when I have only held you a short while?"

"There is a way. In stillness is revealed the depth of
sharing's possibility. To be present in this moment, now:
That is the harbor of safety in our storm of love. A haven
when the boulders crash down inside you so.

"Would you know the greater opening that man and
woman's union has a chance to be, the key to the long
embrace? Then learn the skills of the inner battlefield.
Enter at the gate where stillness waits, where feelings are a

door to wider openness. Sensations once so urgently dangerous shall be your steed to ride the storms of love, gleaning power from intensity. Then the fire need no longer rush so quickly out, as though that is the only way for it to go.

"The light of your attention, when you watch: That is the key. Letting that subtle dance of sensation-awareness take the Thinker's place a while.

"Shall you prevail? This victory must be bought with many battles in the inner life, a victory over noise. For your whole being to open, no longer sky out there and self inside. And you will know: You are the open hand, and no longer need to clutch the little wind you thought you were inside the darkness of the fist you called your self."

The evenings Bellerophon feasted with the Amazons; the nights he gloried in Aristomache's embrace. Letting rare elixirs be released that had forever been inside of him.

Bellerophon also took up the bow and studied hard to know its craft. Each day he stood opposite Aristomache in the long green field with throngs of Amazons drawn up to watch on either side. Each day he sent the bronze-tipped wood so fearfully out, winging in the direction of his cherished one. Each day his arrow missed by a wide expanse, by his design, for he had no skill yet to guide its way. Each time Aristomache sent her shaft into the young oak tree by which he stood. Each night they lay in each other's arms, laughed and talked and wondered at the stars, and loved. An embrace ever lengthening as he learned how.

"Aristomache, such a harvest of power from love's intensity in your embrace! Why do men hurry so, hardly even touching what they may become? Why does death's precipice lure them so, when they might live? Is it that no one shows them what is possible?"

From the captains of archery Bellerophon learned the art of breath, to ride the inner tides until waves of silence joined him to the sky. Learned to stretch the arc of wooden bow til heaven and earth were bent connected at the string, and self squeezed out. Self and target became one. As he had indeed become one with Aristomache, no boundaries in a brightness shared. It was the lightning he fitted to the bow as his proficiency grew and the space of the meadow grew ever smaller for the storm to move across.

How long are we given to walk among these summer woods? How many days shall we own to enjoy love? However long it is not long enough. The heart cries out there must be many summers more. But the golden autumn comes; the meadow's destiny is not eternal green.

When thirty days had gone by and thirty arrows had been launched into the tree, Bellerophon took up the bow toward his beloved Aristomache. The Amazons, the sun, the meadow stood to watch. Ever closer to Aristomache's side he dared to will the arrow's flight, but he did not figure for the wind, those long thin fingers so mischievous! The arrow went too high and fell far left lodging its long branch in Aristomache's breast.

In long frantic leaps he ran to her, held her in despairing arms, gasping tears as she looked at him with one last smile, that smile he loved. "Bellerophon, my great-hearted love. See . . . You have conquered us!"

Bellerophon left Themiscyra then on his great black horse with his fine black plume upon his helm, and at his side his long sword that had so briefly kissed the body of the one he loved. Her blood, like her long kisses, rapidly evaporating memories. Was it not his own blood her heart had shed?

Bellerophon took the arrows and the bow, his skill grown keen enough to shoot the rabbit in its flight, and he rode south. His mood was not victorious.

When King Iobates learned Bellerophon was on his way he dispatched warriors to ambush him, to finish the job at which the Amazons, the Chimera, and the Solymoi had failed. All the anger of Bellerophon was unleashed on those unfortunates. He left them all behind him where they fell.

A tidal wave on the coast of Lycia set King Iobates to wondering: Was Bellerophon guilty of accosting his daughter as she had accused? Iobates showed Bellerophon the letter received so long ago and Anteia's lie was obvious. Iobates in apology offered his other daughter Philonoe to be his wife, so that Bellerophon was heir to the throne of Lycia.

Now you know what happened there when Bellerophon invaded them. As not even Homer did.

Chapter Six

The Journey Is Prepared

I made my way home with the writings I'd acquired, turning the language toward our own as my mother Susa heard — intent on every spear-thrust, every taunt and each response of those who stood to hurl their javelins and meet with swords; imagining each arrow's flight, mourning every hero's wound as though it were some deep-pierced lover's blood. And searching for each reference to what at times appeared, rare as stars in the early morning sky — the warrior-sisterhood of Amazons by the Black Sea.

How Old Are You?

"How old are you, Strax?" strangers sometimes ask.

"How are we to know?" is my reply, "I was raised by wolves."

They laugh! And squint their eyes at me to know if it is true. I seem ready enough for human company, only growling when I sit at meat. Talking to the wind and fire and dancing with the lightning in the summer storms. Later someone tells them I am heir to Susa's throne; that I have created this story about wolves, perhaps to belay the question of who my father was. Then my mother's story is retold: Susa set adrift at sea.

Wolves. Certainly it might have been. Always I have slept outside, snug in sacks of fur to watch the evening sky, breathing in the cold clear air. To watch the circling stars, the ones that stay and the few that fall. Some mornings find me buried deep in snow.

Once I awoke to see a wolf looking down at me! We startled each other and the wolf ran off. But the next morning there were two of them, she had gone to get her mate. We watched each other with delight; then slowly she came near and licked my face. I fed them after that, what my pockets held of dinner scraps, until finally they would run with me among the trees.

In the mornings when I was young my mother cooked me fish or reindeer meat over the fire. Flat cakes of grain, sprouts and roots and seeds. In summer golden cloudberries with the cream of goats. In winter eating from a pot kept always hot. Then outside again to see the blue sky settled on the crisp white snow, to make a perfect fit.

Inge

Of our clan's young women there was only one my desire reached out to touch. Inge. Her spirit was a warmth and a cooling wind, the only one to whom I gave my heart. Inge was a brave warrior too, fighting alongside of me when we were called to go; for our clan has few enemies but many friends to whom we journey in their defense.

How I wanted Inge those years when childhood departs and one begins to become a man. How beautiful she was! We talked and laughed and took long walks and rides. She would not give her long kiss to me though I could tell she wanted to. "If I gave you my whole kiss, Strax, how could I not also give you all my self? That time may be, but is not yet."

Inge dreamed the traditional salt-dream, prepared for maidens to know whom they would wed, making a highly-salted cake to eat before she went to bed. Her future husband would be the one to come into her dream the legend said, with water for her thirst. And yes! I am the man who came to her. I soothed her dreaming thirst. Even so

---

month after month I waited afterwards and dreamed alone. Until the night she came to me.

That night the whole extended clan was feasting at a house nearby. I didn't like the loud after-dinner foolishness the older warriors enjoyed; so when I had eaten I went home, off to bed in my furs out in the snowy field. Better to enjoy the stars and the company of my thoughts, and that deep sky inside when thoughts have fled.

I could hear the others shouting and laughing and breaking things off in the distance of the dark and silver night. Suddenly Inge! Shedding her clothes and crawling in beside me in my furs to lie inside my arms. How good her slender body felt! Giving me the long awaited kiss. I held her close, so happy to have her there with me.

"What made you decide to come?"

She shivered out a laugh and buried her face inside my neck. "Oh Strax! Tonight I have seen Death. It made me realize how much I wanted you, and how little time we each may have."

"You saw Death!"

"Yes, Death came very close to me tonight. Death caught away my hair."

I caressed her head and yes, one of her braids was gone. "Oh Inge, tell me you did not!"

"I did. I knew my braids had now grown very long. So after the feasting when everyone was drunk enough, making long and loud request, I offered myself finally to them. Stood against the wall with my two long braids pinned up to be separated from my head.

"My mother wailed and threw her face into her hands but it was too late for her to interfere. It was time I should participate in traditions of our clan; I would show them I was not afraid. I threw my shoulders back and my brave breasts out, inviting them to throw. I was very calm and did not flinch as the bolts came through the air like fire. And thunder when they hit! I almost lost an ear! I watched the lightning as it flew.

"It was Olaf finally that lopped off a braid and strode to receive his prize, a briefest kiss. Then my mother stormed up to take me off, to save a braid for another day, to many a boo and hiss. So yes, I did. And Death came very close."

"And Death has thrust you now into my arms."

"Yes, Strax. I needed to see Death first, before I could begin to live. Then afterwards I knew, if I had given Death a kiss and been returned alive, then it was also time to have your arms around me in the night, to explore this thing called life that Death has missed. To share with you the mystery I've heard so much about but have not touched, this festival of brightness you've desired so much we'd share. I shall be the crisp white snow to you, and you the deep blue sky to me, to form a perfect fit."

Spring

Mountains, sky, gray against gray. Birds flying fast and dark, as though there were a place to go. Snow has turned to rain.

"Strax! Winter's white bird's let all its feathers fall. It's spring! The world melts to green again, spilling us to put invasions down, to put the fires of evil out. Soon it is time for battle strategies!"

"Oh, Inge. Do not come with me to fight this year if there is war. How I fear some blade shall enter you."

"Through me here? Or here?" Poking at her slender sides. "I shall stand the test, fighting on in spite of such thin cuts. I have blood to spare to sate their blades!"

"You'll throw yourself headlong toward sword and spear. The thought of it gives me despair." I put my head into my hands.

"Do you mind so much that I go off with you to war?"

"It drives me wild with grief! Such a disastrous waste. So much wisdom and beauty, your amazing body squandered, traded for some careless arrow's flight! Let others go this year to fight and bleed."

"And if their blood proves not to be enough? If one drop more may be the one to fill the tide to victory? One heart's drum more to lend its rhythm to the battle dance?" She grasps her high-cliffed ribs. "See how much I have to offer! How strong my drum!"

"If that drum be broken, Inge, so breaks my own."

Sá hon valkyrjur vítt um komnar
görvar at ríða til Goðþjóðar:
Skuld hélt skildi, en Skögul önnur,
Gunnr, Hildr, Göndul ok Geirskögul;
nú eru taldar nönnur Herjans,
görvar at ríða grund valkyrjur.

On all sides I saw Valkyries assemble
Ready to ride to the ranks of the gods.
Skuld bore the shield, and Skogul rode next,
Gud, Hild, Gondul and Geirskogul.
Herjan's maidens, of whom you have heard,
Valkyries ready to ride o'er the earth.

The Voluspa, the 'Sibyl's Prophecy' from the **Elder Edda.** Compiled late 10th century A.D.

Whose Hands Are These

Summer follows spring and clash of arms, with Inge fighting by my side.

Autumn then, and all too soon the winter's snow. What is this water in my mouth as I awake from nodding by the fire alone? It is my tears.

Again the savage memory of Inge last year on the battlefield. Again I feel the storm surrounding us. Again I try to stop the blade that rushes through her body like the silver lightning through a winter tree. Again I am too late.

I kneel down by her and we both look to see.

"Such a small opening, Strax. It is sure to heal," she finds a smile. Looks up at me with those eyes I love as I hold her in my arms.

"My brave Inge! What do you feel?" I watch the urgent crimson stream.

"It is like dreams that almost come before you fall asleep."

"Inge! Do not leave me yet!"

"Strax, do you remember that night when the men stood me up against the wall to throw the battle ax, that night I first came to you to hold you until dawn? How I told you I saw Death? But I did not tell you this: How Death called out to me that night: 'Inge!' so that I turned my head to see; and the ax cut my braid where a moment ago my head had been."

"My sweet Inge. Why do you tell me now?"

"Because now I know, all this time with you, it was all a wonderful gift to me. And because what I see now is not at all like that dark shadow I saw then. Are these the Valkyries, these many horses that I see? What are these gentle hands that reach for me?"

I hold Inge close to me there on the battlefield. But she has gone with them.

———

The Wind and Fire

The sky, the trees, my heart have turned to ice. The fire on the hearth licks at me to set me loose but it cannot. Inge is dead two winters now. How much of me she took with her! At night I lie awake to await the dawn; by day I await the night with hope to sleep again. What have I become? What value has my life? Only the fire and wind respond: "Gray," says the wind, "and cold."

Though the fire has an answer brighter than the wind's response, with intent to heal. "Fire," comes my reply, "Everything I look at speaks of things that might have been. Living is sharp and tears my heart. My life is hardly worth the lives of those that give themselves in trade for it, these salmon, this cabbage, this caribou. Let me die so they may live."

"What would Inge think to have you speak like this?"

"Inge no longer thinks! No longer shares her breath with you or me or with the wind that moans for her outside."

"You have lost half yourself. Will it not grow back one day?"

"It were easier far to lose the other half of me."

"Go then, if my brightness cannot reach to heal, talk to the restless wind of all of this!"

So I go out to have a conversation with the wind. Lie on my back in the knee-high snow, feather soft and cool against my head. No stars now. Only the gray unmoving wall of sky that imprisons me. Soon I know, if I lie here long enough, all the pain will pass and the spark that's grown so faint in me will rise into the wind, to groan with it at Inge's loss. The darkness will enfold and welcome my frail light, and fly away with me. To what? I do not care.

I close my eyes and let my thoughts fade off into a dream. The wind moans and reaches out for me, surrounding that frail spark I am. I go with it.

Journey Interrupted

Sounds, touch, call for my return. "Strax! What are you doing here? Where is your coat?" Young Bror has his hand on my arm, shaking me. "The Queen your mother calls! She is busy with the stories of the Greeks you brought, with questions for you again."

I keep my eyes closed, hope to have my darkening dream go on. My spirit struggles from the icy darkness, upwards toward Bror's bright voice, considering it. Ah. My mother. Wise Matriarch. Patient, loving, fierce. Shrewder of legends, unraveler of mysteries. How she works to bring the past to life again. I have tried that. Now I join the past to die with it.

"Strax! Do you hear?"

Yes, I will go to see my mother one last time. Then return and trade this icy kingdom for the long and peaceful dark. Let someone else be heir of this vast snow one day.

Conversation with the Fire

My mother sits reading in her house of logs and stone, so bright with its great hearth. "Strax. Why are you so wet? Sit here against the fire until you warm!"

I turn to the fire, blow on it to fan the embers up. "That is a breath I know," the fire spits. "Back from your conversation with the wind outside? What did it say?"

"The wind took my spark within its hands, out from the body's labyrinth, spiraling into the darkness toward the distant dawn awaiting us."

"A long voyage to begin. How far did you go?"

"What seemed a quiet-enough adventure was met soon with storms, tempests set in motion from every heart my thoughtless words had stung. So many incidents relived: Every time my heedless pride had ever set aside compassion's light, the many moments lived for self, my lack of interest in the common storms that we all share, all pulled at me to slow my progress forward to the light. When it grew sometimes calm secrets and mysteries would begin to be revealed. But I remember none of them, they all are flown. For someone came to call me back again."

I turn to my mother. Has she heard? I cannot care. "Mother, I have come to say goodbye."

"Where do you plan to go?"

"Mother, when it is day I long for night so I may sleep, so to forget. Then when dark presses in on me I wait for light's thin cheer again. Neither of them welcomes me. Why should I live any longer here? Better I should fly away, wherever warriors go that no longer wish to dream of battlefields, and those who bled on them."

"Oh Strax. Why away so soon? You only begin to learn why you are here."

"Oh?"

"Life is a dance with pleasure and with pain. Shall you dance with one of them? Then you shall have the other one."

"I shall escape from both!"

"You have not learned the way! Until then you only fly to greater darkness yet. To dream your misery continually, sad dreaming in a land where shadows flow instead of light. Where you will remain a worm."

"A worm?"

"Man forgets why he is here, what he may become. He flees from pain, so dark, and chases pleasure, bright and brief, though he cannot for long escape the one or seize the other in his grasp. He eats his way along life's leaf, and tomorrow one leaf more. Can he not see what he may be — the butterfly on its new wings? May he not also fly so free beneath the sun? Shall he not reach for stars?"

"Mother, I am so tired."

"Sleep Strax, here by the fire. Ask your greater dream to comfort you with what may be."

Dream

I sleep, and my dreaming travels to a distant battlefield. Women warriors! Magnificent and strong, fearless as they face the army of men confronting them. An arrow finds one woman's flesh. She falls. The point comes loose, lodged far inside. She grasps the disconnected feathered wood and flings it far from her, then watches as the noble stream pours out. She turns her head to look at me. Such an imploring look. Such sea-green eyes! She rises to face the enemy again. And I awake.

It is late. The coals on my mother's hearth still glow; I breathe to rouse the flames. "Fire, what is this dream of the woman warrior I have had?"

"You are invited."

"What invitation do you mean?"

"To remove the battle's sting, the arrowhead deep-hid in her. A body strong enough for such thin thorns, but what is threatened is her way of life, the oldest matriarchy on the Earth. Long these women have been strong to mend the region all around, far as their circles reached! But now two waves rush over them from east and west. Shall all their ancient clan, all the secrets they have saved, be allowed to perish 'neath that flood of war? They hold so many answers though few think to inquire. So much light, though all be so content with dark. What wisdom the ancient realms once held these women rescued from the dust as kingdoms fell."

"Fire," comes my response, "why must I have such dreams? Is my heart not torn wide enough by Inge's loss? Why did Inge wish so much to go to battle at my side? If only she had not!"

"You blame yourself. Feel you have failed."

"Yes."

"But how? Did you have other choices you might have made?"

"No. Yes. Perhaps."

"You unjustly blame yourself. See, this door — that Inge's warrior-spirit opens now for your release, so that the dream could come to you. A dream to renew your heart, and your mother's too."

"If these women warriors perish what is that to me! Shall I bind yet other warrior women to my heart, to have them tear it from my breast again? To see them fall on the battlefield, then own a deeper darkness where their brightness danced when they are gone?"

Susa's Advice

"Why not go find them Strax?" my mother says when I relate the dream, what the fire has said.

"Two hundred years have come and gone since Persia set fire to Athens; now the embers are fanned to exact revenge, it is Asia's turn to be attacked. King Philip of Macedonia takes his war of retribution to the Persian lands, styling himself as champion of Greece with his son Iskander's help. Philip's advance forces already begin to cross into the east, and he will follow soon with the larger force.

"Your knowledge of the healing arts can serve your quest, to find and join these armies on the move. Make your way by sea to Carthage then to Greece, then across the Aegean Sea into war's dark storm. The Amazons live there, where great armies soon shall meet. Surely they'll have some part to play in this.

"How I wish to know more than this little the Greeks have said of them. Are they wise? What do they guard for the human race? Tell me of the manner they wage war and put themselves at risk, for that is all their passion and the battlefield is their delight.

"Tell them how the ocean saved your mother from the anger of the men; how you are my son who bears to them the spirit of the sea and wind that has protected us. Tell them what the fire has said — you will return with the daughter that I never had."

଼

It is the time in our far northern home to burrow deep into the sleeping Earth; to lie in furs beside the dreaming fire, wondering that summer is so long to come. But I have gone to discover mysteries that time forgot, to encounter women famous for their beauty, strength, and privacy. To mend the broken colors of my heart and shatter them again.

I sail into the mouth of war. So easy to die on this journey I undertake. The women warriors await my quest, but death stands in the way. If death shall move aside, I will discover them. A simple dance, but steps beyond imagining.

The darkness looms wide in me where meaning should have been, the light new wings my mother urged on me, the flight of sun, the quest for stars. And something in me knows, if life is void of meaning death is so very dangerous.

Starting Out

Today I sail. In the small room's shadows I prepare. Clothing thrust into a leather pack. A wooden spoon, a knife, bowl, cup. A purse of gold, a pouch of herbs. What more? Sword and battle ax and cloak. It is enough.

Morning fire flows down the sky. Past forests and lakes to the ice-gray sea where long-oared ships stand by the shore. Sails that wait to fill with sun.

"Strax!" A call on the wind.

Out into the early light I go, then quickly back again to find one precious cargo more almost forgot: Objects bright shining red, short as fingers are, the tears of the sun from the Western Land enfolded in the ancient map I won.

They are to be a "cherished gift," the fire has told me so, "with power to bend the course of storms."

Many come to see our ships set prows into the silver mist. From heights along the shore long horns sound lofty greetings and farewell.

We answer them with our own horns on board, a long and plaintive cry that bids a Northman's spirit meet whatever challenge has been set. A sound that echoes in the soul, summoning ancestors' spirits to meet the horns that plead so long and low there high above. The horns once heard live always in the heart.

Sailing South

We sail south past the great chalk cliffs, the salty brine splashing wild against the face. Turn toward the Middle Sea and the Gates of Heracles controlled by Cadiz, a city settled long ago by Phoenician colonists where I have friends, some of those who sailed with Urfi to the west. They are hoping for our visit, expecting us if we decide to come.

We blow our horns. Soon our friends sail out to us with oranges, figs, olives, bread, and wine, bidding us come ashore a while. We feast much of the day and night, discussing seafarers' lore and news from the Western Land. I tell our hosts of my quest to find the Amazons.

"Do you want so much to die? You've read the stories! They don't welcome men."

"I'll find a way."

"Hmm."

"But tell me, when the Amazons escaped from the overlords on Atlantis long ago . . ."

"To maintain their purity, yes."

"Why did they not bring along some men with them? Men as pure as they?"

"None would! The men were wed to the desire for control, as taught them by those overlords. And there were things being done to males then, too, that the women decided they'd best avoid."

"For instance?"

"Things happen in the male baby's brain when it is born so that the mind becomes a maze to him. Done to maintain him as a slave."

"So then, I, we . . ."

"Yes. We own it, you and I. A purely male situation as it turns out. A bath our brains receive at birth, some substance allowed to pour through it so that a man has two brains now, a right and left, with some thin portal in between past which attention must come and go. While woman has one whole brain, entire, it's functioning far different. Feelings take shape in her more plain; whereas in him sentiments and sensations are too soon bullied out by thoughts, thin shadows that loom only briefly in him beneath the thinker's intense sun."

"There's nothing to be done for it?"

"Oh yes. Gates may be opened. Guardians dispelled. Thresholds crossed. There are skills, strategies, prayers, substances, sounds, help from Creator may be sought. Best is to have a woman teach you what she knows, be with her as that ancient dream she holds unfurls, for both to be fulfilled by it. Few men on Earth are aware what possibilities await. They ignore the legacy woman holds for them; they rush to power as a way of life and build up self into a tower whence they soon fall. Woman meanwhile? She forgets the light she holds that pales to ash from lack of use. It fades, the ancient dream that lives in her. And few know what the promise is that rusts in them."

"So the Amazons, they keep the ancient dream alive?"

"Ha! They own the dream in its bright entirety. And they have arrows too. What need have they for such as you?"

On To Carthage

We bid our hosts in Cadiz farewell and sail on through the Gates of Heracles, eastward along the coast of northern Africa to Carthage, now the major force upon the sea.

My friend Urfi is ecstatic to see me again and welcomes me into his home. I tell him my mission and he ponders it a while, then offers to provide introductions among the Greeks to fulfill my intention. Even go with me to Athens to see to it! "The approaching war with Persia will give you good opportunities for travel east," he says.

Meanwhile he urges me to extend my stay in Carthage. Plies me with tours of the excellent library the Carthaginians have collected with such great care. Urges on me a visit to Egypt first, to see the great pyramid there that he's explored. Warns me of the danger I insist upon.

"You know the stories about the Amazons, Strax! Bellerophon, Theseus, Heracles, Achilles, Orestes: Only these men have met them and remained alive. What makes you think you have a chance of finding them and living out the day?"

"I shall live or I shall not, it is the same to me. My heart is heavy from Inge's death; give me depth enough to sink and I am content to follow her into the dreaming sea."

"Oh, Strax. So sad if you shall fall before the arrows of the Amazons. Please stay here with us!" But Urfi knew that I would not.

My northern escort turn their prows west toward home again rather than take me on to Greece. We will not tempt the Greeks with the mystery we are, phantoms from the north wind's cave. Nor spill out imaginings of that wide secret the Atlantic holds.

Strategy

Carthage. 337 B.C.

Ashore at Carthage Urfi ponders how I might fulfill my quest. "King Philip has already sent an advance force over the Aegean, Strax, ten thousand men on foot and a thousand more on horse. Greece built cities long ago across the sea which the Persians now control — that King Philip and his son Iskander intend to liberate from Persian rule, and throw the Persians out."

"Urfi, are those cities near the homeland of the Amazons?"

"Near enough. The Amazons have many friends nearby, relationships maintained for centuries. Some cities will welcome Philip's liberation force and some may not. Those cities may send to the Amazons for help. Would the Amazons not come to give them aid? Certainly they may."

"I must be there to see it all unfold! That was my mother's plan. How shall we manage it?"

"Greeks will be sailing from Athens across the Aegean to reinforce King Philip's advance Macedonians. Why not travel with them there? You are proficient in the healing arts. Might you not serve as physician, to be on hand in case the Amazons attack?"

Athens

Three days later we are on our way by ship to Athens to fulfill the plan. We lodge with people Urfi knows, then go out into the early evening air. Such a beautiful city! So much to see!

The Athenians are all discussing King Philip's war against the Persian King Darius III. The first wave of Macedonians already liberate the cities along the Aegean coast and a second wave of a thousand Greeks is being formed up now to sail from Athens to meet them there. More a political obligation than much else, it seems. It is with these I wish to sail.

"Where are those who will sail to join the Macedonian advance force, across the Aegean Sea?" Urfi asks, and we are directed to the barracks in a squalid part of town resembling more a tavern than a military post. We find the Captain of the fleet in the loudest part of the tawdry scene, and Urfi goes up to him with me in tow.

"My friend wishes to have passage across the Aegean with you. He can pay." The Captain has never seen anyone like me before with such a sheaf of wild red hair. Everyone is suddenly quiet.

"We go to war. No paid passengers."

"He is proficient in the healing arts."

"What do you give for bad digestion?" the Captain grins.

"Peppermint. Three drops of oil, or some tea," I say.

Everyone laughs when they hear me talk. "What strange Greek you speak! Who taught it to you? Where do you come from?"

"The Carthaginians taught me Greek. I come from far north of here."

"And your reason for going across the Aegean Sea?"

"I go in search of ancient herbal lore I have heard is collected there."

"Herbs? Ha! What do you do for a man with an arrow lodged in him?"

"I give some wine. Then if it has a barb I ask permission to cut it out of him, or to push it through. Or give him a deeper second wound to help him to forget the first."

Everybody laughs. "That's why we drink our wine ahead of time!" the Captain laughs loudest of them all. "Can you fight?"

"When I need to. But I don't anger easily."

"Do you have a sword? Can you use a bow?"

"Yes, I have a sword. I use a bow. And a battle ax if someone succeeds in upsetting me."

"Will you fight alongside of us?"

"I'd rather not. I have no enemies there."

"What if we are attacked while you're along with us?"

"Along the way? Yes, that is fair. But then I shall go on, wherever it is I must."

"Yes you can come with us, as physician's helper. We sail in two weeks. Come back then. Bring your own blankets and sword, and money to trade for food. And your peppermint!" Everyone guffaws again and we go out.

Urfi congratulates me on my success, and we join his friends to feast on lamb and bread and good Greek wine.

"Why didn't he charge me passage, Urfi?"

"He believes you will trade everything you own for food. Or gamble it. That by the time you cross the Aegean all you have will belong to them."

I tour Athens with Urfi the following days, enjoying the sculpture related to the Amazons' assault on Athens before the Trojan War, almost a thousand years ago. The sculptures of Amazons are numerous along the walls of the Parthenon and the Temple of Aesculapius, and to the south at the Temple of Apollo, in the countryside at Phigaleia.

"War had never come to the Athenians on their homeland before this attack by the Amazons, Strax. Long before the Persians came."

"Amazons and Athenians at war? Why?"

"King Theseus sailed into the Black Sea and carried off their princess Antiope. Or else she meant to go with him, it's not quite clear so many stories have been told of it. Once she arrived in Athens she married Theseus and they had a child. When the Amazons invaded Athens to bring her back she fought against her sisters defending Athens against them. And she died."

"Urfi, how excellent this marble statuary is! A glorious clash of arms, the rush of battle all around! So much respect the artists show to these women judged worthy to fight with men, a true test for their Hellenic steel. Such frenzy of energy!"

"It is a frenzy you may know soon enough."

Setting Sail with the Greeks

336 B.C. Iskander's father Philip is still king in Macedonia.

When the day comes finally for the fleet to sail I embark with the Greek soldiers, a surly lot. I am a tall straw-haired mystery to them. Aside from my pack and the clothes I wear I carry only my sword inside its sheath and my single-headed battle ax. And some peppermint I have acquired!

Several Greek soldiers ask to buy my sword, dwarf-forged in caverns deep beneath the earth, beautiful and longer than my arm. But I tell them of that dread curse the sword will bring to any but a warrior of my clan who wields its ornate length, and that keeps their hands off for a while. Even so I sleep on it while we are at sea.

I listen as the Greeks discuss their exploits, telling about lands where they have been. Much of this I decide has no more substance than the air. One of the loudest says he's been outside the Gates of Heracles into the Western Sea. That they sailed out to the great abyss, heard its mighty roar and felt the salty mist that waterfall threw high from its low gorge. Then turned around to live, for they rowed hard.

My words leap out at him on wings too quick, "A gorge and waterfall, out in the Western Sea?" And I laugh at the thought of it. Everyone looks at me. Until now I'd not said much to anyone.

"Yes. An enormous water-cliff!"

"There's no such thing. Or else it only opens up for you when you are there."

"You say I lie?" He begins insulting me and draws his sword. Everyone gleefully carves a space for us, pushing me forward to fight with him.

"I have no quarrel with you," I say. "You like to lie: Is that a sufficient reason for you to die?" But it is little use. How savage the fist surrounding those who take offense! Of course he bellows, "To the death!" Leaving me no choice but to draw my sword, likely the prize he seeks when I am felled.

He charges me and I defend, letting him tire himself and hoping he will decide to stop. But when I ask him finally if he has fought enough he answers me with one more attack and there the story ends, as he forgets how offended he had been.

No one bothers me after that. Some even seek me as a friend. And I still have my sword as the Greek ships disgorge us onto the coast near the ancient town of Troy.

The March to Cyzicus

It will be a three-day march from Troy to the small city of Cyzicus, busy resisting the advance force of the Macedonians like a snail braced inside its shell from the crow's attack. Being liberated from Persian rule must not seem to them the better plan.

"West and east collide," one of my Greek shipmates explains to me, "and we shall be there as they do. The Persians own cities along the Aegean coast that the Greeks established long ago, that pay tribute to the Persian King Darius now, and call him Lord. Darius has set up governors called Satraps to raise taxes; otherwise there is a great deal of autonomy for all those living in this part of the world. Some will side with the Persians, as being the wiser choice of two."

"Why not side with Macedonia and Greece?"

"Some will. Others see us as a momentary stream across their lands, soon to run dry again. And why not? Greece has been an area tempest-tossed with warring city states — Athens, Sparta, Corinth, Thebes. Only in very recent years has any unity been forced on Greece — by the Macedonian King Philip who dreams their dreams for them and schemes vengeance for the Persian attacks on Greece, that time they burned Athens' temples down. Philip feels it is his destiny! One he has taken on himself."

"So the Greeks are Philip's allies, and the war begins. Why don't the Persians mobilize to meet the threat?"

"There must be more pressing priorities for Darius," he shrugs. "Troubles in Egypt, who can say? But that is small excuse for allowing Philip's advance force such easy crossing of the Hellespont. Now our reinforcements are arriving too! It will take a fair-sized force to cast us out."

"So, if the Macedonians are indeed being welcomed as liberators by some towns, why not this city where we're bound? What is its name again?"

"Cyzicus. They have a very Persian-allied government and no desire to be 'freed' by us. The Macedonians will succeed at overcoming them before we have arrived to help, that is my guess."

The Shadows Are Alive

Somewhere between Troy and Cyzicus

The shadows are alive with the horses of the Amazons, archers with lightning set to bows. They watch from the trees as the Greek soldiers make their way along a valley full of woods and fields, the first three hundred soldiers with round shields, bronze helms and spears.

Splashes of tranquil sun slant through the leaves. The men tell jokes and laugh. One swats a fly and swears. One takes a drink and spits. A noise . . . He turns his head . . .

Storm! Women warriors where only sun and leaves had been! They guide their horses with their knees. They loose the lightning from their bows. The Greeks wheel and fall in wild distress.

"Amazons!" Word spreads as the rest of us run up then rush back again to be among some rocks where horses cannot go. Reluctantly I fight beside the Greeks to assist them as I had agreed. How gentle I wish my sword to be as I do my best to defend myself.

The day is hot. The Greeks fighting naked with their bronze helms and large round shields are no match for the Amazons, also mostly naked behind their crescent shields. The Amazons play cat and mouse with the Greeks as their arrows find whatever flesh the Greeks have left exposed. Then as the Greeks fall into disarray the women attack with swords upraised in wild charges seemingly designed to simply provide themselves as noble targets for our bows. Archery and charges alternate and by late afternoon the remaining Greeks are awaiting for darkness in which somehow to escape.

I go in search for water in the woods. When I find a forest stream I drink and fill a flask, then submerge myself in the gentle tide to wash away the battle dust and sweat. How good the silver water feels! I come up dripping from the brook to enjoy the sun, only to be confronted by a woman with an arrow on her bow. There is nowhere I can run or go.

"Who are you? What are you doing here? You do not look like a Greek to me." The finger of an arrow points, one twitch from being loosed, with only air to guard against a flight too swift into my heart. The eyes green ice. The hair a plaything of the wind. What excellence nature has conspired to show me as I die. How beautiful she is!

"I am Strax. From far north of here, chronicler and physician to my mother our queen, sent to be an observer of the conflicts here."

"Strax the North-man?" Narrowing her eyes at me. "What strange Greek you speak!"

She lowers her bow and approaches me. "I may give your body to my arrow's thirst. And to decide I'll have a story from you first in your butchered Greek. Perhaps to know the truth of it, this royal mother it may be you have."

"Of course."

"Why do you travel with these Greeks?"

"For finding you."

"Oh?"

Then I tell her all: How two men had sired me and Susa was cast out to sea. How my mother now rules in our land of snow, accosted by shadows that wonder at her leadership if war should come. Of Inge my lost love and my desire to abandon life now she is gone. That I have come to find the Amazons, for that honorable way to die they surely would provide. One arrow only I'd require.

Thalestris listens to it all.

Then the wind comes briskly up, moving roughly from a distance through the trees as though a cloud flung from the sky. Taking my hair into its hands. "Urfi!" the wind demands.

So I tell Thalestris about Urfi too, and his Phoenician clan. How they taught me Greek. About the wager for the old map I won. How I've brought it as a gift.

"Where is it now, the map?"

"There in my pack," motioning toward the water's edge where I'd let it fall.

"We had a copy of an old map once."

"Yes. That Heracles stole from you. This may be the same."

"Is it so much you know?"

I shrug. "Only the little I've been told."

"What else have you heard about?"

"The Bellerophon tree, with the thirty arrows in its trunk. Is it still there?"

She stares at me. "You bring this across the Aegean Sea — a gift for us? Why would you do that?"

"Because of what the fire has said. The map will be strong to bend the course of storms."

"The fire speaks to you?"

"And the wind. As it did just now.

"If I might see this map . . ."

I cross the stream and retrieve my pack. Set the rolled up map into her hands. She opens it as though some sacred text, and as she does the tears of the sun fall out, all twelve red fingers I'd enclosed in it.

"Tears of the sun," I say, "from the far Western Land. Another gift to you."

"I've heard of them. Wait for me here. Others shall hear these words you've said." She disappears into the woods, my tears and map in hand.

Invitation

I recover my sword and battle ax and clothes. Lie down in the afternoon's last light to rest. And sleep.

When I awake I smell smoke, sense movement all around me in the evening light. Then I plainly see, what had been our private forest is now occupied by Amazons. Some kneel in groups preparing food laid out on fires, their battle-nakedness enclosed now in long robes. Someone has covered me with a blanket as I slept. Seeing me awake Thalestris approaches, goes to her knees beside me on the grass.

"The vanquished Greeks have abandoned you, Strax, fled in all directions to escape. Our mission is accomplished; so we return to Cyzicus to join the battle there against the greater force of Macedonians. You are free to go."

Perhaps I frown. I've no plan for going anywhere.

"Though here is an invitation: To come with us to Cyzicus, to provide your story of the battle here today. An opportunity seldom afforded men, to ride with us. Your honesty and your gifts prepare that place and you are safe with us on my authority. I am Thalestris, Queen of Battle here."

So it is I join the Amazons on the two-day journey to Cyzicus where the fight is underway against the besieging Macedonians. Sitting at the evening fires to hear the stories of battles the women tell, invited to feel at ease with them. And when so many stories have been told and it is late Thalestris bids me come with her into her tent to rest.

"Do you know the long embrace?" she asks.

"The one Bellerophon was shown, that time he came to you?"

"Is it so much you've heard, indeed?"

"I have heard this: Two bodies form a lamp the lightning longs to fill, if time and self are fled and there is space for it. And sparks set too soon loose do not build fires."

"Come, ride the thunder with me then."

Involvement of the Amazons

"What brings you into battle with the Greeks?" I ask next day. "How did the Amazons become involved?"

"King Philip's Macedonians crossed into Asia not many months ago; his dream of revenge on Persia has brought them to our shore."

"They are your enemies, the Macedonians?"

"No. Though their Greek allies were less than friends in times gone by."

"Why attack them then? Are you intent to throw them back into the sea?"

"We might have swept them from the beach like sand before the wind if we'd so wished, that time they began to cross the Aegean Sea."

"Why then did you not?"

"We had no desire to; neither for them or against, nor for the Persians, certainly. The Macedonians made the crossing with their advance force and meanwhile every city along the coast was panicking. The Persian Satrap in nearby Dascylium sent urgent messages to King Darius saying he was overwhelmed with requests for protection. Letter after panicked letter to the King: 'The Macedonian advance force is crossing the Hellespont!' 'Now is across!' 'Now is calling on cities to open their gates to them, to pledge loyalty to Macedonia. What am I to do?'"

"And?"

"Darius sent word back, 'Do what you can; you handle it.' We lived in that Satrap's area, poor man; when he sent out his broad cry for help against the invading Macedonians we said no, we had no interest in their war."

"But you went anyway?"

"A plea for assistance arrived from friends, the town of Cyzicus not far from here, that would not allow the 'liberators' in. Macedonians were stacked in rows before their walls, intent to make an example out of them. So we sent a thousand warriors to assist, just as we sent warriors long ago to Troy."

"Ah."

"When we learned Greek reinforcements were on their way, those you've fought beside, I left part of our women in Cyzicus and led the rest to bar their way, to prevent the Greeks' reaching the main fight. And that much at least is accomplished, a victory from which our only prize is a North-man who speaks strange Greek."

Saving Cyzicus

As we near Cyzicus to join the main battle we receive grim news. The Macedonians have attacked and been victorious. The little army of Cyzicus and the contingency of Amazons have been too small a dam before too strong a stream.

A conference is in progress, a meeting Thalestris attends without delay, introduced as having authority as it relates to the Amazons.

"The Cyzicans," the captain of the Macedonians says to her, "are to be killed, or sold as slaves."

"All of them?" Thalestris asks.

"Yes, all. And your women, for aiding them, shall expect some certain punishment. Why do you interfere with our advance? Are you allied with the Persians now?"

"No. We came to the aid of Cyzicus because they called on us. They have been our friends."

"Now you have one friend less. Go home and interfere no more. For punishment the Amazons shall submit warriors to be weakened ceremonially, two hundred thrust through the body with the sword. Then you may go."

"A just and generous recompense — that will accomplish nothing at all for you," Thalestris smiles.

"Oh?"

"You would be wise to conceive a way to keep us weak continually. Keep us too weak to enter the battle that brews soon with Darius, that king you must soon face, and all Persia that rides with him. Two hundred of us bled, a symbolic sacrifice? Ha! What is that? This victory of yours should purchase for you so much more. Why two hundred? Why not our whole nation of female savages subdued. To keep us weak in future days lest we should stray onto the battlefield again."

"And how might we do that?"

"The Amazons have never drawn each other's blood in practice among ourselves — long a strictly forbidden thing. No more than a ceremony here and there. But you could change all that, could impose on us a sacrifice more dear, even two hundred wounded every filling of the moon, so to punish us continually. To ensure this is our last foray into this world you wish to conquer for yourselves."

"How would you accomplish it, this sacrifice?"

"We would divide ourselves, forming two companies to compete in tournaments, winning laurels against each other in the field. It never has been done before. The whole population will turn out for it! Applauding to see our strongest warriors so vainly used, poured out in competition or practice before gathered crowds. Wide pools of blood make excellent spectacles."

"Why would you do this to yourselves?" came the question of a Greek officer who'd escaped our ambush in the woods, one of those who'd straggled in. "There is something you hope to gain from this! Surely it must be so."

"Of course there is," I smiled at him. "The champions will have the opportunity to fight without ever leaving home. Without having to choose one side or the other in this wide war you bring! Not all the Amazons are warriors; the rest will welcome such new spectacles, to see the blood of the strong released for sport. But more than that, I offer this for the citizens of Cyzicus."

"For Cyzicus?" the Greek officer asked, "How so?"

"To save them. Let them be hostages to what I now propose. Do not kill them or take them away as slaves. You have humbled them, taken away their urge to fight. Let that suffice. If we fail to keep our bargain, do what you will to them. They are our friends; their death would be our greatest punishment. Let our blood be sacrifice for them."

"Interesting. But how would we know you keep the bargain you propose?"

"To monitor these events and provide guaranty the Amazons would take home one of your men with them. This appointed observer we ourselves would be allowed to choose from among any men we have just fought against. One man among us there, to send you monthly messages as he monitors our self-inflicted brutalities.

"Shall you fail to receive adequate messages from him, this man you send to be with us? Then let Cyzicus suffer your full cruelty as it might have been. We will fight and bleed and fall in tests of strength at home — a ransom to let these people live that call us friends, that called on us for help. And it shall keep us weak."

"An ingenious scheme," the Greek captain squints, "Certainly worthy of Odysseus. Do the Amazons keep agreements they have made?"

"We do."

The Macedonian commander ponders it. Eyes boring into me, in search of any falsehood there.

"We are friends of the Cyzicans," I meet his gaze, "*not* enemies of the Macedonians."

"Oh?"

"It is lucky for the Macedonians that we are not! We might easily have prevented your crossing of the Hellespont had we desired. Like waves that reach the sand and fall back again, you would not have arrived here at all, this side of the Aegean Sea."

"Let it be so then," he decrees, "Your reasoning has won your friends for you. Go, pick your man to send reports to us. Then do as you've agreed."

A Choice Is Made

The Amazon officers meet in council to discuss the plan. "Swords through the body would have been a noble and a simple thing, but it would not have saved the Cyzicans," Thalestris says, "neither saving us in days to come if we're perceived as dangerous. If we must have a man with us I know of one that may serve our purposes." She tells her story then, of our meeting by the stream. "What the Greeks meant for our disrepair will instead provide for us new strength. We left him to ride here on his own outside of Cyzicus, so our knowing him will not be evident."

And they agree that of the men available, Thalestris' chronicler Strax would be the best.

When the Greeks and Macedonians hear of the choice the Amazons have made they are dismayed at it, that the tall straw-haired stranger is to be the one to go. They summon me to speak with them.

"See now, Strax, they say," and attempt to buy me off with gold, for which I have no need. With taunts and threats, at which I stare at them and squint. Though several of the Greeks I traveled with by now are there who speak of my courage in the battle we've just fought; so that my selection is soon ratified. We agree I am to send the Greeks reports each month, addressed to the garrison officer at Cyzicus.

When the Amazons set out on horseback for Themiscyra I go with them, contemplating the role I am to play, marshal and enabler of their new sport. Which does nothing for my happiness.

The home of the Amazons is a beautiful area at the shore of the Black Sea, close by the River Thermodon [now the River Terme] with mountains on two sides. Woodlands, meadows, lakes, and streams abound. Our arrival is an occasion of celebration, for their sisters have come home with many stories to be shared and wounds to be displayed.

Walking the Labyrinth

Themiscyra by the Black Sea

Representatives of the Council meet with me to ask questions about my life. My travels to the far Western Land, my friends among the Carthaginians, my voyage with the Greeks, my mother Susa's exile and the new matriarchy where I had my birth, all of this and more I relate to them. They ask if I am content to be among them. I tell them yes.

The next evening there is a ceremony for me to enter their society. The many assembled officers all come to their feet when I'm brought into the hall. There is no movement, there is no talk, there is no turning of the head to see; only the torches' dance on three hundred women standing in their brightly colored robes and the great room's silence as they lead me through the doors.

The audience forms a half-circle around a central space where a great three-sided labyrinth is drawn upon the stage. This labyrinth I am told to walk, to the center through its one opening. As I make my circular way all those watching me sit down and begin to hum, undulating low.

When I arrive at the center of the labyrinth three women dressed in dark feathers arrive suddenly encircling me in a wild frenetic dance. They proceed to remove my clothes, those I wore when I arrived; and they place leafy branches into my hands, instructing me to hold them up with outstretched arms. Into large bowls of wood they place my feet, over which is poured a quantity of sand, enough to cover them.

I stand a tree now, naked save for sand-covered feet and branches held aloft, while those dark dancers flow around me gesturing and shrill, brushing my body downwards with black feathers in their hands and menacing my skin with a gleaming knife.

Now three other women feathered all in white come into view and begin a journey into the labyrinth, winding their way toward me with wings outstretched as though in flight. At sight of these white ones the dark dancers cry shrill and flee, giving no heed to circling boundaries.

The bright dancers swirl around me now and anoint my head with fragrance they have brought. Remove my feet out of the sand and take the branches from my hands. Then with white feathers they brush all of me, with a motion this time from the bottom up. Place white feathers in my hands and with soothing songs lead me from the labyrinth, the steps retraced to be outside. There the feathers are removed and I am clothed with a wine-red robe of silk.

A silver cup is given me to hold which as it comes to view the audience rises to its feet to greet. White feathered hands guide the cup to my lips, and when I have drunk of it all those watching give me greeting, "Hail Strax, among the Amazons!"

I'm brought circling through the hall where many reach to touch my hands, my arms, my robe; a journey that ends in the front row where I am offered a seat as one of them. Song and dance continues then, translated for me into Greek by a woman just behind me where I sit, for all is performed in an ancient language which I have not learned as yet.

My robe is that same color as the one Thalestris wears, though there are many other hues I see around me as I look. When I inquire it is explained, "As a guest among us, invited here to perform a task so sensitive, you are provided the highest rank available."

Every Moment's Possibility

Through pastures filled with animals, through fields green with grain and orchards heavied with their red and golden fruit, past lakes teeming with their broad-winged waterfowl, out to the sea where fish are being caught, I'm shown the women busy, many with infants tied to them by scarves and tending older children as they play. Sewing, mending, planting, harvesting, milking, fishing, busy at their crafts, talking and laughing all the while.

"They are happy," I say.

"Yes. Life moves through them; they are amazed at the dance embracing them."

"Do they ever feel a call to 'something more'? Wonder what else there is to be or have?"

"Something more? They thrill at every moment's possibility, that it ever should have been."

The Fire's Kiss

Thalestris sits with me beside the evening fire, sharing a blanket spread across our laps against the evening chill. I have been in Themiscyra now several months.

Thalestris always enjoys my conversation with the fire, my half of it at least, the part she says she hears.

"There is one that comes," says the fire to me. "Such a dance of light and dark! A king who seeks assurance that he is a god."

"Why does he seek that?" I reply into the flames.

"Because his parents' families were so filled with gods. Now he must be one more."

"Might his father not reassure him of it somehow?"

"This man's father never gave his blessing to him. Though that is all he ever wished for. All he wants now."

"Is that so hard a thing?"

"The father is gone. Now to have a blessing the son must be a god. Then his father's admiration will be assured."

"How will he accomplish it?"

"He will go across the world in search of those who'll honor him. Conquer them as necessary to achieve divinity in their regard. Their refusal he will rebuke with fire."

"Shall he succeed?"

"He shall make ashes easily enough. Such brief bright flames! Not for long shall they provide the glory that he seeks."

"The true glory to be achieved is not outside of him!"

"Even so. The glory he seeks is there within, that spark he holds so tightly closed."

"What shall open it to him?"

"Perhaps woman shall. Woman can enter his private storms, to open his fist with her caress."

"What woman might do this then?"

"She to whom I give my kiss."

Crack! Sparks fly toward Thalestris, landing on our blanket in front of her. We sweep them off.

"What was all that about, Strax?"

"The fire's kiss."

"Whose father? Succeed at what? What shall the woman do? What glory did you talk about?"

"Someone is approaching, Thalestris, a king who wants to be a god. Someone for whom you may provide the key to set his brightness free."

And the Macedonian came indeed. Young Iskander, fueled with his father Philip's dream and off to have his godhood verified.

The night before Thalestris and her three hundred warriors left on their journey east to Iskander's camp the Council of the Amazons convened to see her off. A great energy was there as many spoke.

I was there with them. Wishing only to be listening, though forced to heed the calls, "Strax! Strax!" So that I also rose to speak.

Storm Winds' Ransom

Strax

High on mountain crags I build my eagle's nest and raise a rampart to protect my heart. Here I live secure, at peace with everything. Sun, stars, and moon for roof; sea and mist for moat. Content to feast on beauty's mysteries.

But an army flies at me across the deep. The horizon darkens with their horses' wings, flames for eyes and ice for teeth, fierce to tear the brightness from my sky and fling serenity into the sea for sport. What enemy is this that assaults my walls, that rushes in to cast me down? It is an army of the Winds and all the savage sky that rides with them.

I meet their storm blasts with my sword and with my heart, contend with their encircling howls upon the swirling battlefield of air until their fiendish darkness bleeds away and brightness is restored.

"You have conquered us," they cry, "Now let us go!"

"Not yet, you broad-winged Winds!" I say, "Would you be free to fly again between the kisses of the sea and ecstasy of sun? First you must fulfill the tasks I set. Deep in the caverns of my citadel my forge and anvil wait, and you shall fashion weapons for my heart to wield against such storms as yet may come."

"What work is this that you propose? What would you have us make?" the Winds reply, and rattle at their chains.

"Words! Words you shall prepare for me! That is the ransom I require from you, you who know the secrets of the vibrant air. From your mouths all sighs are born and in your ears are all sounds spent. I know who you are. Your hands mold the shape of fire!

"Primordial words you'll make for me, such as never have been said, that feast on flame and dance in ice. Sighing wings you'll weave for me to fly beyond time's grasp where thought cannot take hold nor sorrow reach. Majestic syllables that require your surest art, to steer and calm the inner storms and mend the broken colors of the heart. Such as these you'll forge, and more, add this! Bring to me the sounds of the sun as it presses darkness out of space!

"Devise sighing subtleties that dance upon the soul and talons winging swift that grip and fasten on despair. Forge utterance the darkness dreads and trembles at, that storms must bow to serve, and this: Sounds that thwart the anger of the sea!

"The anvil waits; so fill your lungs you vanquished Winds, then blow to feed the forge's flame and lick the darkness back with fiery tongues. Hammer strike, and sparks for a worker's song! Call on what allies you have need, for ere this night is past it must be done."

With gusting breath the winds infuriate the fire til their fierce allies appear from other realms to work with them. Dragons grim with rage at being wakened from their sleep and thunder flailing jagged hands. Drippings garnered from the stars are alloyed with elemental mysteries then stirred with hands of steam that travel eons upwards through the earth in hope to hold at last the lofty openness of air. Impurities of skirling shrieks and groaning wails are all skimmed off the cauldron's top as the magma swirls. Then anvils cascade tears as the hammers sing to mold the final shape the brightness keeps.

By dawn the Winds have been reduced to sighs and the words they've made are brought into my treasury, vibrant with eerie radiance, the ransom well fulfilled of all I bid them do.

And that is my gift to you, this ransom-fire the Winds distilled that the tempest fears, fierce-gathered from the huffing hammers' songs and screaming sparks. If ever the savage time should threaten you, to wrench your colors from life's fragile stem, and shadows crowd around your soul, let my words be your arrows to do battle with the storm. Hurl them to blunt the wind's sharp edge when all around you falls."

ช่

Iskander's war swept south of the Amazons, down to Egypt then east to Babylon and on beyond, five years, and we were spared.

Thalestris went to Iskander by the Caspian Sea and then returned. And I have recorded her account in scrolls.

Then Alexander went to Delphi to consult Apollo concerning the success of the war he had undertaken, and happening to come on one of the forbidden days, when it was esteemed improper to give any answer from the oracle, he sent messengers to desire the priestess to do her office; and when she refused, on the plea of a law to the contrary, he went up himself, and began to draw her by force into the temple, until tired and overcome with his importunity, "My son," said she, "thou art invincible."

Alexander taking hold of what she spoke, declared he had received such an answer as he wished for, and that it was needless to consult the god any further.

--- **Plutarch.** (46-120 A.D.)

Chapter Seven

Thalestris and Iskander Meet

Iskander's Hunting Camp Near the Caspian Sea. 330 B.C.

The Meeting in the Tent

"Come inside where it is cool," Iskander invites me to the royal hunting tent. "Meet some friends who've come with me."

It's a large carpeted enclosure with his bed on the far side and cushions and chairs near the opening, with a flap splayed out on poles for air and light. His few invited friends troop in behind us through the tent's flapped door. They pour red wine into silver cups, which I decline.

"Thalestris, Tydeus, Maris, Laontes, Itzak, Hiram, Hector, Thales, Pyrrho. Come all, sit," Iskander directs us to our chairs.

"Thalestris honors us with her presence today. What shall we discuss? Let us each tell our thoughts on some subject narrowly for her to know us somewhat by our words. The origins of things, perhaps?" The men all rustle in their chairs or screw their faces up, as though the subject is not new. They devour me with their eyes. "Thales, you first."

"Thalestris, welcome to our hunting camp, so packed with Macedonian wolves. But I am Greek, named for our philosopher Thales of three hundred years ago. Water is that original stuff Thales said produced the world, as ice takes form from mist, all is water in its forms and will return to it. And I agree with him, with but one change:

Spirit is the word I choose instead to be the basis of the world, of all of us. Not water, but spirit is."

Iskander nods for the next to speak. "My name is Tydeus. What do I think? Thinking is a hard thing to do. But I have heard an idea I like: That all in the universe is an expression, a copy, of ideas in the Prime Mind."

"Tydeus has read Plato finally!" All laugh.

"How did Mind do that, Tydeus?"

"How am I to know? I wasn't there." We laugh along with him.

"Maris?"

"Water in a stream brews bubbles up. Our world is one of them. No more than that." Maris throws up his hands and drinks.

"Laontes?"

"All you see here is by the diversity and change of units of spirit that are invisible. These wage war, taking now this one's part away to add it to itself, and then another one's. The coming together of these units in their various forms give each thing its nature and its shape. And their units' separation causes their change and their decay."

"Laontes, with his mysterious tiny war! Pyrrho, now you."

Pyrrho smiles. "Why involve yourself? These explanations of why and how are futile and a waste of time. You are here to experience, only that. Why meddle the moment with prattle such as this? Your search leads you only to despair, for you cannot hope to know the truth of what you truly are. You can be, and you can see, unless you muddy sight and experience with thought. Seeing, being, let it go at that." Pyrrho leans back and grins.

"Can you see, Thalestris, why we have invited him?"

"To keep you from thinking too highly of yourselves?" All laugh. Even Pyrrho does, loudest of them all.

"Itzak? What do they say in Israel?"

"The Creator makes all that is seen from what is not. Stretches out the heavens as a tent in which to dwell."

"A god in a tent?" Laontes smirks. "That's new!"

"Thalestris, what would you add to all of this?"

All eyes turn to me. Wondering if I have followed this discourse. One so well known to them, so well rehearsed? Shall I make my way along the rival tides of thought, or shall I snag? Shall their test reveal the consternation of a heathen brain? An unlearned savage, as all suspect I am?

It is to Iskander I direct my words. "History is a snake with a long tail. Where shall I begin with it?"

"Is it true you fought at Troy? Invaded Athens before that?"

"We did. Troy was our neighbor, that called on us for help. And as for Athens, well, that attack was a reaction in principle to having our Princess Antiope abducted by King Theseus."

"Though they were wed when you arrived, with children born to them?"

"Principles have momentum which carries them, even when what set them in motion has grown calm. As to Laontes' unseen units, these provide nature's diversity indeed as they come and go in labyrinths too small to see, with speed too great to comprehend, in wide spirals comparable to those planets tread around a star. Units that may be changed, one element transformed into the next, as even the stars would change if we altered whatever orbits them. Transposing matter into energy and back to matter once again, even as fire changes wood to heat and changes the air to rain."

The men sit listening, take it in like the ground takes rain.

Bundles of Energy

"Consider this wood, this stone, what you call solid: It is not. Nothing is. These objects, this, these, all are bundles of moving energy.

"Have you walked out in the summer meadow to see the evening storm? Seen the lightning turn the darkness bright and the fire it kindles with its touch? There is a battle in the meadow! You do not see the blades, only the flash the weapons make, action so much faster than you may perceive. You do not see the warriors, only the flaming shafts they send. Then all are fled and it is dark and quiet again. All these armies with their many horses which in an instant fought are just as suddenly, faster than seeing, come and gone again.

"Now unfolds the mystery! The smaller is the mirror of the larger element. This lightning of the summer storm is given us to understand the smaller lightning flashes that comprise all things: In the meadows of my various elements, my flesh, my bones and blood, these battle-storms are every passing moment waged. Many thousands of tempests in the many tiny meadows of every speck of me each moment crackle and crash in wild storms, such as would take a thousand summers in the many meadows of the wider world to fill one eye's brief blink.

"And this: The body is the battle-brightness that is left behind. This firmness we call flesh is the light and crash from many constant storms, in each moment, in every flake of skin.

"If we could look into this stone, this leaf, this chair, see deep enough into their storms, what would we perceive? Summer meadows so much like our own, trees that spark and smolder from the lightning's shaft. And creatures there perhaps, with hair like ours on their own noble heads. And all around us a sight much like the sky, mostly space, with balls of gathered energy flying free, a host of suns and stars and moons! For the ratio of space to racing energy is the same in the rock and wood and flesh as in the heaven's deep expanse — where all the fiery droplets flow so fast but seem so still, for they are far away."

The Moon, the Sun, the Wind

The evening is setting in. Iskander urges us out among the darkning trees to a blaze that has been lit.

It is a king's fire. Circled by wolves, the thirty friends Iskander has brought along to his hunting camp to meet with me in utmost privacy. Thirsting for me with their eyes as though they'd never seen a woman all their lives. Or none like me.

Then finally when the moon is overhead one by one his men bid us goodnight and leave us by the fire alone.

Alone at last. Iskander's eyes are large as seas, where lightning flows in bursts of storm. And his sandy hair so full of wind, though the air is still.

"A very Macedonian fire," I say.

"Oh? Why that?"

"Well, there's Amazon fires, and there's Macedonian. Yours are big and ours are small. Small fire, we lean together over it and talk, hushed as the trees surrounding us. Big fire, everyone leans back and yells while all the forest's creeping up to watch, waiting til the flames go low to pounce."

"Except for this: All this forest now is Macedonian. It's mine."

"Ah."

There is a silence then a while, til Iskander throws a stick into the blaze. "Thalestris, what news do you bring? What is happening on the Earth now?"

"You are. Only you."

"Is there no more?"

"How could there be? The moon, the sun, the wind all ride with you, to see you take the world into your fist. You yourself are the question on the lips of all. See, how even the wind inquires, 'Where has great Iskander gone? The king who loosed the knot so well.' 'Great Iskander reigns!' the sun replies, and the moon assures, 'Great Iskander never sleeps.'"

"Does the moon say that, Thalestris? How truly the moon knows. As for the knot, I'll tell you what occurred that day."

Iskander and the Knot

Three years earlier, 333 B.C., Gordium, in modern-day Turkey

People crowd to see me along the dusty road to Gordium. Eyes squinting through the wind and sun to see the Macedonian that has put the Persian king to rout, come now to encounter their own town's famous legacy: Rope twisted in a ball, binding a yolk to a wagon shaft, the wagon on which the town's founder supposedly arrived. Shall anyone untie the knot? The legend says all Asia will be his.

Curiosity alone brings me here today. "Make a detour to see the knot at Gordium," they urged, and I almost said no. I shrugged. Asia shall be mine to rule anyway, I knew. And all the world a knot I shall unloose.

If I had been alone, it might have been different. I might have simply looked at the thing, poked about and laughed and gone again. But there are so many curious faces now. Hundreds! Filling all the bright windy space. I have routed Darius once, they know. "Shall this young king prevail," the eyes all ask, "Shall Persia fall to him?" Then no longer Darius but Iskander shall be ruling them! So much tension, to see what I will do today—to watch me as I fail! Ha! Shall I curse and weep, they are wondering, when I have met the knot's defeat? Pout? Stamp my feet? One thing is sure: My failure today is fore-ordained. No one else has had success. So why should I? It is a familiar spectacle, not infrequently played out. A crafty joke at the expense of anyone who tries.

Ah. There it is. Large enough. A thick brown endless snake lying sleeping in a ball. The challenge is to find the end of it, so cleverly hidden in its mass. It begins nowhere; it is everywhere en route. The snake that eats its tail! I kneel to pry the coils apart, to search between. How have they concealed the ends so well? It is a world, like any other. And I shall master it.

I am lost in my task, until I sense whispering, a great viper slithering all around. I look up. The people have begun to make sly comments as they watch, and curl their mouths. One of them sneers. It bites at my heart. I stand, to better see who is mocking me. Yes, a sneer! Faster than thought the lightning from its sheath is loosed, a slender silver storm—I step in his direction with my sword.

The smirk flies away, the serpent finds a hole.

I wheel at these many others encircling me. Startled, they shrink back. Dust and heat rush coiling to my head. Here I am, my sword up in the air. I must bring it down somewhere. And I see the knot. The great brown head bares its fangs at me! My sword comes down on it, unties its snarl easily. Just as that bright edge unties all Asia for me now.

Slow Dance

Iskander cradles a hand to his left arm.

"An old wound?"

"It flares up sometimes. When there's so much water in the air."

""It is a storm in your body's light. Why not let it go?"

"What?"

"Your mind is holding it in place."

"Oh? How?"

"Your mind weaves your body's shape with light. Is it such a mystery to you?"

"Completely so."

"What mind images the body will construct in time." I open my inner sight to let his storms come into view, pale clouds flowing green, blue, violet upon the sea of flesh. Yes, there: Dark whirlpools of disrupted energy. My fingertips reach out to sooth the colors into shape, set the swirling darkness free with light.

"It should be better now."

"What did you do?"

"Painted light where there was none. As you'd spread oil on a weathered board."

"A light you see that comes from me? Why should I presume it's real? Not imagination's dalliance."

"You do not feel the streams of blood that rush inside you. But they do. Bring us a sword, we shall have proof of it."

"Why do I not see this light?"

"You are so full of sky. You feel so little of the rhythms of the Mother's heart, the womb-beat of the Earth. You are uprooted, and the wind comes. Vibrations become dense. The material forgets the spirit that it is."

"The material is spirit?"

"We are spirit into matter pressed."

"Hmm."

"Have you seen the wave that rushes past the rocks, how its form remains the same? You might say it was solid if you'd never seen a waterfall before. But that is an illusion; every instant the wave is filled with many thousands of smallest rushing drops, each next moment replaced by many thousands more. Put your hand in! The drops are revealed against your skin, you discover it is so."

"Yes, many separate drops just as you say, though they combine in form as one."

"Iskander, all so-called solid things are thus. We simply cannot put our hands so easily into them. Rather than a stream of water it is a stream of wood, of rock, of flesh. What seems solidity is a continuous rushing energy and mostly space. We see only the result of their cascade."

"Explain it to me simply then, this light you see."

"The light is the chisel of this form you are. In your mind's hands."

"My mind?"

"Your mind is the architect, daily reconstructing your body from within yourself, directing the light as a brush does ink, by images and thoughts. Over time the mind's images are molded into flesh, this light-made-solid you indwell."

"You actually see this light on me? You can direct its flow?"

"The body is a connecting point for Sky with Earth, a dance to enter when you know how." I put my hand on Iskander's arm. "I simply smooth a storm you might yourself have calmed were the science not unknown to you. Released a jam of logs to clear the flow, no more than that. We learn to do it from our youth."

"What must I do to see all this?"

"Enter the meeting place, where Sky and Earth devise their dance, motion creating illusions of solidity. We need not remain so locked in matter's chains, our energy condensed in this slow state. We have made ourselves slow a while, you see, so very slow to join the dance. But we are not the flesh, we are the flames. And when we're done with such slow dancing we will go."

"We go. And if I would rather stay?"

"The mind decides to go; it is then the flames grow dark. But it need not be so soon."

"You do this? But how?"

"By giving conflict no place in me."

"Are you not a warrior?"

"What conflict is there, Iskander, when light floods over dark? That is the sort of battle that I wage."

Thalestris takes a stick with which to draw. "Do you know to draw the classical labyrinth?"

The Lightning's Child

How does it begin, this adventure you are in?

The body is a labyrinth through which the spirit's spiraling. Shall we draw that flight? Like drawing life itself! From infinite wideness we define a point.

What intention set in motion that first touch, so that you entered matter's realm? What lightning brought you here? Sired by what thunderclap? Will it come in search of you again?

Four directions hem the spirit in. Four winds take flight to set it free.

Then begins the spirit's spiral into flesh, bending circles round in a dance to clothe itself with elements.

Shadows gather as the circles turn. Not yet are you entirely fixed inside, looking out at all the rest. Still the spirit knows: Its home is not inside the point or the circles' flight.

Soon enough the shadows settle in, so much weather now where only sky had been. As you make a nest in darkness and you fold your wings to sleep, leave umbilical enough for dreams to come and go with their thin light.

See what a fist you make! Clutching at the shadows
you have seized, all you decide to call your own.

And here you are inside this spiral-dance you call a
self. Unaware of that first point so long ago. Unaware of the
four winds' dance or the infinite before the shadows' circling
— all obscured, so soon forgot.

Though something in you knows: You are spirit into
matter pressed, a fire no elements can hold for long. An
errant spark the lightning goes out searching for, to unwind
the labyrinth and join you to itself again.

Sleep Comes Hard

"You must rest easy now, with so great a world you've taken in your fist."

"Sleep comes hard for me, Thalestris, just as the moon has said. I have dreams that trouble me. Something that comes at me. Bees. Other things. Bellowing from the depths where it is dark like some Minotaur up from its labyrinth, and I am trapped."

"Trapped? Most people are to some extent. Trapped in fear, since they mistake their garments for themselves, these flimsy clothes of flesh they wear. It's not life's joys and pains that burden and break, but the mind's attempt to chase or flee from them. Clinging and aversion keep us in captivity. To have each moment be entirely new, this is the end of suffering. Have you dammed the moment's stream inside yourself, for tears to pool where they flow deep? It is the spirit's stream that flows from dream to dream. And spirit can grow stagnant here in us."

"Spirit's stream?"

"A stream we share. All of us are united; there is nothing that is separate. All are connected. All of us, one. The sword we wield has a mirrored edge for us as well.

"Life is a path through storms. Some make that journey with the heart, some with the mind. It is a tempest the heart traverses well but the mind must travel slowly through, reaching to grasp the lightning before it will let the thunder go. The mind cannot hold the lightning long, with its hands so full of thunder's noise. But the heart can."

The Hall of Records

"Could the Egyptians give you no help in your quest for immortality?"

"Some. I journeyed over vast piles of sand, through the desert west from the pyramids to the Oasis of Siwah to ask the priests questions that I have. But so much of it is still a mystery."

"Oh?"

"In Egypt there is a Hall of Records, so people say, with wisdom and history of the most ancient times. Thalestris, do you know of it?"

"I know that it exists but could not tell you where. What did the priests at Siwah say?"

"Only terse riddles, that I could not understand:

"Where is the Hall of Records?" I asked the priests.

"We have not entered such a hall," they said.

"Perhaps you have not entered it. But I have heard it mentioned. If I have surely you have too."

"There is one saying that we keep; you may decide if it is relevant. Only to a Pharaoh may it be told. As you are Pharaoh now here is what it says: *The mouse keeps the ancient history. The mouse makes nine holes, to be secure from birds of prey. The holes do not make the mouse secure. But the mouse is.*"

"So the mouse is the Hall of Records?" I asked the priests.

"If not the one you seek, O King, the only one we know about. Is it for you the words are so long kept? Then it is you who must decipher it."

୫ଓ

"Thalestris, help me ponder it. What do you think the nine holes are?"

"Perhaps nine rooms the Hall contains."

"Yes, that sounds right. But I wonder at the rest of it. What about the birds of prey? Why do holes not keep the mouse secure? Why is it secure anyway?" Iskander waves his arms about.

I begin to laugh. Iskander only watches me with his impatient eyes. This makes me laugh more. What is it about woman's laughter that so provokes man's insecurity?

"Thalestris, what?"

"Oh, Iskander . . . It is just that, well, it suddenly became so clear."

"What? The Hall?"

"Yes, the Hall. Think of it: What are the birds of prey? They are the people trying to find the Hall, to seize it for themselves. And the holes give information, how many rooms there are, but the meaning is truly in the mouse, in its security. So, let us decide, what makes the mouse secure?"

"Not the holes, then. What else could it be?"

"Secure goes two ways, Iskander. 'Secure from.' And also secure as in 'securely being held.' Both meanings are needed to tease the riddle out. What does a mouse need to be secure from, other than birds of prey?"

"A cat perhaps."

"Yes! Certainly a cat! Now you can solve it out. Where is there a cat nearby?"

"There must be many in Egypt, I would think."

"Iskander, how does a cat catch a mouse? Have you seen it done?"

"Yes, with its paw. Then it plays with the mouse, lifting the paw and immediately putting it down on the mouse again as it begins to run. Lightning storm, again and again as the mouse tires; runs each time less quick, less far."

"Which paw?"

"Which one? Well . . . The time I saw it, the right paw as I remember it."

"Exactly as I have seen it done by cats I know. Now, consider the other meaning, 'Secure by being held.' Secure, the way a cat holds a mouse secure. *The holes do not make the mouse secure. But the mouse is.* If we find the cat, may we not also find the mouse in its nine holes, held secure beneath its paw?"

"And what cat shall we choose?"

"The cat in the story must be very old. In Egypt there is a famous cat I've heard about. Have you truly seen the great pile of stones with its four gleaming sides, the pyramid? Then you have seen the cat that crouches there."

"The Sphinx! And the Hall is the mouse, held secure from birds of prey beneath its paw!"

"The right paw, if this cat is like the others that we know. And you ought not tell anyone, Iskander, lest on your return to Egypt you find those nine holes already opened by someone else. By some other bird of prey than you."

A Legend of the Amazons' Origin

The fire thins its last colors out. Through the trees the moon is full.

"Tell me, Thalestris, what are the origins of the Amazons?"

I laugh. "There is a legend I could tell. Of women born to the clan as each was bid to come, separating themselves from the rule of men, each at her own heart's call. A process we still celebrate: Women who encountered the fist of war and the closed hearts of men, and maintained their light. The open hand is so vulnerable to the fist, to marauders who prey on those who live in peace. What are those who live in openness to do? They learn how well the open hand can stop the fist!

"If what I tell you now is myth, yet do we still treasure it."

༄

Villagers were defending themselves as best they could from marauding bands that pillaged all the area with their violence. When the village was repeatedly attacked and husbands killed, some now-single women claimed they would lend their assistance to the village's defense and requested weapons so they might train to join the men to keep the invaders out. They were women but they were angry and they were strong.

They were also beautiful, so that the men in control of the community's defense suggested they take other husbands and go on about their lives. But the women insisted, they had made up their minds.

Seeing the women persist in their plan the men tried to dissuade them with taunting now, asking how one might know they would be brave in battle and not simply run away, thereby endangering everyone. "The battleground is not the place for undiscovered cowardice," the men said. "There is blood and confusion everywhere."

The women replied they would prove their resolution and their courage to them somehow. The men said, "Fine," and thought that was the end of it.

The women, twelve in all, after much discussion decided on a plan, rather bold, and called a meeting on a certain day. When the men were gathered one of the women, Melanippe, spoke while the others stood beside her in a line.

"You say that because we are women we will be frightened by the threats a battle holds; that we will be afraid of pain and terrified by blood. That we will balk at

146

the risk of having wounds. That we are not to be trusted lest we run. Why do you decide such things? It is so little you perceive?

"Our husbands' spirits have flown and we are content to go to them, but not until we have avenged their deaths and fought this plague of violence. Our blood is no concern to us, for we've decided to consider ourselves as already dead. All we desire from you is weaponry so we may train, to fight alongside you.

"We have at your urging prepared a test meant to persuade. It is our intention, we must tell you, in consideration of the blood you think us loathe to shed, never to give thought to protection for ourselves. Seldom to wear armor nor often to bear shields; for our bodies shall welcome the enemy blade and we are prepared to bleed. Now behold, we provide for you our test."

The women let fall their garments and stood naked before the assembled men. The sudden disclosure of their fine forms caused quite a stir.

Melanippe spoke again. "Our only weapons now are slender knives, such as this I hold. With it we propose to show you we are not afraid of wounds nor hesitant to draw another's blood. Each of us shall offer her body to be opened, and each of us shall wield. Those who survive will hope to join you in our town's defense."

Melannippe motioned to the woman in line next to her who slid the knife she held along Melanippe's skin in a long red line beneath the high-held ribs. There were murmurs from the men as the blood ran down. Then another woman took the blade and cut the offered flesh of one nearby. So on down the line until each one received a shallow line across her body for the blood's release.

Then the knife started on again with deeper wounds this time, thrust in, removed, one by one until the seventh woman received the blade deep in her side — and the men asked them to stop. Courage, they saw, would be no reason for concern.

The men made comment on their bravery and dedication to their plan and promised delivery of weapons and instruction too. If they intended to be useful they might indeed join in, as long as they'd obey the officers.

So the women received their weapons and instruction, forming a small fighting force. They showed valor and skill and when the village was attacked they fought and fell. Thinned ranks were filled with new recruits and the camp moved away from the village to an area some distance out.

Their honor, they decided, was their blood's release and their wounds' display. In compensation for their recklessness they studied the healing arts, herbal mixtures to make the opened flesh close up and mend rapidly the deepest wounds' distress. Many women joined them as news spread and the marauding bands soon went in search of weaker victims and less brave.

But some village leader became consumed with prideful arrogance at last, making demands of the women warriors with a will for controlling them. Harsh and angry words were said and the women moved their camp farther away yet, depending less and less on the village for their needs.

The people round about learned that the warrior sisterhood could heal their wounds and the many problems of the sick, and they came to them for their healing work. In return they left gifts of food, weapons, gold. And left their daughters of all ages too, as better able to survive among this warrior clan than where they were at home—another mouth to feed in a poor and savage land, exposed to wandering bands with the constant threat of being noticed as desirable, so to be taken away to some chieftain's lair to be a slave for pleasure and for daily chores.

Death had ruled the area for a long time; now in an ever wider swath these women reined brutality in, buying safety back for everyone with their strength and skill so that life might find its way past fear a while — freedom from those who come to plunder what they can, living for power and lust and self, oblivious to treasures the heart can own.

All this is a pageant now that we enjoy with re-enactment every year. An honor to be chosen to perform in it, to receive the several wounds, to be among the twelve.

Daughters of Ares

"Though it's said you are daughters of Ares the God of War."

"Yes. Directed to the enterprise of war so very long ago, so the overlords could see us fight for their amusement's sake. It was in the far time in a place far out at sea, one no longer existing now. Those you call 'gods' gathered our clan of women warriors to be 'Daughters of the God of War,' as you've heard said. Though we escaped from them."

"Because?"

"Because they had no love for Earth; control was all their love. Nor took delight in us, save to see us as we bled. We did not mind the wounds, skirmishing among ourselves or with men as they'd decide; wounds were a noble thing as they still are. Though for their lacking compassion's fire and love for Earth we grew dissatisfied in serving them. Came away with treasured concepts and life-stratagems, a legacy we keep for all humanity when it is time. Till then we train ourselves for strength, so to safeguard what we hold."

"What gods were those?"

"Not gods at all. Powerful enough of course. Wishing to have one think they come from planets far from here, or one that comes near from time to time. Though they do not."

"What then?"

"They cross dimensions, as fish do when they jump into the air. Ours is not a dimension in which they belong; interlopers here, no less than the marauding bands I spoke about."

Penthesilea & Achilles

"My ancestor Achilles fought your Queen Penthesilea at Troy, the stories say."

"That's true."

"Why was she there?"

"Troy was guardian of the approach to us on the westward side, sentry to the Black Sea's entryway. You know that well, as it's there you came ashore on your mission to defeat King Darius."

"Indeed," Iskander grins.

"The Trojans called on us for help. The presence of our women turned the tide a while against the Greeks and Penthesilea met Achilles there, just as you say. They fought, then loved. As to who was defeated, well . . ."

"She died! Is that not defeat enough?" Iskander's sea-sized eyes shed sparks. "As to the story that one hears, what happened there . . . That Achilles loved her . . . When she was dead."

I smile. "It is a more subtle tapestry our Amazon stories weave. As for defeat, it may be seen both ways, since Achilles was out of action for a while again for grief at what he'd done. First losing Briseus, poor man, then this. Back to his tent to sulk!"

Iskander screws up his face, incredulous.

"Have you not heard it said, a lovers' kiss may unify two souls, their brightness joined, when one of them has flown on that last breath?"

Thus they performed the burial of Hector. Then came the Amazon, the daughter of great-souled Ares, the slayer of men.
— **Arctinus of Miletus,** *The Aethiopis.* Writing 750 B.C.

Amazons at Troy

Troy, in present day Turkey, about 1200 B.C. Perhaps a century after Bellerophon's journey to the Amazons.

The thirteen Amazons arrived at Troy to join the Trojans' ranks against the Greeks. Amazon energy and weapons made the Trojan courage swell.

The twelve who rode with Queen Penthesilea were Alcibie, Antibrote, Evandra, Antandre, Clonie, Polymusa, Derinoe, Bremusa, Hippothoe, Derimacheia, Thermodosa, and Harmothoe.

Daily they offered noble targets as they abbreviated the numbers of the Greeks. Penthesilea's beauty offered an urgently proud mark Greek archers bent their bows to reach, but no arrows ever found her flesh. Those who approached to try her sword wished they had not.

Achilles at that time was keeping apart from battle in his tent alone, angered by injustice at King Agamemnon's hands, who took the captured woman Briseus from Achilles to be his own war-prize instead. So Achilles sulked and would not fight. Then his friend Patroclus dressed in Achilles' armor, thinking to raise the morale of the hard-pressed Greeks, though Achilles was unaware of it. And Patroclus died.

Out from his tent the fierce Achilles came with grief enough to forget King Agamemnon's pride. Slew great Hector, as Homer says. Then Achilles went in search for more.

Who is this, Penthesilea wondered as she watched, that easily fells so many Trojans, any that come near? They are the grass, and he the wind! Achilles danced upon the blood-soaked plain and drenched it with his every stroke, and Penthesilea admired him instantly.

Penthesilea had never known her match in war. Those Greeks that sought her sought their own hurt. Their desire for her, fighting naked with her helmet and her shield, was their last lust. They were moths and she the slender silver consuming fire. But now half-god Achilles strode toward her across the crimson field where the bodies of Trojans he encountered lay in heaps. Seeing him her muscles turned to wax, her sword stood heavy in her hand, her crescent shield inadequate. One foot upon the body of the Greek she'd just torn she stood watching him.

Achilles was the lightning where only wind and sky had been. Was this his spear that tore into her side? She felt its flash but she saw only him. Achilles stood back to watch the red stream out. He'd not fought with women before this.

"I am Achilles, King of the Myrmidons. Who are you? Your aspect is noble. How do you know the art of war, so that so many Greeks have fallen by your hand?"

"I am Penthesilea, Queen of the Amazons, come to aid King Priam against the Greeks, not for love of him so much as to protect our western boundaries. Shall Troy fall? That breached wall allows new violence to enter in, where we have worked so long to create peace. I fought well til I saw you, but now my sword is heavy on my arm and I receive your weapon's kiss."

"Your Amazons," Achilles said, "defend these loathsome Trojans, whom I might indeed have left in peace. But now they have killed Petroclus my finest friend, and shall repay his loss with an offering of a thousand, not one less. But you are beautiful and fair; with this brief wound now be content and stand off from the battle; do not interfere. These Trojans are the dogs I seek and I shall send them to their shallow tombs!"

"Son of the goddess Thetis, is there no way to slake your thirst for war? It is my duty to my people's destiny to guard this citadel where Priam sits. And yet . . . You are the first that I have met whose spirit opens me. My body says my purpose coming here was to find you: Is it for war, or for some wedding of our destinies? I urge you to make peace with Troy! Find room for peace within your hero's heart. Set these weapons down and let the spirit's wings unfurl, with peace to fly, with tenderness to touch. Yet stand against you guarding Troy I shall if so I must. If foe or friend you wish for me to be, you may decide. See: I turn aside my shield; consider all of me. For yourself or for your spear, with love or blood if only that shall ease your rage, come drink from me again."

"You talk of peace," Achilles made response, "So nobly offered! But you still stand armed, to be a wall between me and these Trojan dogs! My spear has tasted once and thirsts for you again!"

Higher in her now, by the high-held ribs Achilles sent his spear a second time. She clutched at the long wood as she went down to her knees, then to her back. Achilles tugged out the lance, then took the helmet from her head.

Had the body been fair? The face was fairer yet! Wed to this face was a grace that held his heart. What was it she said? Had she urged peace? Achilles raised her with his arm to watch the uncapped fountains flow where his twice-drinking javelin had been.

"Why aim so high here by my heart, Great King? Some kinder thrust more low had been a gracious offering and soon repaired. Now I am rapidly poured out."

"How beautiful you are."

"Would that your love had drunk of me, and not your spear. Quickly now, fulfill our spirits' possibility! To these wounds add that kinder one that makes us one while breath still flows within this flesh I was! Connect our spirits by a last kiss. Do you know that lovers' kisses join their souls when one of them has flown on that last breath? The winds fan your spirit now to ever higher flames, while mine are embers that await your touch to give them flickering life again."

"Penthesilea . . ."

"The spirit door closes, come! Join me there in that bright shadow where I go. Make our bodies one! Then kiss me as I die. Noble Achilles, I came for war and death and now I shed my tears that finding you I cannot stay to live."

Were these his lips against her mouth or were they tears? Was this his strength she felt merging as her life poured out? So much motion now where emptiness had been. The doors were shutting, darkness closing in.

Yes! Her spirit flowed with his.

"What are these many warriors in the sky? What these radiant shafts of light? But see — you are here with me!" her spirit to his spirit said, "Astride this smoothest floating horse on which we ride."

When her hand let go and her lips no longer sought his own Achilles lingered yet to feel her body one with his, this woman whom he barely knew but knew he loved.

His spirit joined her own, some part of him a motion on the inner wind, flung toward some distant light on a great wild horse they rode. Was this the moon that welcomed them? Were these the stars that streaked across his face? Penthesilea was flying off with part of him, bled out against the crimson sky into the evening sun. Part of him with her — and the other part still on the battlefield, terribly alone.

The great Achilles felt the darkness that had almost been the light, stirring in the shadows of the ashes that had been his fiery heart.

You Need Not Fall Into That Pit

Thalestris and Iskander.

"Pharasmanes, King of the Chorasmians, has spoken to me of you."

"Indeed? What did he say?"

"He offered his services to me, to overcome the Amazons and the Colchians near the Black Sea."

"Colchis? Where Jason sailed so long ago? The Colchians are peaceful folk, except when someone goes to plunder them. It is a wonder Jason got away! He only escaped because he won a woman's love."

"I believe the true goal of Pharasmanes is to conquer the Amazons."

"Are a race of women so dangerous to him?"

"He says you sacrifice all strangers who are washed onto your shore. Is it not so — even as the *Oresteia* asserts, in the story of Orestes and Iphigenia? He says your raiding parties menace all the area, going out in search of men to take as slaves after you have slain enough to cool your battle lust."

"I suppose Pharasmanes would be named governor of all that area when our lands are overrun? If you ask his neighbors you will learn what is really going on, how he invades to raid their stores of grain when his run out. The women he seizes as his slaves, out of their very homes. Then ask those same neighbors to tell you the intentions of the Amazons. 'There would be no peace in a wide area if not for them,' they'll say. 'Only marauding bands who constantly plague the area.'

"Do you know, Iskander, Pharasmanes sent an army against us some years ago thinking to take an easy prize. Oh! We had fine sport with those uninvited guests. No female slaves for them that day. They would need to await some greater champion to lure him into joining them in their vile cause."

"And Pharasmanes hopes that will be me?"

"But you have a way of finding out the truth of things. And battle with the Amazons and the Colchians, as Pharasmanes desires, will certainly draw the Scythians into war, down from north of the Black Sea. Surely you know the history of the first King Darius who tried and failed when he marched against the Sythians. How he wished that he had not! Week after week of wandering across the endless wastes, hoping for the pitched battle that never came. Scythians preening the edges of his force on their fast ponies, never closer otherwise than the horizon's edge.

"Finally the Scythians sent Darius that famous message in a box: A mouse, a bird, a frog, and five arrow shafts. It took him part of a day to solve its meaning out: Options for him to choose. If he could not burrow into the ground like the mouse, or slip beneath the water like the frog, or fly into the air as does the bird, then the arrows would be his fate. He turned around and fled, leaving his sick and wounded as rear guard.

"The Scythians, north of the Black Sea, are the friends and brothers of the Amazons. Our allies when we fought at Troy and when we invaded the Athenians! And they are the friends of Greece as well, shipping quantities of grain to them with Greek wine in return. They will be as worthy enemies as they now are friends.

"Why would Pharasmanes lead you to that pit? Why hope you will fall into it? Is Pharasmanes indeed your friend? Or is he the agent of those farther east, toward India, who tremble when they hear of you? 'Lead Iskander away from us!' they plead with Pharasmanes perhaps. 'Lure him toward the Colchians with their gold-flecked streams and to the forests of the Amazons! Remind Iskander how his kinsman Achilles fought the Amazon Queen, so he will want to fight them too!'

"Is that what is happening, Great King? But you need not risk the Scythian pit — nor forego your conquest of ancient India. Here I am. Fight with me now. A Queen for you to battle with as Achilles did so long ago, who found that queen's rare beauty much too late, only as she lay dying in his arms. Shall you pierce me now, my wounds as wide as Penthesilea's were? Come! Test your fist against the goddess strong within my heart, that offers you her open hand! See here beneath my robe," I flared it from my flesh, "no armor deeper than the skin to bend aside a blade."

Moved by the spirit of my words and by my sudden nakedness Iskander takes me up into his arms. I sweep my windy hands all through his hair. How great a fire I have unleashed in him. How ravenous his thirst! How fine a battle in the moon's thin light.

Better Things To Do Than Die

The combat ends. The conqueror's head upon my breast. Silence long; then deep-dredged speech.

"Thalestris . . . Your beauty is the sea inside my hands. With each touch I call your mysteries mine; then the water goes through my fingers back again. This terrible beauty that you are escapes my grasp. How shall I hold you --- all of you at once?"

"Peace. It will seem a paradox. But peace provides the only way you might hold all of me. And peace is a place inside yourself you do not know. The other side of a silence you have never found."

"You can lead me there?"

"Perhaps. If peace is indeed your goal, and a vision of a peaceful world."

"Tell me your vision, then, this peaceful world."

"What if there were peace? No war? Then iron would be for tools, to dig the fragrant earth, and not for spear and shield. The fire for warmth, to bake the bread, and not to swallow cities up.

"What shall we do with peace when we give up the sword? Then we shall love! Enjoy the bounty of the ground. Dance beneath the stars and walk upon the wide green Earth, as though this were indeed our home. As though we had better things to do than die."

Desires

Iskander groans. "I live inside a fist. Only in battle am I free."

"Will you not open up your hand, to live?"

"Here with you, Thalestris, yes. Then when you are gone I'll fly to war again. I am free there. And for a while now in your arms."

"So much freedom to be found! A grand purpose to fulfill, as much again as you have done. Why not return to Egypt — you are Pharaoh now! If you desire my company we could search the ancient scrolls that tell of long-lost realms. Boat down the Nile. Swim among the crocodiles! You shall vanquish me with your wild battle lust; and I shall guide your journey through the storms that fill the mind."

"Battle is my way. But it is easy to forget that plan when my whole self explodes with you at longing's end. How ready I am to rest, and not to go. All I am is so poured out in you."

"What you give to me you receive double to yourself again the other side of that brief death. Pleasure restores as does a sleep."

"Pleasure's death forebodes mortality! Not a feeling gods should have. See how mortal I am here with you. If only death shall be as kind as this oblivion inside your arms!"

"Why would you fear death? Does Earth hold you so, that you shall hesitate to go? What does your spirit crave so to keep you here?"

"Battle! Beauty. Are not your own desires the same?"

"To be here now with you is enough for me, to drain the thunder from my heart. And deep inside of me our battle's sweetness lures the spirit of a child to us."

"A child. Is that immortality enough, in woman's world?"

"You crave reassurance of eternal life. But you fly on the wings of death to discover it. Why not take your place upon the Earth and let death fly away? Learn the fire you are, and not flow out on sparks?"

A Dance With Storms

All in Nature wishes to survive. And does it? Not in the form it's in. Other rhythms claim each shape. Collected patterns reduce to smaller elements again. Within the root the leaf lives on.

Nature plants in me the urge to guard the limitations of my form as long as possible --- as long as Nature wills it so. For Nature is capricious and a dance with storms. Everything in Nature wants so to remain the same, but only with constant change is Nature ever satisfied. Therein the paradox! In releasing my claim to separate existence I join all things.

Change is the battle into which I charge. Now I dance within the storm; now the storm's dance is in me. Shall I hold too tightly to my form? The wind shall tear it from my grasp.

Am I a leaf? Autumn's new colors come; I leave the branch, I fall! I lie upon the ground. But what is this? I join the complexity of earth. My leaf is rich to feed the root, where grows the tree on which I danced within the storm.

Guide the mind to step outside itself. Why should I fear lest this form be reshaped? Shall my spirit not take wings to fly? I am today a song with lips, tomorrow thunder of the sky. This shell in which I move shall decay and split apart and shall become a tree. The seed lives in the leaf again. We simply mistake ourselves for this small form we're in.

Consider that country where I go to dream, to watch that other world unfold before my dreaming face. I recognize who I am there no less than I do awake: Dreaming's drama on the spirit's stage complete with music, dance, pathos, mirth, solemnity; one moment true to the landscape that I know and in another all the seasons out of shape.

Is dreaming not a sign to us? When my self that lives in daylight dies my dreaming self lives on at night. In the morning I die to dreams, often when I wish so much to live, waking to the me that walks within the day. So much dying! Am I not now used to it? Why should dying be a strange surprise? Which one is more real? Do the dreams not have a strange eternal feel?

When in some battle the arrow finds my heart, the dream here with you shall end. My spirit shall fly to that new waking day and all this shall be the evaporating memory of the sky's wide face upon the windswept surface of the sea. "What was all that?" I will say as I awake. "Who was that strong warrior there with me, with the wild sandy hair? What this clamor of war, what these many shouts? That wide forested plain, that river green, the fire, the willow tree? What was that he said to me? I still feel the care I have, feel the pounding of my interrupted heart.

How I wish to reclaim my dream! To better understand it all. But it fades from view. The new day dawns. A whole new sky so bright around my head.

Iskander Dreams

When half the night is past there is a storm beside me in the bed. Iskander dreams.

"Back! Open! Let me in!" Pleas that shatter dreaming's boundaries. He wakes awash with sweat. Thrusts his face between my breasts.

"The dream again. I fled. From what dark fear or cruelty I cannot say. There was a door tight closed that barred my way as terror set its urgent course for me. And what if I did not wake? Would I be held forever dreaming there? What great door is this that blocks my way? My pursuer nears as I fumble at the latch. Pound on it with panic at my heart. What are these shadows in whose jaws I'm held secure? What is this that chases me in dreams?"

"The darkness inside of you."

"Help me understand."

"What light you are is buried deep inside your fist as you fly across the Earth, throwing obstacles of kings and armies all aside, whatever bars your way. But on your inner battlefield that dreaming door requires a key of light; and darkness enwraps the spark you are to put it out. You can build a road out through the sea to take a fortress in your hands. Will you not build a path into your self, to rule your dreams?

"You cry for greater light to thrust the dreaming darkness back. You strive and strive and have no peace. Shall you see to rule all this outside and have blindness overtake the greater life within? Fear has no hold on you here in the day, on the battlefields of Earth; you have proven it! But on the spirit battlefield that darkness shuts a great dark door you cannot pass."

"What is behind the door?"

"This moment is. But the past and future bind you from its entryway."

"You have no darkness pursuing you inside?"

"I am open Iskander, unfastened as the flower is. My openness calls on the ally of a greater light. Have you not heard? It is the flower's kiss the sun has come to taste. It is the flowers' tears the dawn has hurried here to wipe away. Light floods over dark. That is the battle you must wage. You shall consider its place one day and the darkness shall not be."

"Does this light bring power when I make it mine?"

Power

"Would a man have power? Let him harvest integrity and feed on truth. Say truth. Do truth. Let truth come live in him. That is the foundation on which power may be built.

Opportunities to be tested, to be false or true, provide a battlefield in him. Shall he fail? He shall live on in light a shade more pale, for truth in jealousy has escaped from him, so jealous he preferred falsehood over it. Shall he prevail? Power is the banquet spread by truth inside his heart.

"There are those who do what is right because they say there are angels observing them. But what if the angels turn their backs? The battle would be lost! The banquet never tasted. The treasure of power never held.

"Is money power? No. Possessions weaken a man when he starts to depend on them. Or rulership? 'To rule is power, certainly!' you say. Though if truth is compromised to rule, what then? Only position will remain, and what is that? A throne on which there sits an empty shell. With so little power within it takes so little pressure for that empty shell to crack and break.

"Integrity brings mastery over inner storms. Weather these and you shall rule the outer ones.

"A man's intention is his ship. Until his cargo is truth and his pilot is honesty his life will sail an unsteady sea, with no course set when weather's fair and no anchor when there's storm. His craft will smash onto the reefs, and though he scrape loose from there he will be back again. He'll be selling feathers to the wind. What harbor shall his brief wares find?"

It Could Be Arranged

Elsewhere in the camp, Maris and Tydeus meet privately.

"Oh Tydeus, how I tire of battles and philosophy. I wish we could go home to Macedonia."

"You have more mountains to climb before that, Maris. High ones. Up to India."

Tydeus drinks. Maris puts his head into his hands.

"So, my friend Maris, what do you think of her?"

"Beautiful. Intelligent. I liked the stories she told us."

"Though I doubt her portrayal of small worlds inside a flake of flesh."

"As for these Amazons, Tydeus, I think I would like to fight with them."

"Ha! Maris, you would find an arrow in your chest!"

"We've survived arrows before this."

"Perhaps it could be arranged, to have your battle with the Amazons."

"What do you mean?"

"Here is this Amazon, visiting Alexander. Why?"

"Why indeed? Does she come to turn Alexander toward India?"

"Is it so well you discern? Ha! She will succeed! See, how she has taken him!"

"Yes, how distraught he looks. What moon-snarled medicine does she pour into his soul? Surely she will feed his dreams of India."

"She must! Her home lies astride our homeward path."

"I wonder, Tydeus, can it be she knows Pharasmanes has come to us? Are they indeed the savages he portrays? I begin to think that they are not."

"Savage or no, it is her own homeland she cares most about! She meddles! Keeps us from going home!"

"It has been suggested to the King why she's here, but he doesn't seem to care."

"Maris, are you indeed intent on going home to Macedonia? Enough to arrange some tragedy for him?"

"What could we do?"

"Something that appears to be the work of these savage Amazons."

"It could be arranged?"

"Look."

"One of her arrows. How did you . . ."

"Easy enough. She left them by the tent door. She will be with him constantly. Riding here and there. How hard can it be? The tribe in the hills, what if they were offered gold to take more than the horse this time? The rider too."

"No!" Maris goes to the door of the tent to look outside, assuring himself they are alone. Whispering now, "Look what happened last time, Tydeus! When we arranged for those tribesmen to take Bucephalus. What a disaster!"

"How was I to know?" Tydeus matches the whispered intensity. "I thought Alexander would simply pay the ransom for his horse! Half for you and me, half for the mountain tribe! But no. Alexander said he would rip their forest up until he found his horse again. They looked down next day from their hill and what did they see? An army down below with axes in their hands, crunching down the trees in swaths."

"You were among those who took the word to him, that the horse was gone?"

"Alexander was furious, of course. Yelling. Doing his 'disappointed act' I hate so much with his face inside his hands. Telling us to get the message out to them, even if we had to go ourselves. Meanwhile he sent the army out into the trees to clear a path into the hills. It's not the tribe's fault. They did their work well."

"You used your stableboy to communicate with them?"

"Yes, Bren; ambitious boy. He's even learned some Greek. His father is a leader of the tribe, it was through him I set up the plan to take the horse. And later sent word to them to forget it all, that no ransom would be paid, and to send the animal back to us."

"And Bren is still around to carry messages?"

"We could do it right this time, Maris! And soon be home again."

"Shall the tribesmen kill him, Tydeus? What then?"

"We would make it seem their work, these Amazons! What are their intentions, really? Who did due diligence for this little meeting in the woods? Have they come here to deprive us of our King? To end his rampage out across the Earth? Are we not the allies of their age-old enemies the Greeks? They have reason enough to wield the blade, it will be easily believed. Our army will be grief-struck, hastily accepting that explanation as certainly the best. Swiftly overcoming those few women she has brought with her then striking west to the Black Sea before ever grief has cooled."

"These Amazons are fiercely beautiful. They would make good slaves perhaps."

"Once they are tamed. And if not let them die, a noble sacrifice to bring us home again."

"And Alexander? Shall we be sad that he is gone?"

"Yes a while. But Alexander's mission is fulfilled, to punish Persia for attacks on Greece. That is why we came with him. Now he considers no mountain too high to make us climb. For what? So he can prove this image of himself, that he is a god?"

"For his own sense of immortality! For his 'world plan.' Already he entertains Persians within the army's ranks. Makes officers of them! But it is our blood, Tydeus — Ours! — that brought us here so far from home. It is time, my friend, that it should end. Time to return to Macedonia."

"Shall we turn theory to action, then? Shall I send Bren, contact these tribesmen, offer them the chest of gold we've brought with us? Are you with me? Shall we do this thing?"

"I am with you, yes. Still . . . Are we not his friends? Shall conscience tear at us?"

"Yes we call him friend. And how many others are our friends as well, whose trust he betrays with his plans for India? How many hearts cry out to go home again?"

"But see how many adore him still."

"Then let us rest, play the loyal officer and watch. Complain into our wine as others do. Spill our blood to climb the mountains up to India. For him to claim the little ribbon of some most-eastern sea."

"No. We have these women with us here, to take the blame for it. Let us strike now."

Reaching Deeply Into the Well

Thalestris and Iskander

"What elixirs for longevity do the Amazons know about?"

"Those elixirs are within you already, now, waiting to be poured out. Many hold the cup, but few do more than put it to their lips. Poured out as man and woman meet to achieve the harmony nature intends for them. To embrace is easy, but nature's deepest possibilities are overlooked when humans fly by default to what comes easiest."

"Nature's possibilities?"

"Nature provides a primal source. Until we learn to drink from it thirst joins us on the journey of our lives. Men and women drink of what each other have, but their reach is shallow in the well so their cups run dry. Missing the wider pleasure to be enjoyed and the elusive harmony. Tell me, Iskander, what is the course of a man and woman's love?"

"Well . . . Each is drawn to the other's form and energy; they embrace to begin a dance of desire and touch. The woman's beauty excites the man and her passions also grow, so that she opens to him and he enters her. The fire of their sensations builds until the man reaches a peak of excitement and flows out in release, in an eternal moment of oblivion. Then he lies quietly with her as one dead, floating back to earth from some great distance he's been thrown."

"And what of the woman — when the man is flung so far away, and is settling back to earth again?"

"The woman? She could have loved another hour, throughout the day, and again at night. But what man is capable of that? The man has fallen, his desire is spent. The woman dances without him in the air a while, then glides slowly to the earth again. And by that time he sleeps."

"Iskander, for shame! The woman does not 'glide slowly to the earth again!' With the man's brief passion spent the woman is abandoned to an interrupted dance; left hanging there, let slip by her partner down the mountainside, barely having tasted pleasure's promises."

"Yes. It doesn't seem quite fair."

"Iskander, a man can prolong the act of love a great deal longer, if he so decides. It takes practice, and a decision to explore the wider distance on the path, the journey few explore: To hold the woman, to be one with her, and not flow out."

"Not have pleasure take its course?"

"There is a wider pleasure possible! Though he seems to deny himself, he discovers a subtle pleasure he would not have imagined possible. His woman's satisfaction reaches out to wrap him in a joy they share. No longer is he desperation's prisoner, knowing he leaves his partner unsatisfied as he goes off to sleep, desire wrung out of him. No longer will they meet so briefly then be wrenched apart again with violence as the man expends his energies.

"The one flesh man and woman are meant to be is reality when they learn this pleasure born of peace instead of violence, a sensuous melting into a unity larger than themselves, long moments of eternity instead of lonely spasms that pass for love. It is a journey so few take. A filling so many miss, so very eager to be poured out. To learn this is to control the mating energy, one of the five wild things in the inner life.

"And you who are skillful in battle must surely understand, this also is a contest, one with forces in yourself, that is to be achieved. Would you explore the greater opening man and woman's union brings? Learn stillness then! In stillness the depth of life may be revealed. That is the key to the long embrace — and to the spirit battle in your dreams."

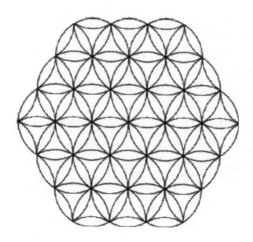

The "**Flower of Life**" from the wall of the Temple of Abydos in Egypt.

Dreamer of the Spheres

Thalestris and the philosophers

"So then Iskander, what does Aristotle claim holds everything in place here in the universe?"

"The Prime Mover, that moves and others move it not. But what is that?"

"The Dreamer of Spheres perhaps."

"Spheres?"

"What dimensions do we know, my Prince?"

"The linear, the flat, the solid, as Plato says. As in the line, the circle, and the sphere."

"And the others?"

"What do you mean? What others could there be?"

"What is your starting point? Draw the line for me."

Iskander puts his finger to the table top.

"Stop! There, where your finger touched. Why no mention of that point? Does it not precede the line?"

"Ah."

"And even before the point, what then? Why did the finger move, what was that motion's source? Where in you was that desire to have it done?"

"A dimension of the creative act?"

"Is it in that dimension the Unmoved Mover first set it all in flow, all this universe we see? Now let's draw a circle. Then make six circles more, all around the first circle's circumference, each of the six moving through the center of the first circle and the centers of the circles on each side of it." I draw it as I speak.

"And we could draw wider yet. Those farther points where the six circles meet, on each make one circle more." I begin to draw them in.

"I have seen this!" Iskander say, "In Egypt, on the wall of the *Osirion,* the temple of Osiris at Abydos. The *Flower of Life* is the name it's given."

"Indeed. Consider these circles, each of their spheres, each with its own center, its own identity, its own point of view; each with its own life, though also intermeshed with all the rest. And how did it begin? With the Prime Mover's first desire!

"All proceed with their own realities in a fabric they all share. You and I, my Prince, are we not included here? Are we not points of view, both connected and set free within the design of all?"

"It goes on and on, as many spheres as we might make!"

"Oh yes. Each one capable of its own infinite creation through imagination's force. And why? To be enjoyed by the Prime Mover! One great life from many points of view. Drops spun from a central sea, each with its own skin to wear."

"Of course!"

"We are circles the Prime Mover makes! Though we forget. Rain drops wondering at our skin, blinded by an inner mirror we hold up and refuse to set aside. Forgetting we are the sea. Forgetting the great movement to form the first circle, then the others that fill all dimensions of the universe. Forgetting the First Desire that sent us out, units of awareness connected to every other circle and their source. Within each of us a similar inner point, an image of that First Cause, spinning our own circles out, a creation of our own."

"Why does the Prime Mover desire the circles' flight?"

"The desire to experience! Do you think it is only for you, all this, the great adventure that you are?"

"Experiencing through me?"

"Through all of us! One great tapestry of one great dream. To know our gladness and our suffering. Shall Prime Mover be content with but one dream alone? Why not so many more, those that flow in all of us? As many as there are points of view! All of us wandering through the great labyrinth of the Prime Mover's dream, that holds all the circles with its own."

"What dimension is the next, beyond our own?

"Some say Spirit is. A dance intention casts, that ripples up the edge of dreams and harvests all our inner storms. There thought creates or else destroys, to bend the circles all askew."

"And then?"

"Then Prime Mover's pulse brings the circles true again. Cleanses what becomes unclear, to make the colors of the dreaming bright."

"How?"

"What happens to the wagon's wheels, league after league?"

"They turn; they wear and break."

"Our interwoven circles, so connected each to each, also have their shape skewed in this three-dimensional dance of solidity. It's then we merge with the Prime Breath. Merge our own breath with Spirit, and our intention too.

"*Intention* reached out to make the point as you began to draw. *Movement* was born with the curving line. *Distance* was defined as the circle was brought round. With each sphere's addition relationship let *gravity* grow. Intention, movement, distance, gravity, disassemble any one of these and all the intersecting spheres would come apart and be no more, bubbles pricked and burst that flail shards of gossamer. The waking of that first point to marvel at its retreating dream of spheres as dawn comes rushing in and breaks that dreaming shell."

The Unraveling

"Thalestris, is there no longer life designed for these bodies we have?" Iskander says to me when we're alone. "Must death come so soon for us, though something in us cries out so it ought not be?"

"The ladder goes only so far to the stars; we climb, we fall."

"Is poetry to be your answer then, and nothing more?" He shuffles in his seat. "Can the ladder be prolonged, repaired? Our span mended somehow with outpoured life? Why must death be?"

"It involves each *unit* of us, as Laontes says."

"How so?"

"The fabric of the body comes unwound. The ends of the threads splay out and no longer hold the pattern tight."

I pick up two cords. "See how I twist these cords, making spirals as they meet. Each of us has such a twisted cord in every speck of skin. Of hair, of bone, of spit. Of egg, of seed. And when a man and woman meet to make a child their turning cords entwine to dance — one cord of hers and one of his is their offspring's inheritance; thus does the child take shape from them."

"Two cords entwined? How do you know all this?"

"Part of the legacy we keep. And there is more. Give your arm a rub. See how the worn skin shuffs off? Each unit-speck replicates itself before it goes, taking shape by that pattern it owns unique to you, half from your mother and half from your father long ago bestowed. Those spiraling cords administer the building of new specks, replacing them before they fall. It is too small to see, hidden in the deepest storms, over and over again reproducing themselves until there comes a day finally when that speck shall be the last to form, with no new one grown to take its place. Speck by speck our bodies waste away."

"Why do they stop their reproducing work?"

I release the ends of the cord I hold. "Unraveling."

"It cannot be forestalled?"

I present the twisted cords to him. "What will you do to prevent their coming loose?"

"We do it with the laces of a boot, maintained tight with nubs of wax, or tiny caps of silver if a prince's shoe."

"Yes, nubs! And that's the key. The nubs rub away with use so that the cords unravel and a speck no longer recreates itself. Firmness into wrinkles, speck by speck, the fragile legacy of years.

"Each new speck of skin has new nubs at the cord's ends, and each next nub's less strong than the one before. After so many years, so many specks replaced, too much of that nub-cap's gone and the laces come undone. The speck no longer remakes itself, an obsolescence fashioned into us."

"Is there no stopping it? No way to safeguard the binding-caps? Why else would you be told such a legacy, if not also to be repairing it?"

"Ha! How you drain the mystery from each cup I pour! There is indeed a knowledge we safeguard for humanity, when it is time."

"Not now?"

"There is a key we hold. But no door to receive it yet."

"What? What are you telling me?"

"The science is not developed yet that can effect the change. It is an operation we have directions for but no knife small or sharp enough. There is a map, but no landmarks to know our position on the sea we sail. It's a treasure we hold for a future time: Why the cords become undone and what to do so they will not."

"How did you learn all this?"

"We rescue knowledge from the kingdoms as they fall. Fallen into dust or fallen in the sea, they feed the snake of history. That snake is long. And we have held it by its tail."

The Mysteries

"I've a curiosity, Iskander."

"Yes?"

"If your desire is to have acknowledgment of your godhood, was that not satisfied when you went to Egypt to be proclaimed 'Pharaoh' there? Each Pharaoh is considered a god by the Egyptians, yes? But that seemed not to have sufficed; you still needed to trek across the endless dunes to see the priests at the Oasis of Siwah. What did you hope they would provide?"

"Initiation in the mysteries."

"People were created for a great purpose, Iskander, to make our home in the wideness of the universe. First Earth then all the rest, an immensity to journey in. And this you'll consider irony: That journey begins inside of you. Propelled by what you'll encounter there where all is still.

"What am I? What is Prime Mover? Are we meant to have relationship? Questions long the domain of priesthoods and temples, etched in massive stone but in few hearts. Certainly not the hearts of humanity toiling dawn to dusk in fields, urging grain up with their sweat. And never told.

"And why? Is it not their birthright to know Spirit's plan for them? That the Creator is not out past the clouds somewhere but awaiting them in the quiet inside. For them to be loosed as life intends, set free from the chains of time as that relating starts.

"The priesthoods were created to keep the wisdom safe as the dark age came and the light of wisdom dimmed; then decided to keep it for themselves. And why? Why deny spirit-power to the rest? Did they feel overwhelmed at the massive job of educating them? Or was it something else, the realization that closely-held secrets make control more possible?

"Did they feel justified in doing that, taking control into their hands? Did their 'good intentions' somehow allow for it? Though even with the best of intentions the fact remains: They were holding Spirit back; and Spirit has intentions too, with freedom and power and wholeness for each of us. Shall the priesthoods set their hands against the sea and not be drowned as they attempt to stem its tide?

"There are stories meant to be told us on our mothers' knees. Unlocking possibilities. But mothers forget; and the priesthoods are not reminding them.

"Consider the ocean of Spirit with your body a wave on it, a finite form that's risen from its depths. The wave, so eagerly involved with separation's dance, proceeds to forget its source. Yesterday and tomorrow lock us in smallness, tight, though we rattle at our chains.

"The wave decrees itself a name and a history and self and from that brief wake creates a 'me.' Declares it is the only sort of dream there is, though a dream that melts and flees. The wave forgets the sea whose dance it is.

"There the solution is: As a wave we are the ocean too. As we wake to that inheritance we bring the entire sea into the life of the waves we are and a new quality of experience unfolds for us. We're still waves; but wave-life has a whole new feel once we know we are the sea and our little dramas no longer possess the same urgent relevance.

"With silence deep enough it becomes real; the ocean's depths are soothing us with, 'Now, now, be present now with what is happening.' That Spirit from which we're sown is urging us back toward itself with, 'Wider, be ever wider yet!' So that the qualities of what we know as self are changed as we grow toward greater possibility, a journey to something more than what the body's little history can hold.

"The sea we are remains and we can be connected strong to it, though we're waves still. We'll leap to catch the sun! And bring all the sea into our flight."

"More mysteries!" Iskander throws his hands aloft.

I stare at him. "You invite me to loose you from the chains of time. And I would; save that the lock is one you've fastened on yourself, though you forget. And the key is in your hand."

Integrity

I build the evening fire. A smaller one this time. "Peace allows integrity to be found."

"Integrity?" He takes a seat by me.

"Another word for honesty, with its root-meaning 'one,' as in integral, whole, not divided. When I realize my unity with you on some deep level I'll not soon be cheating you. The end result, one becomes 'responsible.' Community becomes a possibility."

"What of those who take the other path, away from unity?" Iskander throws a log onto the fire.

"Those who remain body-identified? With no interest in community they become smaller yet, caught in time's net and lured by surface storms. Their sense of separation increases in an ever-spiraled life-for-self, embracing the destiny of waves, that they shall end."

"Though they seem to prosper so!"

"As waves prosper, yes. With no care for integrity, responsibility provides no pause to their debauch. Regrets will soon wear down their confidence, shredding their self-assurance with each misstep. And the future-fear shall claim them certainly."

"Why no interest on their part?"

"They'd take interest a while for power's sake. Though the sort of presence I speak of is a connection to Prime Mover's source, that too-bright power from which they've taken flight. They belong to the noise of fear, and it's no mystery why: That time when the wave shall crest and break is foremost in their minds, for the wave is all they chose to be."

"So simple from your lips."

"Though it is not. Not easy to be quiet, not at all, with a distraction formed in us by Nature at an early age."

"What distraction's that?"

"One Nature thrusts on us, to have us serve the body's continued life at a time when life hung by a thread. A plan to assure survival, even at the expense of peace and happiness. Have you not discerned? Peace is not the agenda of the mind."

The Infant's Wordless Reasoning

"Consider control. So important to you, yes?"

"Of course."

"Can you control your thinking, so not to be at the effect of it?"

"What do you mean?"

"The thoughts that give unpleasant feelings birth, might it be you aren't in control of them?"

"Not in control of what I think?"

"That's it."

"Of course I am!"

"Oh? Perhaps when you decide on going left or right. Whether to eat a date or else a fig. Otherwise well . . ."

"What an outrageous thing to say!" His face flares red.

I lean forward in my seat, not quite whispering, "Shall I prove it to you, then?"

Iskander flings an arm, get on with it.

"Can you decide on silence as you choose? Will to have no thoughts at all?"

"Well . . . They keep coming back again."

"Where are they coming from? If you're not thinking them who is?"

Iskander scowls.

"Humans are fraught with sorrows and regrets. Are you heir to those?"

"A few."

"Though you banish them? That's odd. Who allows them audience, those thoughts you'd just as soon neglect?"

Iskander's eyes scroll thin.

"They keep coming back to chew on you? That must be annoying." I choose a date from a silver bowl of them. Slowly eat it bit by bit.

"And?"

"Perhaps it's best that I not say, Great King," I wave a dismissive hand, "You wish to think you're in control. Why not go on thinking it?"

"I wish to know the truth!"

I face Iskander. "There is a creature in you doing it. That's where the thoughts come from, the ones you'd rather be without."

"No!"

"Yes."

"Who put it there?"

"You. When you were small. For your survival's sake, or so it seemed."

I choose another date from the bowl of them.

"The creature produces thinking. And makes it seem the thoughts all come from you. Though they do not; not the true you that holds Prime Mover's spark and meant to learn and share its will. It is a phantom self that's been devised."

"A phantom self?"

"Tell me, are you often drawn to the past and the future, obsessed with what's not happening?"

"As much as other people I suppose."

"Do you end up feeling better from all that? The worry, the regret?"

"Obviously not."

"Why do you let that happen then?"

"Well . . ."

"Don't you have the power to remain present, where your power is, in what is happening now? Why not exercise the will to stay?"

Iskander begins twisting in his seat. "What does that have to do with it, this creature you speak about?"

"Because that's the task the creature has! The creature thrives on thoughts that keep you in anxiety, ever fearful you will break. And declaring no matter what is, 'It shouldn't be this way!' Intending to distract you from this moment, now. From your power and from your peace. From your allotted portion of eternal bliss."

"But why?"

"Because survival depends on our distress."

The Philosophers Gather

"There's a transition to be made. It's time to take your power back, all that creature stole away."

"You've done this?"

"I am a cup the Creator fills then pours into the sea. Deep silence welcomes me and bids me stay. My spirit wings are wide. Though not always so. We all begin as waves intent on being separate."

We can see Parmenides on his way to the tent, arriving early for the meeting of philosophers. "I want to hear more about all this," Iskander says, "Might you explain this to Parmenides?"

"As you wish. Let him talk and I'll bend the subject round."

"I heard a strange thing today," Parmenides takes his chair.

"What's that?" I answer him.

"That there are entities that feed on fear."

"I suppose there's quite a feast for them these days!" I laugh. "Did you ask what entities those were?"

"No. Though obviously it's doubtful . . ."

"Why doubt? I know it's true! And not least fierce are those inside of us, that have control of our emotions and are squeezing them. And the curious part is, that's the job we've given them."

"Why would we do that?"

"For our survival's sake!"

Parmenides lets his face contort.

"And why fear only when regrets will do as well? Shame, blame, guilt, regret, the whole sad dialogue. Energy enough to feed a multitude. What better way for entities to access unlimited supply than take control of our emotional lives, to prune and nurture that grim harvest as they will?"

Parmenides gives a glower.

"Shall you ask why? Did nature leave the inner door ajar, perhaps, for progress as you grew to render you susceptible? So thinking when it did appear — was seized by them! Their tool. Not so many, though. Only one. What you choose to call the mind."

Parmenides pours himself wine. "I suppose you can explain all that, how fear and regret help us survive."

"Tell me Parmenides, what is more natural for humankind, to seek revenge or to forgive?"

"Vengeance, certainly."

"Ah. And is it natural to forgive themselves? Or is regret by nature just the same?"

"Ha! It is. A mental plague of self-vengeance assailing them."

"A plague of regret certainly. Is there some source of it? Let's think it through. Regret must have some reason to exist or we'd not be doing it. What reasons can you find?"

"Well, we're trying to improve, I would suppose."

"Improvement. Good. What else?"

"So much inner wrestling! A quest for 'why,' as though to renew one's self-control."

"To keep or regain control. That's two. One more."

"Tell me." He shrugs.

"How does it feel, all that rummaging about inside the past, the urgency to improve somehow and revive self-trust by recovering control?"

"It feels bad."

"Yes! Feeling bad. A third reason we have regrets."

"But why?"

"So we'll survive! Just as I said. It's an original survival plan we have in place. A feel-bad habit we're stuck with, developed during infancy for survival's sake, still functioning. And it's time now to dismantle it!"

Pyrrhus, Thales, and Itzak

"More on their way," Iskander has a view through the tent's open flap. "Now we have Parmenides involved let's start again with them."

"Good. Let them talk a bit, then I'll begin."

Pyrrhus, Thales, and Itzak arrive and take their seats.

"How does Thales today?" Iskander asks.

"Trapped in thoughts, somewhat."

"Though desiring to be still?" I take up the thread.

"Um."

"Tell me about your survival strategy."

"My what?"

"You know, the plan you have in place so you'll survive."

Thales thins his eyes at me.

"Are you truly 'at cause' in your life, or simply making a crazed effort at controlling everything?"

"Wait, wait!" Thales waves his hands, "We began with stillness, shifted to survival and now we talk about control?"

"Peace comes with control, once control is truly yours. Tell me, can you control thought, stop thinking when you want?"

"Well, the thoughts keep rushing back."

"You go into fear a lot?"

"As much as anyone."

"And thrash around with old regrets?"

"Yes."

"Well, there it is."

"There what is?"

"You're not in control. Fear is. Fear is your survival plan. Not a protocol I recommend as being very practical, though folks seem so content with it."

"Fear helps me survive?"

"Why would you be going into fear so much if it didn't seem to serve somehow? As for the regrets, that's fear as well, you know. 'What's wrong with me that I did that?' Stirring mistakes in hope to soothe your withered self-esteem. Sleuthing your tattered respect-in-self in a way that just keeps shredding it. Which doesn't seem to address the goal too well."

"What goal?"

"Survival. That's what we're discussing, right? Tight control is central to your present plan, though a plan you have scant handle on; and fear is its choice of tools."

"What other plan for survival is there then?"

"One you may develop when you're quiet enough. You'll have options then."

"Oh?"

"Noisy stuff, all that regret and fear. It pushes you around, you're 'at effect' of it. You don't embrace every person you pass by but you'll accept every thought that comes! It keeps you from what else there is inside."

"I'll just say no to fear!"

"Of course you will. And easily too, once you know fear's origin. The way it got the helm of your life's ship."

"Which is?"

"A process quite natural as it turns out. A hoax Nature plays on us, that no one's told you of and you've not deciphered yet. But you can do that now. Access is meant to be assured, winding down past thinking's noise to peace. I'll give you clues."

"All right," Thales says, "I'm ready for the clues you have."

"Whose ship is it?" I thump my chest.

"Ship?"

"The ship of the body. Whose ship is it?"

Thales squints at me.

"See that tree out there? That's Life's tree! Life's flower! Life's body too," thumping again. "Life streaming every moment through, fresh and new. With its own agenda. With Life's own protocol. Its own survival plan! Life's voice awaits inside of you to connect you up with it."

"That I can't hear for all the mental noise?"

"Yes! And whose noise is it?" I thump again.

"The body? It's the body's noise?"

"Yes! The body has its own mind! One that develops as it grows. It's what I call the 'body-mind,' though 'Tyrant-mind' is a term more true! The source of so many thoughts you think of as your own. The body developed its own fear-based survival strategy before the year of two. Though it doesn't work, not very well devised for life as an adult, and still in operation even so! Such noise! Though there's another option, one that Life provides."

"How does that work?"

"Someone should have told you long ago. You'd not have let the body keep control, feared yourself into an early grave."

"So how . . ."

"No, no. I'll give you clues, the rest is up to you. First clue: How did the body get the helm, take control of the ship of Life?"

He shrugs.

"You've met control-obsessed people right? Why would someone develop in that way? Why would such an urgent desire to maintain control be so imperative? The end-all of existence."

"Hmm. After they'd been helpless, I suppose."

"Yes! After a time of helplessness in the extreme. Trying to gain some semblance of control, any little shred of it — when there was nothing to be had! None at all. No wonder control was such a big concern to them. Then finally they found a way."

"Ah."

"So tell me, has there been such a time for you, so lacking in control?"

Thales looks off past the open tent flap as he ponders it.

"Consider life's progress in you. I'll wait. Here's another clue meanwhile: Start at day one."

"Infancy! I was a baby in the crib."

"Indeed. That's when your survival plan was put in place. There you were, blissfully being. No sense of time. No thinking. No sense of self. Only conscious contact with events of the moment, now and now and now. The world was radiating love and life was kind. But you got cold and wet and needed food. So you put out a call for help. And life provided! Life seemed a well-run institution set on meeting your needs in a quite amazing way.

"Though it could be slow. Wordlessly you wondered, 'Why does it take so long? What am I to do to have help come? Must I improve somehow?'

"Whenever help did not arrive in a timely way the discomfort became increasingly intense and you were feeling worse and worse, until — suddenly the remedy! Had little

You accomplished it, improved sufficiently? Or had you finally felt bad enough, a simple cause and effect scenario?

"That was the only data available; and a system was set in place that was based on it: The First Survival Strategy. From that time on you've been goaded with the imperative to improve, a situation that conflicts with 'contentment now.' And there's a perpetual propensity for 'feeling bad' since that's when help arrives — as confirmed by your experience! Wasn't feeling steadily-worse the pattern that precedes release?

"The body developed a mind of its own, and when thinking came on board at about one year of age the body-mind took charge of it and is still wielding it today, employing thoughts to do its will: to have you feeling bad so help will come. Help from outside, of course, and never looking in."

"So that's what sends the thoughts," Thales asks, "fear and regret and all the rest — the body's private made-up mind?"

"You're getting it! The body-mind means well, working to keep the body intact by protecting it with fear's blunt tool. Meanwhile its vestigial voice proclaims the body's little wave as all that is; that with its demise all is despair and ruin, and stark oblivion. With no will to see beyond."

A Portal to the Quiet

"What's to be done?" Thales asks.

"You find the portal to the quiet, where one thought stops before the next begins. A first-level peace awaits we're meant to know, that arrives as time-based cares subside."

"What even greater peace exists?"

"You must discern. Prime Mover in search of you, perhaps, deep in that inner sea; and you are meant to meet once the tyrant-mind lets go, as a shadow does when the sun appears."

"Ah."

"It may help now to play a game. Tell me what you notice going on," I motion toward the hills. "Even the most subtle of events."

"There's a lot of motion in the sky, clouds . . ."

"Yes, but let's ignore the weather in the sky for now."

"Very well. There's people walking about."

"Good."

"Wind in the trees, there on the left. Smoke from fires."

"Yes."

"Bird . . . Butterfly . . . Squirrel . . . Hawk . . . Bee . . . Bug."

"Very well, you have the idea. Now peace shall be our prize! Tell me this, is peace a feeling or a thought?"

"Well, more a feeling I'd say."

"Then it's in feeling's realm it's to be found. Feeling is the gate through which we'll pass to peace: Where one thought ends and the next begins, an opening. Now another game to discover it.

"In our first game you placed attention on the landscape and ignored the sky. This game is similar: You'll pay attention to feelings but ignore the thoughts."

"All right."

"Close your eyes. Discover feelings that arrive. Thoughts will too, but no need to respond to them or push them aside. Just let them come and go of their own accord; it's your energy of responding that keep's them there so long.

"Thinking becomes faint, and the calm arrives. Be aware of the feelings in the body that emerge instead. Like sitting quietly beneath a tree to let the forest come to view. Simple awareness, effortless."

I watch as they all begin.

"Allow what awareness brings without resisting it. A tingle on the arm, an itch on the foot, the breeze against the skin. The sensations require no labeling. Absence of words in the head allows sensations to proliferate. If a feeling seems intense breathe into it and await the next; allow them to morph and coalesce until a whole-body peace has a chance to come, subtle as spring to take you by surprise.

"Leave the weather thinking stirs at the surface of the sea so high above as you experience the ocean's quiet, a depth of silence long ago forgot. Deep inside the body's shell of form dwells the sea's voice to be heard. On the other side of silence, the sea's soft song."

The Lost Name

"Such a wonderful feeling," Pyrrhus says as they open their eyes. "And a feeling that I know."

"Oh?"

"There are times I've escaped the flood of words inside. Where noise had been there's sudden awe."

"When did this begin?"

"With a name that's lost. When the mind went off to look for it."

I only smile so he goes on. "One day in mid-thought there was a person's name that wouldn't come to mind, entirely irretrievable! So the mind went off in search of it.

Awareness was left alone, staring into nothingness in expanding wonderment. Out on the ledge with a whole new inner landscape coming into view.

"Then suddenly the mind returned, lost name in tow. 'What are you doing out there? Come back instantly!' And I went back in of course. Though when it happened next, some word mid-sentence suddenly absent and nowhere to be found and the mind away in consternation at its loss, I went out even farther on the ledge, the better to view the vista of pure being's realm, calm and clear and bright, no words in sight."

"And then?"

"When the mind returned to call me in I turned a deaf ear to it. No matter it pouted so and stamped its feet."

"Luring you back into its game of time!"

"Yes. I kept looking forward to the next occasion of forgetting, the pure presence it offers me. Now you've shown me how to enter feeling's realm instead of thought — so I can come and go in it at will!"

Clearing Muddy Water

"What are we to expect in the inner life as we become aware of the body-mind?" Parmenides asked.

"How do you clear muddy water?"

"By not stirring it!"

"Of course. The normal way to handle muddy feelings is to stir them with our thoughts. Then we wonder why it just gets worse! A thought breeds a feeling, to which we summon yet more thoughts to mull the feeling out --- in a circular trap. It can happen very fast, in one big blur. Feelings breeding thinking, round and round.

"But not you. You have a new procedure now, the simple observing art, to be with feelings as they come and go and detach them from whatever thoughts are causing them.

As you sit with a feeling to experience it in its purity, not labeling it or feeding more thinking to the mix, the thoughts slow down enough to recognize each one and ask, 'Where did this come from? What is the intention of the thought? Is it to have me feeling bad?' And the feeling has a chance to change.

"It comes down to this: Can we decide our survival no longer depends on feeling bad? Can we entertain a thought as though to guide or warn without having it become anxiety? Can we begin to reassume control, say 'no' to fear and decline the invitations to regret? Yes? There begins to be some silence where the noise has been. We take our intention back! Free to develop some more tenable survival plan."

"Does the body-mind simply capitulate?" Pyrrhus asks. "Does it concede to this superior wisdom you devise? Relinquish the control it had the childhood mandate to acquire? Shall it give that power up?"

"You'll take your original intention back! Consider, what you brought with you here when you were born. With what did you arrive on Earth?"

"Well . . . The body of course."

"Yes."

"Awareness, knowingness."

"Go on."

"The will . . ."

"Intention, yes. That the body mind has commandeered --- serving its early mandate, for the body to survive. Not so bad as intentions go, though a short-sighted one, and the survival plan formed round it is unfortunate. Our innate will can be reclaimed.

"You can retake control, reclaiming intention's role for the will to serve the steadily emerging true-you at last. Be calm; watch. Ask where the thoughts are coming from and what intention they perform. Additional options come to view and the body-mind's short-sighted urgency is evident.

190

Understanding what is happening has been the key to being free of it. You've let the water clear. Whatever higher authority is yet to be discovered, you are at-cause then for the quest."

By What Authority

"Higher authority," Parmenides leans forward in his chair. "How are we to determine that?"

"Ah," I smile. "Who are you, really? By what authority have you come here? Tell me that and I shall answer you."

"Spirit then? You spoke of 'spirit-wings.'"

"Spirit? We know as much of that as fish know about the air! Shall you find wings broad enough to fly in that rare element? Be sure you know they'll hold your weight when the body's gone!

"This much is sure: The mind thinks you are a body, no more than that; and the process of becoming free shall never be complete until you become convinced, persuaded in your most inner knowing, that you have moved beyond that self-definition and thoughts of the body's demise no longer trouble you. That you are immune to its urgent plan to rescue you in its body-centric way. Till then the body-mind has hold on you, for anxiety to interrupt your peace. You're 'at effect' of it."

A New Heart

"What of Itzak?" I let my smile inquire.

"It is a peace I also know, as when I am at prayer. Making request with thoughts; then silence for listening, a stillness deep enough for boundaries to be loosed, the Creator and me no longer separate, no more than a raindrop when it hits the sea. Continuous prayer then, and continuing relationship."

"The infant's survival strategy makes sense to you?"

"Oh yes. A spark of the Creator's Spirit-fire exists in every human born, ready to grow by relationship with him. It is with that relating I have replaced the body-mind.

"It's as the prophet Ezekiel said: *A new heart will I give you, and a new spirit will I put within you; and I will take away the stony heart out of your flesh, and I will give you a heart of flesh.*"

Angry Dreams

The philosophers go out, to their own talks by their own fires.

"I am so tired." Iskander rests his face inside his hands. "So many angry dreams that come. No way to escape their rage."

"Angry about what? What makes you angry in your dream?"

"Too many shadows. Too many people with no face, no name. Anger storms up in me. What causes such distress?"

"As to the rage you feel, it has its roots in time. Once you understand its source an opening can appear to that realm where silence waits. The one we have discussed today."

"Oh?" He wrinkles up his face. "So I'm causing it myself?"

"Consider how much you've taken on yourself, that you yourself have never caused."

"What do you mean?"

"Have you taken on some other person's dream?"

"Whose?"

"Your father Philip perceived the Persians had 'deceived and cheated' Greece when they burned the temples of Athens to the ground, so that he dreamed revenge. You have taken his dream upon yourself. Then claimed godhood for yourself, for a god's justice-making to be your own; so to wring the dreaming circles of their right and wrong, to make them clean again by your own strength.

"In your life-dream you fling their subdued circles round yourself, these many nations of the Earth. All the pressure that the center point must be so strong to hold you shoulder to yourself, as Atlas shouldered all the world.

"So much conflict you distill, waging war on battlefields, your chosen way of making circles straight. It comes back around to you in dreams. You face a conquest you'd not thought to have, an adversary you'd not thought to meet, the one inside yourself. From outside vast sandy empires call to you to take frail ownership of them, but so much more awaits where you might rule within. The conquest of the mind's fierce guardian."

He stares at me. "Your remedies are for normal men. Does the mouse call it evil that the hawk has claws, and strikes? For the mouse it's true! But I am the hawk, and I bend Nature to my ends."

"But what of so much bending *you*? What of your father then? His spirit's claws still clutch at you. You can be free of it. It is a stream of dream in which you need not drown."

"Why must I go into that?" Iskander snarls, "I have closed it off from me!"

"It closes you away from life!"

"No! Why torment me so!" Wheeling round, hands to his head.

"It is a stream dammed up, a pool grown stagnant-deep. How shall you be free of storms, so chained to them?"

"This world is mine, if I go conquer it! Talk to me of freedom then!"

"So much weather, stirring waves inside of you."

"I am the wind! A storm the world does battle with! And you," he gnarls his face at me, "What am I doing here in your embrace? Soothing me with such soft words, distracting me with pleasure's calm! A woman from — where? From a clan of women that fought my kin! Who may even be my enemy. You make a journey here to take control of me, so my companions say! Is it not so?"

"Iskander . . ."

"Is my army one great band of intruders you detest? Is that what I am to you?"

Iskander wheels about, throws wide the tent's thin flap. Calls for his horse that's saddled instantly for him.

Then he's at a gallop down the path. Hurrying past trees that gather beads of silver from the swollen liquid sky.

Iskander's men are clumped to watch, turning to the tent to look at me. I shrug at them. What Macedonian has not had lover's quarrels of his own?

I call my horse and slowly take the direction he has flown. Thoughts tear at me that search for feelings' cause, requiring some solution, any foothold from despair. What have I done? So many thoughts that reach out for reply, to snag me in the Thinker's labyrinth. The mist stirs heavy on the air. I welcome the hoof beats' song to slow the breaking savage drum.

Three Sentinels

On a hill near the camp three Amazons sit as sentinels among the trees. They watch the morning's brightness grow. Hear each bird that calls, each song that sends response. Aware of every path of doe and boar and fox. The wind goes down the valley touching all the trees, caresses the three sentinels and shuffles on again.

"Something coming."

"Horses."

"There! The trail that leads into the road."

"Twenty at least. I go to the Queen!"

"Wait! One horse more, running fast along the road out from the camp. The rider races to a trap!"

"Iskander! Why fly so? Why all alone?"

They watch as Iskander is encircled, given blows and returning them with his bare fists, hemmed in with spears and staves. They seize the horse's reins. Back through the hills, taking him with them.

"Come! We follow them!"

Lightning You Are Playing With

For how long I ride I do not know, when suddenly an Amazon rides toward me on the path. "Thalestris! Trouble! Iskander! Taken prisoner!"

"How?"

"Mountain tribesmen came into our sentry-circle. We were about to come to you, then saw Iskander at a gallop racing toward their trap. They took him off into the hills."

"Did you follow them?"

"Yes, two are there and I am come for you."

"We go!"

At their village the other two Amazon sentinels watch at a distance as Iskander is tied to a post. The tribesmen laugh and menace him with spears. Then an argument breaks out. "Let's kill him now!' says one.

"No, we'll ransom him," another's voice.

"Kill! That's the agreement we made, what Maris and Tydeus said to do." Iskander hears; two names he knows.

"You heard what Bren said!" Pointing to the boy nearby. "We must make it seem the work of the women who have come!"

"No, not yet! We can get more gold from the Macedonians than Tydeus and Maris offer us. Do you know how much gold the Macedonians have acquired? All the gold of Persepolis!"

"Let him go." A quiet voice. The men turn around to see the women standing there.

"Go home," the men say, "We'll handle this."

"We won't have a home soon, if this goes on. Let him go. Apologize to him."

"Be quiet! Or go away!"

"Where are we to go? Shall we stay here to die with you? Where shall we go far enough to escape what you bring down on us? Let the Macedonian go. It's lightning you are playing with."

But the men turn away from the women and their pleas, back to their arguing. The women snatch their children from the scene, go off a distance and hold their heads inside their hands.

The argument goes on. "We have this arrow we're to use," waving it about, "to have it seem the women's work. But we have no bow."

"We make a way for it with this," a man unsheaths his knife, approaching Iskander at the stake. Raising the blade to strike . . .

"No!" Thalestris and the others come from behind the trees, arrows on their bowstrings, taut. The man stands back, let the knife fall.

Thalestris unties Iskander. "I have made you upset," she says, "and I am sad for it. I have come to say goodbye."

"Please don't go. I've been so arrogant. There are things I wish to say, about my father, since you ask. So much I need to know; the winds inside, do you believe their raging could be stilled?"

Iskander's horse is found. He reins Bucephalus where the group of women and their children stand, weeping, terrified.

"Here boy," he reaches out for Bren the stable boy, pulls him up behind him on the horse. "I shall send him back, if he knows how to tell the truth. I am sorry for you, that your men have failed to honor you. For your sake I'll let them live, for the courage that you've shown. Greed is a plague the whole Earth shares. I knew the cities were its home; I had hoped better things for those who live among the trees."

Vision

"There was a vision that came, Thalestris, while I was tied there to the post. I was in a sphere, one connected to others, each to each, so many circles curving away from me toward that First Central Circle they started from, the Flower of Life, the one I'd seen at Abydos. So many circles bent, flawed, out of harmony. Just as you said they'd be.

"Then a voice came. 'Give the anger to me. Send all that broken energy here, where the circles all convene to touch, here at my heart. I shall make the circles true again, shall take the anger out for the energy to run pure once more. This is justice, bringing the circles true again. That is what I do. Justice proceeds from me. Not you.'

"I gave all the anger then to the circles' dance. It flowed through me and I was calm. Again the voice: 'There remains one thing for you to do. The 'you' that has been hurt, that place in you that's been a battleground and you were wounded in the fight, give up that injury as well. Give that dream of separation up, that tears your circle from my hand.'

"So I let all the hurting go. Anger and expectation fled. I found my breath again. And the hurt was gone."

Tydeus and Maris

Back at camp Iskander takes me with him to his tent while he speaks with Bren. Then calls several officers to come in as well.

"My friends, you are called here now to be a court. Tydeus and Maris have very nearly got me killed by tribesmen hired to ambush me. Thalestris and her warriors saved me; I owe her my life. These tribesmen tied me to a pole intent on doing violence. I heard them speak two names: 'Tydeus and Maris,' they said. One of you go now, bring Tydeus in to us. Tell nothing to him of what it is about, nor anything at all to Maris yet. Do you understand?"

"Yes."

They go and return with Tydeus.

"Tydeus, there is treason in our ranks. We have had unpleasantness with the tribesmen from the hills. There is a name they spoke while they had me tied up to a pole: 'Maris' is the word they said. I know Maris confides in you at times, that his lips are loose. What have you heard of this?"

Tydeus goes pale. "Maris? They said his name? I know the love he has for you. Oh, frustration does occur, so homesick for Macedonia. He makes jokes, says stupid things. Then laughs as though it were a jest. I hardly thought it serious enough to be alarmed, and decided to come to you if he should seem truly intent on some ill deed. But you are safe! How glad I am!"

"Tydeus, you should have brought me word of it instantly. For that I am upset, though with Maris more so. Go to your tent, await my call to come to me again."

Tydeus is escorted out by an officer. Then Maris is called in. Maris provides words almost the mirror of what Tydeus has said. Then Tydeus is led in again. The two men look into each other's eyes, wondering what each one has said. Wondering what to do.

Iskander motions and Bren comes out of the shadows, crossing the floor to stand at Iskander's hand.

Tydeus and Maris throw themselves face-down on the ground at Iskander's feet.

"What am I to do with you?" Iskander sadly shakes his head. "Would you kill your king? To have it be blamed on these innocents, our guests? So their homeland might be overrun to avenge my death while you stand back and laugh? What sort of justice, what sort of civilization have we brought with us across the Earth? What! Is it so vile? Should we never have set out? Yes, I heard two names today as I waited for the taunts to cease and death to come. Names of two I had considered friends. Has evil found such a welcome home in you? What did you hope to gain by all of this? What am I to do?"

"We deserve to die," the two men simper.

"Yes, of course you do. As I also do for the anger I displayed, racing off instead of facing this life I'm in. Shall I judge you before I judge myself? See . . . I weep for you. Is it Macedonia, you desire so much? Go then! I send you back to Macedonia, there to explain to my mother and our countrymen what you have done. Let them be the ones to judge you there! With letters from me as to what has happened here, in which I shall plead for you, for mercy, as I must also hope for it myself. 'It is Macedonia they loved more than me,' my words shall say. 'How have I failed them? I who thought I held them in my heart?'

Tydeus and Maris do not look up to see the tears they hear.

"The tribeswomen in the hills came to my defense. Women! They played the part that you, my friends, were sworn to do. How much gold did you offer to betray your king? Let its weight in stone be tied to you as you make the journey home to Macedonia on foot, so to remind you of my heart's heaviness, so heavy now at having two friends less."

Face to Conquering Face

We go to Iskander's tent and sleep. When it is dawn I feel his hands on me again, circling round my waist. I fill his arms and we are in an instant one. "What will be thought, Iskander," I spread my hands against his chest, "when you return without having hunted lions?"

"Ha! Are you not lion enough to hold? A lioness has conquered me! Though it seems we do indeed have a lion nearby as I learned yesterday, and we must go in search of it. Shall you come hunt with us?"

"For sport? Shall lions not have a right to live as well as we? Such noble beasts!" I run my claws down Iskander's skin and purr, beseeching him on the cat's behalf.

"I feel the same way you do concerning it! But this lion has crossed the lines one sets as boundaries. It was attacking sheep in the villages and soon afterward the goats. Then the dogs, which one would hope have the sense to run. Now it has a taste for small children it finds playing out of doors."

"A problem, yes."

"And as I am the conquering king in residence here it falls to me to lead the party out."

"When do we go?"

"Now. Will you bring your bow?"

We join fifteen of Iskander's men and ride east with several of the local villagers as guides. The men carry spears and shields. I have my bow. On the way Iskander explains the plan to me.

"When the lion is first sighted we will dismount and form a long line, separated from each other by a short stone's throw, and with that formation proceed through the trees and grass until we see the lion again.

"Each time the lion is started it will run and we'll pursue in our long line. The lion is strong, such fine muscles wrapped in fur, but becomes winded easily, accustomed to brief streaks to attack its prey, not running distances. We'll run close behind after each sprint and catch up to it each time it rests. The lion will run a third time and perhaps a fourth, but not much after that. Then it will stand to fight it out."

"What happens then?"

"The easiest thing would be to send you on up to make short work of it."

"And the other options?"

"Actually, the men would be disappointed not to take a hand in it. See how they have begun to shed their clothes, to allow the claws to find the skin. Such an honor to have scars to show from the battle we'll be in."

"Of course," I smile, "Why should fine clothing be torn when it is flesh the claws come close to find?"

"Indeed."

"So. It becomes a brave bloody snarl? How glorious! Do you have knives?"

"We do; here is my own. But first we employ spears, throwing them from behind our shields. I know that is the lazy way but custom dictates it."

My clothing I also shed, as the others have. The men make futile pretense at propriety as they mill about like gnats to look at me. "So the lion will run a time or two?" I say, pretending not to notice their huge eyes.

"Yes. Then it stands for the last time, in the thickest grass it has available. We'll make a circle surrounding it and begin to close the circle tight. The lion will roar at us and wait, at least while we are far enough away. We draw the circle tighter yet and the lion is loud and lunging with its claws as our circle ever smaller grows, with our spears held out to hem it in. Finally one of our hunters will be sent to move toward it — they made me agree not to be the one this time."

"Because you have a guest!"

"That's right. One hunter ventures ever closer to the lion, taunting it. As the lion prepares to jump at him the other hunters come closer poised to strike.

"When the lone hunter is too close the lion will spring at him. As the beast flies through the air his own spear may be too frail to stay the beast and he'll be knocked down by the great paws while everyone else closes in to finish it. He'll be the first one with wounds to show. But see! We have found our prey!"

It is a male, with a great mane and reddened mouth from some recent prize it's won. It makes its first run away from us. We dismount and form our line. I take my place with my bow at Iskander's back, as I have no shield.

The chase develops as he said it would. We follow after it until it tires and stops. Then the lion runs a second time and we catch up again. No more running after that, the big cat stands and turns on us as the circle forms and the men close in. The lion roars at the lone hunter coming slowly forward to make it leap.

But this lion does not follow all the plan; it leaps too soon, going suddenly past the one that approaches him, intent on escaping the ring of spears and swatting at the next closest Macedonian. Then full at Iskander, knocking him to the ground and reaching for Iskander's skin beneath the shield, paws moving fast and quick, a cat that digs a bug that hides beneath a shoe.

The circle is too wide to provide help. I am the only one nearby, with an arrow on my bow that I send swift into the great beast's heart. The lion goes limp atop Iskander, face to conquering face.

We pry them apart, red streaming toward each other's wounds, the mingled blood of kings.

Light To Cleanse

I tend Iskander's wounds. Bind them up with light. He is amazed to see them heal so well beneath my hands. "It hurt?" I ask.

"Some. Not as much as the things some people say."

"That pain is released as you forgive."

"That is a concept I find strange when feelings rage. Taking off a person's head most easily restores my own."

"Iskander, would you be free or bound? Your thoughts of being wronged are chains. They open you to spirits that stand ready to feed on you. It is a simple strategy for victory, this: Make the choice to unilaterally heal the wound, no matter what any other person does or thinks. Being strong takes you beyond their pettiness."

"That quiets the fire of hurt?"

"Your exterior has been scruffed? So has the other's, just as much. 'Others should be strong enough to accept our most blunt comment, whatever we may say,' we think; though we ourselves still crumble at the slightest quake. You must be the stronger one, to introduce the gentleness."

A Request

"What may I give to you to keep, to remind you of this time we've shared?"

"The gift of this time with you is all that I desire, Great King."

"But you give so much. Saved my life. Twice. Is there nothing more? Surely there must be."

"The libraries in Egypt and in Pergamum are your domain. I would accept the invitation to have certain scrolls and stones and walls be copied for me there."

"Of course."

Before the day is out I am presented with a letter providing all I've asked. Next day he also takes me to a tent where with a sweep of hand he presents to me a heap of scrolls he's had brought in. Some that survived the fire at Persepolis and others retrieved from Tyre and Babylon.

"Here in your hands let their dust secure a resting place."

"How royal a gift!"

"I hope you will tell me what you find in them."

A Gift for Our Child

"Iskander, though it cannot compare with your gift of scrolls . . . Here is a small golden gift for you."

"The four-headed leopard! It's me!"

"Yes. With its four heads and delicate four wings."

"From the prophet Daniel's words that speak of me, that they showed me in Jerusalem!"

"Yes."

"Thalestris, tell me . . . Is gold highly esteemed among the women of your land? Do they jostle for it? Does it corrode their dreams?"

"Oh, we prize it for its workmanship. But we do not fill our thoughts with it. Do not live for it, to amass our own self-worth as it grows in piles. And our care for one another replaces the idolatry commerce can become."

"When I first invaded Asia I had no idea how I would pay my men. Just in time I would overtake some city with its treasury. I kept nothing for myself, rewarding generously all who fought alongside of me. And now I have a thought . . . You have a strong force here with you . . ."

"Three hundred warriors, all armed with bows. Strong and tested, bled in battle with marauders or in tournaments."

"I know you are not my enemy. You have saved me twice when you might have let me die. And of course there is the knife beneath my pillow as we sleep. Surely you would have used it were you so disposed.

"And here is my true problem, though a happy one: I now possess vast amounts of Persian gold. The treasury at Persepolis was full when I arrived, they were not expecting me so soon. Such a great hoard of objects awaiting me, the equal in craftsmanship of this fine leopard you've given me. And now, you believe you shall have our child?"

"As women are able to know these things, I may tell you it is now accomplished, yes."

"Will you be custodian of some portion of this Persian gold for me? Where could it be more secure than there with you? An island of sanity in a sea of bewilderment! A nation where strength is prized to achieve the peace. I know you love me well and the gold shall be there when I have need of it. A gift for our child, to keep in trust for her. Will you do this for me?"

"You honor me, this trusteeship you propose."

"We can sort through it, to choose what you'll take to safety with you, secure by the River Thermodon. Oh, I have sent some west; but those men I place over my cities and my treasuries begin to sport themselves as little kings and dream that I shall not perhaps return. They become despots as they see, then hold, then feed on the gold I send to them. One even has his own little army he is gathering. Such a plague of temptation I heap on them! What am I to do? I cannot drag all this gold across the mountains to India and back. Who knows what foul weather we'll encounter there! Why can't gold be a lighter thing, like fleece or feathers, or the frost? All this gold . . . Dug from the edge of time. You'd be disgusted to see it all! I distribute it to the men but it weighs them down, the army becomes a treasure caravan! Best it be spread around for commerce to grow and be fed on it; but not at the expense of weighing down our march. I shall have it brought to us in wagons, for us to make pleasant evenings of it, separating what is fine and rare from what is merely weighty with solidity. And you shall take it when you go."

"How elegant a stewardship you place on us! How excellent a gift for your child to have."

"We must find you another two hundred horses and a lot of leather saddlebags. See how because of you my plan has been revised: When the world is mine the nations will no longer grind each other into dust, nor any more the Earth, to extract whatever pride and gold may be acquired from it."

"May it be as you desire, Great King."

"And there's something else I'd like for you to have. In Persepolis I made distribution of treasure to my men, which they tired of carrying and began to bury at night along the route as the hills grew high and numerous. With trusted friends I sometimes did the same, chests of it returned to the ground awaiting my return. And as I did I produced a map. One I wish for you to have. Come see." We go to the tent.

"This is a copy of my original. Can you read what I have written there?"

"Parts. It seems that there are codes . . ."

Iskander carries it to the desk and brings out ink. "Take notes on each site as I explain." I make notes about locations in the margins as he speaks.

"And a question now: How well known do you wish it to be, the existence of our child in Themiscyra you'll have? If anything should happen to me . . ."

"I see what you mean. Let's keep it hidden, at least for now. I'll send a message back to you when I'm part-way home, notifying you that I have died."

"Yes. And use the password I'll write here: *Eagles that do not fly.* From an old song my mother sang. That shall be our password too. Any messengers should bear that too. *Cannot fly, won't fly,* something similar concerning eagles' flight so I know what's truly sent from you relating your presumed demise."

"Agreed."

"So then. We're done. Where will you put the map so it's secure?"

"My quiver perhaps? If I take the arrows out and peel away the leather lining it?"

"Yes, that works." He watches as I wrap it around inside and place the leather molding back again. The arrows back in next. "Good. So never to be far from you."

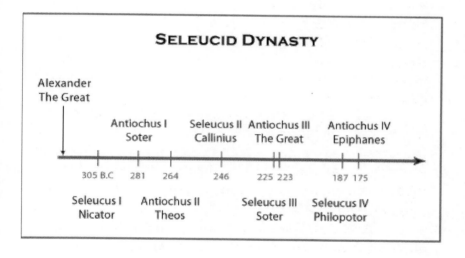

The **Diadochi** (from <u>Greek</u>: *Diadokhoi,* meaning "Successors") were the generals, families and other associates of <u>Alexander the Great</u> who fought for control over his empire after his death in 323 B.C. The <u>Wars of the *Diadochi*</u> mark the beginning of the <u>Hellenistic period</u>.

Chapter Eight

The Search For Heirs

Sharif and the Sultan

Mint tea arrived for Sharif and the Sultan.

"So then," said the Sultan, "Thelestris made this account to Strax and he wrote it out. Was there a child?"

"The manuscript says there was. Svea was her name. Someone history knows nothing of."

"What became of her?"

"Iskander went to India and returned to Babylon and there he died. Do you recall what happened to Iskander's lands after that?"

"Of course. His generals divided his world among themselves, tore it like a piece of cloth! Antigonus took Asia, Seleucus obtained Babylon and Cassander kept Macedonia. Ptolemy seized Egypt, with Cleopatra the eventual end of his long Ptolemaic line. Then wars broke out as those generals fought."

"Add this: With a hunt for any heirs, lest any such obstruct their plans. What if a threat were sent to the Amazon women demanding Iskander's heir be given up, just in case one might be there, as one would shake a tree for fruit? What would the Amazons' options be?"

The Sultan set hand to chin. "A demand they surrender Iskander's child? Ignore it, I suppose. Prepare to fight. Or give up the child. Or have her sent away, out of harm's reach."

"It's there my story shall begin. The manuscript says Svea was eight when the threat arrived."

The Threat

Themiscyra, home of the Amazons south of the Black Sea. 322 B.C., one year after King Iskander's death.

Fifty women make their way to the council chamber, called to gather by their battle queen. Thalestris moves to the front of the great half-circle hall. Waves a crumpled scroll above her head.

Iskander died a year ago. Now his officers divide his world. The general they call One-eyed Antigonus claims we live in his domain. He sends this demand to us:

Alexander is dead. All this area now is mine. Deliver his child to my officers in Ephesus by the solstice next. Or I shall come to you with force.

Thunder in the council hall! Thalestris waits for quiet.

"To whom is Svea such a threat? Do they imagine her at some army's head, seizing her father's kingdom for herself? There is no kingdom! Only a long trail of fire and tears. A childish message written on the sand that says, 'This is all mine; I have subdued and mastered it!' Sand the waves shall feed upon and the wind root up, so unimpressed with pride, until that sandy message of a moment has all flown away."

A murmur fills the room.

"Why should they think this child exists? This surely is a bluff and they will never come. Even so I feel responsible; it was my decision to go to him eight years ago. My daughter Svea knows who her father was. She has no fear. She is ready to go to them."

"No!" The women rise as one.

"We shall not give up a child to suit the whims of men!"

"We shall meet the Greeks again, as we did at Athens and at Troy!"

"We shall play the ocean's part, show them how fragile sandy empires are!"

"We shall set the lightning to our bows!"

Travelers Here are Rare

Along a road somewhere south of the Black Sea. Two months after the threat from Antigonus arrived.

The summer woods are golden green, alive with thunder's shadows moving through the leaves, a storm of archers eager for their lightning to be spent. Watching soldiers on horseback along a dusty road, Macedonians on their homeward march, about a hundred with their spears and round bronze shields. They've pillaged a village and eaten well; then taken hostages for sport, captives that now walk along behind.

One captive woman goes too slowly, stumbles, falls, is dragged along behind the horse. The man yanks at the rope he holds. He hears a sound and turns his head to see . . .

Storm! The men are eddies in the torrent's rushing sweep as thunder reaches for their hearts. So few see more than shadows as the lightning falls. The man that held the rope lies on the ground, clutching at an arrow's shaft.

An Amazon dismounts to kneel by him. "Who are you? Why are you here?" she softly asks.

"We are Macedonians," he blurts past his distress. "We fought with Alexander against Persia. Now Alexander is no more."

"Has someone sent you here? Is there someone you are sent to find?"

"No. We serve no one now. We make our way to the Aegean Sea, then home."

"Ah. But you are too far north, too near the Black Sea. Has no one told you of the dangers here? The legends abound that should have warned. And now you go plundering villages. Our friends! Is this some necessary part of going home again, pillaging the homes of others as you pass? Are those living here such barbarians, indeed, fit for nothing in the scheme of things except to be your slaves? This woman you drag behind your horse, why would you treat her so? What redeeming wisdom have you brought to share with us, to offset this plague of violence you spread?"

The man stares at her. The wind replies.

"You have nothing more to say to me?"

"I . . . I didn't know!" the words rush out.

"Not knowing. Not knowing has brought all this on you? Who takes a journey without knowing where it is they go? Look! You even had a guide available!"

"A guide? What guide is that?"

"This woman tied behind your horse! Better you had let her lead your way! She knows the area well enough. Her wisdom could have saved you from all this. But you wanted slaves, not friends. Better your King had stayed alive to lead you on to glorious victories, down through Africa and on across Arabia. You would not have found such mischief to be in. And instead of women you might have met on your last battlefield with men."

She stands. Notches an arrow to her bow.

"We're only traveling through! Is that so wrong?" On his elbows, wild to find excuse.

"Travelers here are rare. Some come to search the ancient histories, exploring what we've rescued from the dust of empires as they fell. But they are far more kind than you have been and their humility announces them. No, you have no interest in the light. You 'travel through' as most men do their sad brief voyage of Earth, hands clenched to strike. Soldiers of the fist! You bring the darkness here with you. That is who you serve. And to it you return."

It Rains
Themiscyra. Three months later.

The Amazon they call Scyleia sits indoors by a fire she's made. It rains. Soon others come to be with her.

"I knew it. She ought never to have gone to him."

"The Macedonians we encountered were going home, no more than that."

"There will be others as they flow west. Do we attack each band, as though they are invaders come in search of her? We'll become their enemies soon enough if we are not."

"We've been spared Iskander's storm til now. Shall it arrive here finally, to take his daughter up with it?"

"Are we to be another Troy, to withstand a ten-year plague of Macedonians? Can't you see? Svea is the horse. That fatal gift the Trojans brought into their walls. Even as we have now!"

"What's to be done? You heard the Council's will expressed. 'We will not give the child to them!' A consensus loud as it was clear."

"An emotional first outburst, natural enough. But this truly endangers us. Deserves to be thought out. Shall the storm arrive to find the cloud it seeks? At what high cost to us? Shall we not rather be the wind, to send the cloud off to the storm before it comes?"

"And her mother? What of her?"

"Thalestris will realize where the little cloud has gone. She can follow her into the Storm Kings' labyrinth if that is what she wants. She knows how. She has gone to visit kings before."

Will They Come For Her?

Four months after the threat arrived. Thalestris walks with her younger sister Mara by the Black Sea's shore.

"Mara, what child should they expect is here? Would they truly fulfill their threat? To come for her shall cost them much."

"The Macedonian soldiers will settle where they are or hurry home, worn out and old from conquering a world. Iskander has no other heir?"

"I am told his Persian wife Roxanne has birthed him one, conceived not long before he died. Mother and child have been hurried off to Macedonia, imprisoned there. Not likely to live long when the feuds break out, so vulnerable among those warlords with their controlling games. Shall that not be Svea's fate?"

"To whom did Iskander leave his lands, all this vast conquest, Greece to India?"

"His generals questioned him in Babylon as the fever — or the poison! — took its course and he grew weak:

'When shall we celebrate you?'
'When you are happiest.'
'To whom shall the dominion pass, to rule all this when you are gone?'
'To the strongest,' Iskander said, and died.

"Now they carve his world among themselves. Soon wars begin, as boundaries overlap like seas. His generals poisoned him, Mara, I know they did!"

"As for this demand from Antigonus, Thalestris, it seems to me it is a bluff, no more than that. Look at the letter's words: 'The child' — rather than 'the girl.' They probe the legend of a meeting only rumored at, near mythical.

What do they have to lose? A bluff costs them nothing and may gain much."

"They believe we'll comply if a child indeed exists; simply give Svea up to them. And when she doesn't arrive? They use it as excuse for doing what they want to anyway."

"Why is she worth a war to them?"

"She is an heiress in their eyes! Heir to all her father's clod of world, one they take into their fists to crush to powder now. And for power, a useful pawn."

"What can you do?"

"Meet each moment as it comes. Meet them if they come with it. And one idea."

"What?"

"I'll send Svea away."

"Away? Why? Why so concerned about an army of these men? You shall meet them with the sword and bow if they shall come, and with the battle ax!"

"No Mara, it's not the men I am concerned about. It's something else. A shadow I've seen as evening falls, and heard its whispering."

"Fear."

"Yes."

"Ah. How then? Where shall Svea go?"

"Away with you and Strax. To live a while in his far-northern home."

"Strax? Ha! Twelve years with us. He'll not want to go."

"You must! You two are the only ones I can entrust this to. When you take Svea out start out to the north, then turn your horses south instead, down to Phoenicia to board a ship. You'll cross the Middle Sea to Carthage where Strax has friends. They will arrange your passage to that snow-white realm from which he comes. Wait there for the storm to pass."

"So far to go . . ."

"You must leave soon, the sooner one day to return."

214

Farewell

Thalestris bids farewell to Svea, Mara, and Strax.

I shall look for you upon the sea, for your return to us one day in your long ship, calling out to me from above the prow in the swirling mist.

Each day I'll search the sea's gray sky for you where the water reaches high to look for you as well. Each wave shall lift its head to look then put it down again with that long lapping sigh that says, "Forget . . . Forget . . ." But I shall not.

"The snow holds me now," I'll hear you tell the wind so far away. And the flakes of snow that fall to you shall be the kisses from my lips; another, yet one more. See how like mine they melt and come again.

"Come home to Themiscyra!" I shall plead upon the wind; nor ever cease to look for you though the wind have no reply. My eyes shall never cease to search beyond a sea of tears.

Already in me, this bird in snow you've fed so long is wondering at the feast no longer there. Soon that bird takes wing to search, circling ever higher as its songs turn into cries, not finding you. How ever faster the wings are rising, falling, drumming frantic on the sky! How quickly darkness closes in to thwart its far pursuit, going in wide search of you within the storm that is my heart.

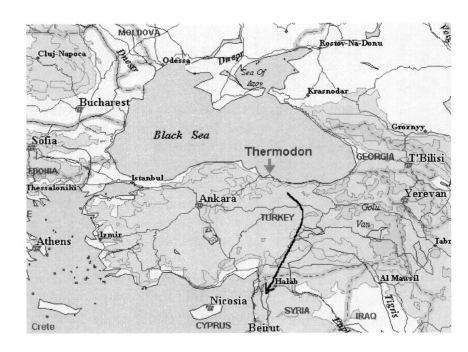

Leaving Themiscyra

Strax reports.

How I wish to remain here now, to ride with the
Amazons against the men if they arrive to fulfill their threat.
The wind, the sky, my heart, all are pleading with me not to
go. But that is not to be. My farewells I make with heart and
eyes when words no longer come. Soon even heart and eyes
no longer serve, for my heart lies in a heap and my eyes
drown.

I fetch along my sword and battle ax, so long unused;
and Svea brings her bow, trading her child's quiver for some
larger one she finds inside. Then out into the dark we ride,

the three of us, swept out upon the night. Rushing through the green-gray urgency of trees not trusting even stars to know our route. Every noise an enemy, each branch a claw that reaches out for us. The night wind makes armies of the leaves, those we must believe are abroad in search of us.

How ever more solid the specters grow as the light grows thin! We avoid the roads, preferring to share the path of fox and deer where trees grow thick enough to shield our flight. South toward the Middle Sea we ride to seek passage on a ship, to only breathe at last when the sails are full, swept out upon the freedom of the sea.

Only when the woods are thick enough to conceal us from the road do we grow bold to talk and make a fire. I set aside my sword and battle ax and the bow and arrows I've snatched from a peg to bring along. Remembering Bellerophon and feeling very much as he must have felt when he left Themyscira that time long ago.

"Svea, what was your first pet?" I tend the little blaze.

"My little horse?"

"No, the next."

"My two-headed snake."

"Tell me again, how did you decide which head was boss?"

"I dangled a mouse over it. The head that ate the mouse was the smarter one. It happened every time. I feared the other head might die and held food close for it to have."

"Svea, we must play a game a while. We are the mouse and a many-headed snake is sent to search for us; one we must avoid. Even aboard ship we'll use other names. We shall go far from them, and fast. Then return one day when all is well."

"Snakes. Are there any out here in the dark?"

"We'd surely hear them hissing, wouldn't we? Don't they sleep at night and hunt by day?"

"You've never had a pet snake, it's clear."

"Svea, are you comfortable in your bag of fur?"

"Yes. I'm tired. Will you and Mara travel in your dreams again tonight? How I wish that I might go along with you."

"We'll reach out for you, Svea," Mara smiles, "Look for us on dreaming's wings."

"Will you be hard to recognize?"

"We shall look the same, though brighter possibly. And Mara may become a swan, or butterfly."

"Will I get in the way where you fly so high?"

"How useful you shall be!" Mara laughs, "To brush the stars out of our way. And disentangle us from clouds."

"And save us from the moon, when we charge at it like drunken moths."

"Are you quiet then, Mara, as you dream together through the night?"

"Do you mean Strax, the way he growls and snorts?"

"Ha! You are far noisier than him! So many sounds you make, like small desperate animals."

"Spying on us as we sleep? Tonight it shall be quiet. Each of us in our own furs."

"How black it is here in the trees," Svea surveys the labyrinth of limbs. "Strax, will you take me on a voyage into my heart, to quiet the inner winds? Tell me the 'brightness inside of us' again?"

"Yes, Svea, close your eyes . . .

ॐ

"What brightness is this inside of us? The lamp of the body is beautiful and the work of it complex. So quiet within its corridors the inner rivers swiftly rush unfelt to feed the flame. This light you call your own, has it been borrowed for a while? What meaning places you in so wonderful an instrument? So finely made, what are you meant to do? Life sprouts in you, grows higher as you stand beneath the sun. What bright tree has left you as a seed upon the landscape of this world? You move among the colors on the many-shadowed leaves you call your life. Weather wanders through the branches of your sleep. You wonder what is really yours to keep. What drama unfolds here? What hand has stirred the spinning world? Shall it topple finally, to fall and burn amid the stars? Where shall the swirling spark of your own spirit fly to then?"

My story's done. Mara moves closer to me in the dark. "Is she asleep?"

"Perhaps . . . Yes."

"Purr."

"Snort."

"Strax, you noisy beast. Where do you find these things you say to us?"

"The words are written on my heart. And you are the light for me to see them by."

Figs

We ride many days. Now less than a day from Sidon and the safety of the sea. Traveling near the road but always off of it, tonight we rest behind tall rocks. Mara and Svea ready our furs for sleep while I tend our nine horses, the three we ride and three led on by each of us.

"It's a fig tree Mara, over there," Svea points. "Near the road. I know it is."

"Where? You know I can't see far away."

"There, by those big rocks."

"I'll go see if it has fruit. Don't tell Strax. He worries for us so."

Yes there are figs, fine ripe purple ones. Mara gathers some and eats a few, opening them to marvel at the gold and crimson nectar they contain.

Suddenly three men. Soldiers! She starts to run but the men are fast. One catches her. A struggle. Screams. Laughter, coarse.

The leader holds her while the others tie her hands and throw the rope across a branch to stretch her tall. "What a pretty one! And what is this? A pendant? The double-headed ax! An Amazon? Is that what you are? What are you doing here? Where are your friends?"

"I'm by myself. On foot. On my way to Egypt, to see the pyramids. My horse has run off. It's always doing that."

"We've been told to look out for Amazons," a second soldier says.

"There's sure to be rewards!" the third one grins.

The leader reaches out for Mara's robe, tears it open to expose her skin. She squirms and screams again. "Such spirit!" he says, and slaps her face. "Who do you think is hearing you?"

From the shadows the swift answer comes, my battle ax. One soldier less. Another meets my sword as he turns toward me. But the leader puts his knife to Mara's side, beneath her ribs. "No closer! Drop the sword! Or she will die," his blade against the golden skin. I let fall the sword.

"And who are you? I think I've found what I'm looking for. You're traveling with a child, yes? I think you should bring her to me now."

I stare at him.

"Now!" The knife presses in. A thin red stream starts down as Mara pulls her ribs up higher and her belly in.

The soldier opens his mouth to yell at me again but no words are coming out of it. His eyes are open wide. The knife falls from his grasp. He turns around to encounter Svea with her bow.

Now I can see it, Svea's arrow in his back. He gropes for it just out of reach, not believing what he sees as she calmly delivers another to his heart.

I rush to take Mara down and hold her in my arms. Then Svea also, the three of us, delirious, happy to be spared.

"How was my aim?" she asks.

"We're very pleased with you, Svea! Very proud indeed! This story shall be told by every fire forever in our country so far north. No one shall ever doubt your true warrior's heart. And Mara has a fine new battle wound to show. My warrior, brave!"

"Can you forgive me, Strax?" Mara is contrite. "I wanted figs for you. Now I doubt I'll ever eat another one."

"It's just as well, Mara. They don't grow well so far north where we now go."

Svea gathers figs, suddenly ravenous, as I saddle the horses once again. We travel through the dark to lend some space to these events and Svea is soon asleep at our new resting place.

I celebrate Mara's wound with her. A wound she never thought she would receive this side of dreaming's battlefield.

Does It Bother You?

The next morning is warm. We ride, then rest among the trees.

"How do you feel about it, Svea, the battle you won for us last night? Does it bother you that you killed that man?"

"Some."

"He was already drowning, Svea, in a whirlpool of choices and actions he had made. A natural procedure in which you became a participant. Simply that."

"Whirlpool?"

"Svea, do you see these rings in the tree's old stump? How it sends its circles out? Just as you also do."

"Circles? I am sending circles out?"

"Yes, Svea, to everyone. Then they curve back to you. As with us all! If the soldier had been kind it would have brought more kindness back to him as Mara's spirit circle flowed through him, and his through her. But cruelty left a jagged edge. His brutality bred a kink in it, so that its journey through him was no longer smooth but left him torn. Your mother explained it to your father that time she went to him."

"What did she say?"

"I've written it for you. Wait." I go to a horse and release a scroll from its coverings. "Your Greek is good, let me hear you read." Svea takes the scroll in her small hands.

Circles

Thalestris and Iskander by the Caspian Sea, 330 B.C.

"This Dream of Earth is one we share, Great King; all of us are united here. There is nothing that is separate. All are connected. All of us are one. The sword we wield has a mirrored edge for us as well."

"Thalestris, so ever mysterious! How shall you explain it's true?" The king reached out to find his cup, and stared at me with his deep eyes.

"Circles of energy connect the spirits of all here. A bright spirit-necklace that links us all! So many subtle circles you send unseen. So many rings of others on their cascade to you, that you return more golden or more gray, hindered or sped along their course. Each person's ring is in your care to be polished or made rough, bent or straightened as it flows through you.

"Shall you transgress, hate, betray, lie, steal from me? Then my ring no longer passes smoothly through and your light-body tears and bleeds where my roughened circle makes its broken way. I may not ever know what you have done but the circles do. As do they all, any you have harmed, all storm against you with their question, *Why?*

"First breezes that inquire, then a great tempest's gale. As the storm grows fierce you hide, weaving stony darkness to enclose you round, to seal and soothe somehow the pain that throbs as the broken circles turn in your deep spirit wounds."

"So Thalestris, might the offended person be convinced to die?" Iskander grins at the sure solution he has found. "Then the circle goes with him!"

"Ha! The barb is trenched in you though the shaft be gone. Pooling stagnant where the darkness breeds more shadows like its own. With that person's pardon it might have been dislodged, the light restored. But now that healing source is gone."

He glowers at the cup he holds. "Shall we not wake from these spirit-circles finally, as from a dream, and find them gone?"

"Wake? There is the mystery: All the rings must run smooth and true again before this dream of circle-weaving may be folded up and woken from. For us to pass into that wider sky where we are meant to be. For this brief curtain to be flung aside to an ecstatic dance we join, tearing off these clothes of flesh. No longer to live in bubble-worlds with dreams no broader than our skin! No longer to be this tiny grain. The seed we are shall bloom, our smallness the memory of a moment and then quickly gone."

"A wider sky in which to live?"

Ah. That immortality he craves? "But not all of us."

"Why not?"

"How shall a drop of rain climb back into the sky again, to soar, if prevented from its journey to the sea, hidden in some crevice where no water flows? It must forever dream of that expanse where it is meant to go, and it cannot.

"If only we could see the circles on their course, how the rings all pulse to be straight and true again, to work the destiny out, this great journey that we are. We would be so careful with the energy of others as it flows through us, holding them with gentle hands to soothe; and also that great circle of the Earth that holds us to her breast. If only we could learn to love, then we would need no hiding place, escaping what we've done, looking for a place to lie asleep, when we might live."

I leaned back, my thought complete.

"This is woman's talk! Conscience has no hand to hold a sword. But I wonder," leaning forward in his seat, "What of curses others put on me? What validity has that?"

How wide a curse-sown furrow there must be. Half a length of world!

"Yes, a curse comes on you. But not from them. You have accomplished it yourself. You have wound their jagged circles tightly round you as a bandage for the pain. What shall deliver you, for the circles to run true again that are so out of shape? What hand shall free you from that brackish pool in which you hide yourself away, dreaming fretfully of storms? How shall your journey be restored for you to wake, hastening toward the sea and the sun that call and call for you to come?"

Iskander is silent for a time before he speaks. "What then? Is there some hope for it?"

"There is. Easy to be had as waking is. But who has care for it? See, how so many sleep, let slip the opportunity of Earth. Shall they hold brightness enough within themselves when time's steel cage is sprung? Shall they know they own wide wings, to fly? 'Look,' they will be told, 'The prison door is open. Up, away! The sky is yours!' Shall they not blink at the sudden sun, so bright? Clutch the shadows to themselves and ask, 'Where is there to hide from so much light?'"

ऀ

"So, Strax," Svea lets the scroll roll closed, "Because the soldier was cruel to Mara her ring no longer flowed so smooth through him?"

"That's it. Her broken circle tore a jagged hole through which his life poured out. Not always so fast, but it is sure."

After the fig tree incident we journey at a greater distance from the road, ever south through the Lebanon toward the coast and no more soldiers do we see until we arrive at Sidon's port on the Middle Sea.

Passage Arranged

I arrange passage for us west to Carthage on a ship, paying with our nine horses and a small bag of gold. The sea is calm, as though it does not know the wind that goes in search of us.

The ship's captain is a stalwart Phoenician merchantman, burley and pensive with deep dark eyes. I hope he will consider we are common folk, no more than that, and leave us to ourselves. I can only wonder what he thinks of us. "We must tell him nothing!" I counsel Svea and Mara, "None of our personal history! We dare not guess whom we may trust."

"What are we to say?" Mara asks.

"Only tou and I shall use our names. You shall say you're from the countryside near Troy. I am from Carthage and Cadiz. And you Svea, say you are the 'Daughter of the Storm.'"

"Daughter of the Storm?"

"Yes, only that for now. No mention of Iskander or where we're from. If you say more they'll know us sure."

We are presented a cabin to which I lug our many bags aboard, heavy with my scrolls and our hoard of gold, part of the gift Svea's father has provided her. Svea totes a bit of it about, a linen bag heavy with small golden animals to play with as her toys.

Several days out to sea we stand with Svea up on deck to watch the sun descend into the ever-reaching sea.

"Out there somewhere is Egypt," I point beyond blue water toward the coast of northern Africa, color of ripe lemons in the sun. "They crowned your father Iskander as the Pharaoh there. And the priests all hailed him as a god, the son of Ammon-Ra."

"Was he really, Strax?"

"You must await the answer in yourself, to feel it there. And ask the Earth and the Fire, for they shall surely know."

"They may know, but they don't tell. Why did it mean so much to him?"

"Seeking equality with gods? So to escape their wrath! Outdistance that great blade the conscience is. And the blood of gods was in him, so they said: Achilles on his mother's side, and from his father's veins the blood of Heracles."

"And my mother . . ."

"Thalestris opened his fist to let the darkness fly away, as much of it as he allowed to go."

The strand of shoreline lemon turns to orange and sea's deep blue to dark. Svea points with glee to every flame's transition into ash across the western sky.

"What shall I say, Strax, in my new northern home — when someone asks me who my parents are?"

"Tell them you are the 'Daughter of the Storm.' Even then at destination's end! Watch their foreheads furrow as they try to understand. Then tell them of the king who wished to be assured he was a god and went to take the world into his fist to prove it so. Of your mother the great Matriarch who set the lightning to her bow to bend his tempest from her home. And you, that bright spark she harvested."

We watch the trailing salt on the dark sea and soon enough the moon. "I see clearly Svea, it is for you I've written all the scrolls, for you to own the answers when they ask you who your parents are. All remembered there for you, as your mother told it all to me: The thirteen days with your father by the Caspian Sea."

Chapter Nine

The Ship Captain's Letter

The Captain Writes A Letter Home

*Aboard the 'Pegasus' on the Mediterranean ('the Middle') Sea.
322 B.C..*

Beloved, I have passengers I must tell you of.

I remember the sea, so calm, the day they came aboard my ship in Sidon's port. Beautiful Mara, wondrous wise, with amaranth eyes and freckled cheeks and whole histories inside her head, the origins of many realms. A tall man with a head of rusty straw named Strax. Truth rules his voice, and laughter from a heart the thunder shares. And a sky-eyed little girl with them whose smile could teach the brightness to a summer day.

Simple robes could not conceal their obvious nobility. Escaping royalty was my first discerning thought. I'd seen enough of such those days Iskander passed twelve years ago, the high-born escapees, always paying well and nervous until we were out to sea. But these are different. Their royalty grows from deep within, far past money's surface jangle and earth-bound pedigrees, the sort that's bred of journeys' distance crossed and hard storms fought.

One day when we were six days out from port I spoke with sun-haired Svea as she sat against the rail at play with shiny objects, little animals that seemed made of brass, but which on holding them, feeling their heaviness, I recognized as gold.

"Interesting toys," I said to her, surprised at what rare things I held.

"This and this are from Egypt," delighted at the interest I showed, "But these are even older, from Persepolis," pointing to Persian dromedary, dragon, lion, elephant, "that my father sent to me."

Confused suddenly I glanced at Strax and Mara across deck absorbed in talk. His hair so rusty and hers so dark, and the child so golden fair. "Your father sent them. Whose daughter are you then?" handing her golden playthings back to her.

"I am the Daughter of the Storm."

Encounter

I encountered Strax and Mara the next day, my ship's crew behind me armed with staves. "You are the parents of the girl?" I asked, and scowled.

Surprised, they shared a glance, then squarely faced me. "No."

"I thought not. Where have you acquired her, then?" Only their silence answered me.

"Stealing children is not something I condone; I have children of my own. We're turning back to Sidon's port. The authorities there can decide your fate." Then to my men, "There may be rewards, so watch them well," and I turned to go.

"No, wait," Mara called me back, "Do you bear the Macedonians great love?"

"No. I am Phoenician, after all. They trampled through my world with their brass feet."

"Then why so eager to be serving them?"

"Why would I be?"

"Because they'd pay you well for her; then enslave her for their pride, or kill her when they can. Is that the freedom you intend she have?"

"Why do you think they might?"

"Because of who her father is. Because they think she is a threat, though she is not."

"Her father is a 'storm,' the girl said."

"The story's not a simple one," Mara's eyes flared fire.

"It seldom is." I flashed fire back.

"The storm has spawned her; now it seeks her for itself again."

"What storm is that? 'Daughter of the Storm': Who is her father, then?"

Mara looked full into my face. "Was there not a storm here, just a while ago? Did you not feel it, so great a tempest as it passed? Overcoming armies, kingdoms, all that encountered it!"

I gasped to realize what she meant — whose daughter I might have near me. "Iskander's child? But how . . .?"

"We have it written down, for you to know the matter's heart. For the Heart of all the Earth went out to that young god, to show him what a man might be."

"Svea? Heiress to the empire he subdued? Who are you people? Tell me plain!"

For answer they equipped me with a scroll.

Meanwhile I've sequestered their weapons, bow, arrows, sword, and turned the ship around, back east to Sidon's port again. I'll let the authorities decide their fate; they'll know what reports of recent have been made. As for their story, surely it's a fable they've made up!

Though if this is the Macedonian's child indeed, well hid these eight years' time, what then? Beloved! How I wish I had you with me here for your wisdom's clarity.

It's seems they've stolen the child, this woman Mara and her man Strax. Whence, from whom, I cannot tell. They wish for me to "know the whole of it," so I complete one scroll each night for them to provide me one more yet. As for their stories, imagination's realm is wide, and I am tending toward my narrow incredulity.

Is the girl the daughter of two monarchs, truly so?

It comes to this: I must be alert to clues as to the veracity of what they're telling me. And in their favor, one clue came.

Zhirus

Among my crew aboard the *Pegasus* is Zhirus, a pole-thin man with eyes of a crocodile. Zhirus likes to gamble but is not good at it, and I have rescued him from agitated creditors so that he serves me now, mending fishing nets he pays out long behind the ship and hauls back in again, to win whatever silver fish may come between. Rumors dredge much history for Zhirus, but the past is put away now we are out to sea; he has escaped all that, content to brew the future up, as the horizon brews up storms.

Zhirus is working at the nets with half a heart, one eye on the storm that settles toward us from the north and one eye on young Svea, at play with her heavy sack of ancient golden toys — left unguarded at the ship's rail as she's called by Strax and Mara across deck to watch the sky throw out its long black net and its fierce claws, feasting on the horizon to grow fat from that thin sustenance.

When the waves and wind grow high enough the three of them descend to go below and secure the doors — bag of golden playthings left behind — as a heavy storm comes bristling up with quantities of rain.

Zhirus quits his nets. Hefts the deserted hoard of golden ornaments into a compartment where the sails are stored and hides it well beneath the canvas shroud. A moment more, the lightning flails and the waves crash hard against the bulwark where the linen pouch has lately been.

Below deck they nest like happy moles, Strax reminiscing at his scrolls, and Mara and Svea sharing the mysteries of their healing arts.

Dawn is ozone clear and purged with salt next day as Svea comes on deck. But her tote-sack of heavy gold is nowhere to be found. The waves were high and loud all night, she knows — bending over the rail to look, as though to spot a somehow glimmer down below.

"I have enough of gold," the water whispers up to her, "What need have I of yours?"

Svea says nothing. But she begins to look more carefully at everyone. Deeper, as though to peel away the skin and go beneath the colors of the spirit's dance. At dinner she regards me, shifts the light inside her head to see the circles come to view, now a few and soon strong storms of them, rings entering and flowing out from me, some golden and some gray, some silver-smooth and others torn. And there as well she may discern her own, a circle bright and fair and glad; I hold her spirit sacred, it is clear. It was not I that took her gold.

For the other crew it is much the same, each one's storm unique to him, circles flowing to and fro and returning to them crushed or smooth. As for Zhirus, Svea sits a long time up on deck to watch him throw the nets behind the ship and bring them in again; so many spirit circles flowing torn and rough through him, streaks of pain where they transfix him barbed. And among them there her own.

Svea sees her circuit gouge at him, and many other circles claw him too as they flow landwards to their source: This person cheated, this defrauded, this coerced. She sees, and she is sad at it as she sits on deck against a pile of sail to practice her subtle mudra dance, her hands the nets that seine for far-flung energies.

Zhirus watches her with wizened eyes. Pulls in his nets. One fair-sized fish at last! He takes it in his hands, flapping slippery and wet, eyes unblinking wide, gills pumping terror from the air.

"Let me go!" Svea listens to it plead, but Zhirus does not hear or does not heed. The fins flair out, spikes fierce to find unwary flesh — that enter Zhirus' palm, a deep long slice. "Ah-eee!" he wails as the blood spouts up.

Svea runs to him, unties the sash from about her waist to secure the gash. Sets her hands to his wrist and palm as he glares at her, that wide stare of the river horse when the crocodile has come too close.

A moment more . . . Svea unwraps the cloth. The blood is staunched, the wound is closed; only a lavender lip of scar survives. "There. It's better now," smiling up at him, that brighter smile than any summer owns.

Zhirus begins to sob. Weeps as though to claw the lightning from his eyes.

Next day Svea comes again at dawn into the open air. Her sack of golden toys has reappeared, as though spewed from the ocean's depths. She bends across the rail in wonderment, looks down into the sea.

The water smiles at her and lifts its hands, "See, these new jewels I have," showing those bright tears that Zhirus shed, "So much long-stagnant that is free again."

The Sultan and the Emir Meet (Turkey, 18ᵗʰ century)

A meeting with the Sultan could not happen soon enough for the Emir. "So you met with Sharif? Was I right?"

"Sharif confirms the meeting did occur."

"Excellent!"

"He even knows most of what went on, all thirteen days of it. From some manuscript he's seen. I'll hear more of it tonight."

"There was a child?"

"Likely so. Svea is a name he gave. And it only seems natural, as you've discerned, Iskander would have sent her gold."

"So we can begin to plan . . ."

"Though you ought to be aware," said the Sultan, "whatever gold was there may now be gone."

"Gone? Gone how?"

"Gone with the child. Some of it at least. As you may recall, when Iskander died his generals divided up his world, then went searching for any heirs that might slow them down. The Amazons received a threat and according to Sharif's manuscript the girl was spirited away for her safety's sake. About the age of eight."

"Where?"

"By horse south to Sidon, thence by ship to Carthage, ultimate destination the farthest regions of the northmost part of Earth in the protection of trusted friends. So to escape the generals' claws. And some of the gold may have sailed with her."

"Though there may have been so much of it! More than a horse or two could hold!"

"Nine horses, Sharif says they had. We'll need to think it through."

"Why trust each detail of this manuscript?"

"I do my best each moment to discern just that." The Sultan threw his arms aloft. "For now it's our only confirmation of there being any child at all! And as it is the source of Sharif's comment to you . . ."

"She sailed on a ship to Carthage, then she went north?"

"Far north. Though Sharif isn't sure she actually arrived."

"Why think she might not? How would we know?"

"Excellent question." The Sultan shrugged. "Perhaps if there were some place named for her."

Why Believe You've Been Anywhere?

322 B.C.E., on board ship. The Captain speaks to Mara and Strax.

"There's little reason to believe it's so," I shrugged at them when I found them next to return their latest scroll, "That you've been anywhere at all, much less across the Western Sea. All this is bred of fables that you've heard, no more than that!"

From behind the silence of their sea-deep eyes they simply looked at me.

"You want me to think you've crossed the Atlantic? Ha! That you've been to the women warriors by the Black Sea, the ones that kill all men they find nearby? Why would you survive?"

Strax glanced at Mara and she gave a nod. From a pocket of his robe Strax brought small objects out, put them in my hand: Thin as fingers, smooth and shining red.

"Tears of the sun!" I sighed to see them, holding them as precious jewels. Began to look at them with other eyes.

"You have heard that Iskander may have had a hand in his father's death?" He said.

"Oh yes. If not directly, his mother had it done and he acquiesced."

"This next scroll will supply your curiosity with details."

Tormented

Iskander and Thalestris

"Thalestris, you ask about my father's death. Each night I am tormented, though I may have acquiesced to it, no more than that. Hideous creatures pursue me through my sleep. How shall I escape?"

"It is a ripple in the circles. It can be stilled."

"How open I become, Thalestris, here with you. As I wish my father and I could have been, but never were. How I thirsted for my father's praise! I excelled in riding, wrestling, fighting, every sport. How little attention I ever received from him! Increasingly he turned against us, my mother Olympias and me. Then he took yet one more wife, his fifth, and the slender threads that held the three of us together came apart."

"Why then?"

"He'd taken other wives and my mother seemed not so much to care. I was the one she gave her attention to; my fate as future king was all her desire and every thought."

"Your mother lived for you, Iskander. Only you. The future you would have."

"Yes. My father grew fearful of us. Rumors of impending assassinations were readily available when he wished to hear. His only mistake, finally, was the one my mother would not tolerate. Philip let it be known that he would marry the niece of the nobleman Attalus, to sire another son to be his heir, replacing me. He'd heard the stories and had decided I . . . That I was not in fact his son."

"How terrible! At the very time he planned his invasion of Persia, across the Aegean sea, when he would need you most. How rash."

"Yes, it seems ill-timed. And the wedding festivities, you must have heard what I said then, and what I did."

The fishermen wondered whether Alexander were truly their king, the son of Philip, or the son of the God-Father [Zeus], born out of the witch woman Olympias.

— Harold Lamb. *Alexander of Macedon.* 1946.

Philip's Wedding
337 B.C., seven years earlier. Pella, in Macedonia.

This should have been my twentieth birthday festivity, Iskander muses as he lets his wine go untouched in his cup, half listening to the long toast his father is loudly offering the assembled guests.

She's pretty enough, my father's new wife, but very young. His fifth? Why is he doing this? To spite my mother? It's all so terrible, so sad. I don't like these people. The music is bad. Why am I here? To watch my father limp around on his one good leg, peering at everyone with his one good eye, showing what a half-man he is to his new "family." My father. Is this the man descended from Heracles, whose love and acceptance I sought so long and never had?

Bored. Iskander spins the cup of wine to see the red sea circle its silver shore. Wine so much like blood.

The girl's uncle Attalus gets to his feet to speak, the man who's here to give away the bride, addressing King Philip with his own well-chosen words.

" . . . And it is our hope for you that at last you may have a *genuine* heir for the throne of Macedonia . . ."

The words jolt Iskander from his lethargy. Swift as storm he's up from his seat and crossing the brief space, hurling the goblet's clinging brew full in the face of Attalus.

"How dare you say that!"

Is it a smirk he sees through the red streams? "Poor boy . . . Are you the last to know?"

Now King Philip is up, fist clenched, sword drawn, rushing toward Iskander, not so steady on his one good leg after all he's had to drink. Half way he stumbles on a bench, cluttering face-down in front of everyone in a great flailing heap.

In the sudden silence Iskander is the one who speaks. "That is the man who intends to cross the Hellespont, to conquer Persia. But he can't even cross the room."

Going North

I left the wedding festivities then and hurried north with my mother, urgently, where we had friends. "What are you feeling, Mother," I asked.

"Sad. Yes sad as much as I am afraid. Afraid for you, Alexander, I think most of all."

"Why be afraid for me?"

"Nothing matters now, not Philip, not anything — except that you be king one day. One day soon!"

A long silence.

"Alexander, do you remember that time long ago when you struck a boy, because of what he said?"

"The one who told me my real father was one of my mother's snakes?"

"Yes, that's the one. Were you so very upset, thinking you might not be Philip's son? Was it for your father's honor that you hit that boy?"

"No. It was for me. And for you, somehow. Your honor. Ours. Why do you mention it?"

"What other stories have you heard? Of who your father may really be."

"Ha! I stopped taking them seriously. Something one expects when one's father is the king. Let's see. There was the one about the Egyptian that visited Macedonia the year before my birth. But I hardly look swarthy enough to have Egyptian blood."

"Alexander, how many stories have you been told, about the Greeks and their god Zeus? What Moses wrote and all the rest — how they mated with the daughters of men to breed half-gods? What they call *Nephilim*."

"Many such; and the goddesses do the same with men they see and want. My ancestor Heracles on my father's side, and Achilles on yours are said to have such origins, to be half-gods. Though it's also been a convenient thing for a woman to say, giving birth when the husband's off at war, away from home. 'The child?'she says. 'I was visited by the god!'"

"What does the god look like, Alexander, as he takes her up into his arms?"

"No one has said."

Olympias looked away. "The god glows. With bright ivory-marble skin and blazing eyes. Ecstacy is in his touch; and all her will is water, urging that she drown in him, a living sacrifice. No enticement can match that invitation to be joined, so that her whole intent floods out to him, so much desire she never knew she had. Urgent for this brightness that he is to fill her now, all that space she used to be. Eager to go if he will take her in his arms, away with him wherever it is that he may go. And his embrace! Like those mysteries of Osiris they say the Pharaohs are provided by the priests, to know the spirit unchained, soaring beyond the body's boundaries. To know, yes KNOW that one is more than this frail flesh. Deep in her the god's seed is consuming her with urgent beautiful fire — the husk of her body left behind so easily like a sack of flesh outgrown as she is soaring up with him into the wind, the slender flame she is. Entwined with his."

"Mother, how do you know all this? Has some god provided this to you?"

"Alexander, what do you know of the god in Egypt they call Ammon-Ra?"

"What Aristotle has said, that Zeus is perhaps the same. The Athenians have built a temple to him, calling him that name; and I have seen his statue in Macedonia at Aphythis. There are priests serving him in an oasis at Siwah far east of the Egyptian pyramids. Why, Mother? Is my father truly that great god? Not Philip, as the rumors say?"

"Philip. Ammon-Ra. If not the man, perhaps the god. Alexander, it was so long ago. How am I to know?"

A Father's Displeasure
Thalestris and Iskander

"Thalestris, can you release the furies' plague? For me to sleep again?"

"It is a darkness you allowed as you set your father as judge over you. You cared so much what he might think."

"Oh yes, wanting him to think well of me, and he so seldom did. His words stirred storms in me, threw my world into despair. I imagined I displeased him, though he was likely simply displeased generally. The feeling penetrated me; I wrestled with it to throw it out. So tiring that constant wrestling was! Hoping for some sign of forgiveness for whatever it was I might have done to work such unhappiness in him. If not love acceptance then, that would have been enough. But it was only worse the next time and the next.

"When I could not throw the painful darkness out, I let it stay there finally. Let it live while I picked my way around the edges of the sharpness that became my life. Not caring. That was the narrow path on which I made my way, encouraged by those rare times he gave me scraps of praise, as he did the day I succeeded in riding Bucephalos when no one thought I could — those were the times I'd open the inner gates to let the sparks of brightness in.

"But by then the gates would no longer open very far. By then anger had been mixed with fear. Not only for myself but for my mother, the treatment she was receiving at his hands. The insults, the savage eyes. I came to hate my father every bit as much as I had wanted to be loved. Hate, fear; one darkness exchanged for another one. Or else enlarged, two pools of poison mixed.

"At least I, myself, know how to give encouragement, to give the praise my father never did. My army lives for me! But the pain remains. And the darkness lunges out from me sometimes, dark claws to my companions' throats. When what I meant for them was love."

No Fetters on the Heart

"Soon after that wedding my father was killed during his grand entrance to a great gathering the whole Greek and Macedonian worlds had been invited to."

"And the assassin was quickly silenced?"

"A man named Pausanias. Not my doing. Though people say my mother put him up to it."

"What do you say?"

"It is all so terrible to think about. My mother would bring the subject up, 'Philip must die!' But I didn't want to hear. It disgusted me, even as I wondered if it might indeed be possible. What I heard her say I immediately determined to forget again, not even daring dream of it. Now it is in the dreams I hear my mother's words. Dreams so dark! 'No!' I scream at her, 'No! Not my father! Not until I conquer the world for him!' And there are others, too, that enter my dreaming. Spirits, hideous!"

Iskander buries his head in my breasts and begins to sob. I run my hands through his hair. "Iskander, why so sad? What could you have done?"

"Something! Anything. Might I have warned him? He might have lived."

"No. You could not have warned him, even if you had determined to. Think. If you had warned your father you and your mother would now be dead. For all you knew your mother was only talking anyway, as women do. How sure could you be that she would turn the thought to deed? You had no control of what your mother did! Yes, you would become king in your mother's dream, because of what she'd set her mind to do. But it was her dream, not yours; you were only a player there. Your father sealed his own doom, quite thoroughly; there was nothing you could do."

"He did?"

"Your father sealed his fate when he thrust your mother from his heart. Yet she was patient with him many years. He might have gone on like that, lover after lover, wife after wife, but he said words finally that thrust a dagger through your mother's heart: that you would not be king. In your mother's dreams, Iskander, already you sat upon the throne and ruled. She would allow nothing to topple her plan for you! Philip threatened the dream in which your mother's true self lived, where you sat as king; it's then he sealed his fate. It was time for Philip to wake from the nightmare he'd created for himself, to release the fist and let the light go free — the light of his wife Olympias whose heart he had so often crushed."

"Nothing I might have done? I'm not an accomplice in all this? The Furies, those spirits that avenge a parent's death, pursue me through the days with vicious claws and flood my dreams at night, condemning me. Only on the battlefield am I for a moment free."

"Iskander, this is your parents' fiery dance! You were caught in the middle of its flames. Would you be free of the Furies now?"

"How?"

"You must forgive your father all his wrongs. Yes. You can do it now. It need not take long, swift as the bird of thought across the ocean of despair. A decision to let him go, for his spirit to go free. Then gently send him on his journey with a wish of love. Love's bright spiral sets you free as it does him, for you to proceed upon your course. What you do not release keeps you enchained.

"When you have forgiven Philip you have one more: Your mother. Forgive her too, send her the releasing love. Forgive her that she removed your father from your dream too soon. Tell her, in your mind, you know it may have been the only way she knew. Tell her you know she did it all for you, for you are all the world to her."

Out of the darkness, up the burning throat, up into the eyes where the light awaits, the sordid histories are distilled. He weeps.

"Iskander, forgive them. Do it now."

"Yes, I forgive. I send them love." The tears are spirit's wings to set him free. The fist is opening, the shadows flowing out. He sleeps.

I watch over Iskander until the Furies come for their usual feast of his dark grief. I watch them searching for the chains they've taken in their hands each night to wield as whips against his heart. Watch their surprise at finding no more fetters there.

They glare at me and I smile, which makes them furious. Spinning yellow wasps incensed, so resentful that he's lost to them.

Chapter Ten

Intentions

The Captain's Letter

"A fine imagination someone has," I returned that last scroll to them.

"Define 'evil' for me," Mara said.

"Doing what's wrong."

"As so many do. Have they purposed evil's course? Or simply gone bad, like rotting fruit?"

"Doing what is right involves intention."

"Ah. Intention takes the helm to stear clear of evil. And without intention one is evil by default?"

"You might say so. Evil comes most easily for mankind it seems, as though by nature's own design."

"How is this intention achieved, you say one ought to have?"

"One encounters evil and is intent upon avoiding it."

"Was Iskander evil?"

"In evil's hand, assuredly."

"Not responsible then?"

"Well . . ."

"And if intention is the standard as you say, what then? Though Iskander be thrust 'neath evil's paw, shall his intentions have no chance to speak for him?"

One more scroll provided me.

The Intentions of Kings

Itzak joined us by the fire one night.

"It is my opinion Itzak," I said, "that the Persians would have attacked Greece again if Iskander had not come east to conquer them."

"It pleases me to hear you saying that," Iskander smiled.

"It amazes me, the way the Greeks resented you and King Philip for your efforts on their behalf. Forcing you to conquer them in battle before they'd consent to unity for Philip's plan. Such a waste!"

"Oh yes. And Thebes! Do you think it gave me pleasure to put their insurrection down? Ha! It tore at my soul."

"Your intention was to maintain control for what you considered a lofty end. Intention, ah. Increasingly a word that guides my opinion concerning those who wield 'control.' The Persians on the other hand. What good could possibly come to the Persian kings from their attack on Greece? They simply wished to hold it, as a child desires to hold a toy some other child enjoys. And when prevented, to plunge the toy beneath the foot."

"As they did by burning Athens down."

"Your intention is to bring what is best in Greece as an offering to the world. To join the world in one great unity, in commerce sweet. Creation and destruction. Two intentions. Two ways of rulership."

"Indeed."

"Two examples of kings that work to take control. Two different intentions. Two paths for the future to take."

"What do you foresee?"

"That evil will prevail a while, for the basest of intentions to rule the world, thriving on chaos and delighting in disarray, not caring what they destroy in order to achieve control."

Chapter Eleven

The Ancient Map

Iskander Has Been Told

The Ship Captain's letter continues

"Are our story-telling skills so frail?" Strax asked when we next met. "We fail to convince, and why? Though it's urgent that we do."

"Because?"

"Iskander learned what you'll think unfortunate: The secret of the Western Sea. He was shown the map."

A moan welled up in me from somewhere low. "Iskander is no more. Did the secret die with him?"

"It may be the case."

"Let us hope." My groans would not abate.

"Iskander swore he'd tell no one. Though it's you yourself who've let the secret out, once they question us on shore. Because of you the entire world will know! Your cherished secret you desire so much to safeguard from the Greeks. There's the irony, you see: Your secret lives in us, available for anyone to squeeze it out. You are permitting it!"

I stared at them.

"Whatever we know, those who interrogate us will discover it. Is that what you want? Best you decide, and soon, what we know and what we don't! If it's a mythology we create you need not have concern. And otherwise?" Strax shrugged. "What are we to do?"

"Iskander knows . . . Tell me the details."

"You think that we cannot! How would we succeed? You demand we verify it's more than gossip that we've heard or story we've contrived. We have no solid map to put into your hands. So inquire this of us: If we clearly know what it alone can show."

"What's that?"

"The true route of King Solomon's silver fleet. The ships his friend King Hiram built at Aqaba and why he built them there, so far from the Western Sea. Would that provide some proof for you?"

I glared at him.

So they placed another scroll into my hands.

ಐ

Atlantis was the way to other islands, and from these you might pass to the opposite continent which surrounded the true ocean. — **Plato. Dialogues**. (Born 428 B.C.)

(Alexander's mentor Aristotle) did not believe, as Plato had, that out upon this Atlantic portion of outer Ocean extended islands known in legends as the Blessed Isles, or sometimes as the lost island of Atlantis. He did not believe it for the simple reason that he had come across no evidence of it. Nor would he waste thought upon a lost Atlantic civilization — pointing out that civilization seemed to have advanced from east to west, not the other way around. — **Harold Lamb, Alexander of Macedon.** 1946.

ಐ

The Unknown Seas

Thalestris and Iskander by the Caspian Sea. 330 B.C..

"The day of small city-states is past. The world shall be one when I have conquered it. No more east, no more west. When I am master of that streaming sea surrounding all the lands of Earth the nations of the world shall be my own; by that circular road of Ocean I shall hold and nourish them. Already my plans begin: In Egypt the new harbor-city of Alexandria, and at Babylon a port to berth a thousand ships."

"Persia now is yours. Soon India."

"Yes. To stand on Earth's most eastern shore shall be to know I hold all Asia in my hand."

"And when all lands are yours? Then peace?"

"That time shall come too soon. Conquest is my life and battle is my joy."

"What a cruel master you serve, Iskander, this spirit that propels you on to war. Needing to find ever newer realms you never knew were there to occupy your lust to conquer them. Or subdue again and again these few you own."

"Once I feared King Philip would leave no lands for me to overcome! Now I fear it of myself. Soon enough I shall seize the western lands as well, Carthage, Italy, for them to hail me as their king. Then out through the Gates of Heracles into the Western Sea, up to the north and later down the coast of Africa."

"How envious your ancestor Heracles would be, who formed those two great gates with his own hands where the Middle Sea greets the taller western waves. But Heracles was too short to see beyond the western sky, what lies hidden there. Are not oceans so much like sleep? So many strange uncharted dreams within their midst. Believe me, there will be lands enough for you."

"Uncharted lands? Beyond the Western Sea?"

"Can it be you do not know, you who subdue so many kings?"

"Know what?"

"Yes, there are lands far to the west. And vast. It is a journey some make."

"A journey where? Who is making it? You must tell me all you know!"

"It is a secret never told the Greeks. Shall I betray a trust to give the information out?"

"I shall tell no one, Thalestris, unless you agree with me that it is right to do."

"I have your word on it?"

"May they pull out my claws!"

"Very well. Far beyond those western Gates of Heracles there is a land to know. And not simply little islands as you might surmise. A land that is immense! Weeks or months to arrive at it. A journey of years to go across! Why do you give me such a look? I know a man who has been to it! When you return from India perhaps the two of you shall meet."

"He has truly crossed the Atlantic Sea?"

"Several times. And shall tell you all, as he has also told so much to me. He is from those cold lands where the North Wind dances with the snow."

"Surely my teacher Aristotle would know of such a western land!"

"Iskander, I am convinced that he may not. The Carthaginians, who now command the gateway to the western sea keep the Greeks from going out, lest crossing the sea they find the land of which I speak. It is a secret guarded well. 'There is a precipice over which ships fall into a great abyss,' they tell the Greeks.

"But the Carthaginians and the Phoenicians have been going there for centuries; though the Hyperboreans from the north were there even earlier. Now you have a secret that the Greeks have never known. You must not tell them as we have agreed."

"I shall not. But how am I to really know?"

"Have I myself not told you so?"

"Can you provide some proof? Can you do that somehow?"

"Proof more than my word? With what treasure will you bury this insult," I smile, "when I have verified all this to you?"

"The half my kingdom if it is true!"

I bring a bright blue bottle out. Glass blue as the sky above the Caspian.

"What's that you have?"

"Something from that far western land."

"Really? What?"

"These are the tears of the sun."

"The tears of the sun?"

"In the far south of the western land the weather is hot and life can be cruel. The sun is so sad to see the people living in a land so harsh with so little water and so few trees, though so thankful for what little food they do receive. 'We do not blame you that we are so dry,' the people tell the sun, 'We are grateful for the light and warmth you give.'

"The sun's great heart is touched by their gratitude and sheds fiery tears which falling to the land spring up as plants bearing red, yellow, and bright orange fruit — the powder this blue bottle holds. The people harvest the pungent crop and add it to their food, the plant's dried flesh with its spicy seeds. It brings the tears of the sun inside of them for strength. It gives them joy."

I raise the bottle and reach out for his hand. "These are the tears of the sun, Iskander, that fall upon that hot southern area of the western continent." Red powder falls into a smallest pile into his hand, then also mine. "Yes, taste."

Iskander lowers his tongue to it. "Hot!"

"It's good to season lamb and bread."

"How did you come by this?"

"My guest from the far north brought them to us. Those he met in the western land made a gift of them to him. Like bright red fingers before being dried and ground."

"Good for the stomach?"

"Certainly so, if taken raw. And to cake it on a wound will stop the blood. But there is a question you have not thought to ask: Might you not inquire, 'How am I to know this comes from the far western land? It might have come from Africa or India's unknown realms.'"

"You are good to enter my heart, Thalestris, to see through my own point of view."

"Nor would I wish to provide you less than full assurances. Do you not deserve as much, for half the tears and flames your kingdom holds? Tell me, Great King, did you conquer the Phoenicians?"

"I did. Sidon opened to me in peace. But Tyre would not. Egypt was my goal, to which I hurried south. Tyre's fortress would still float free among the waves but for its arrogance! They threw my ambassadors from their high walls and laughed, out on that stone-island where they lived, a league off from the shore on which I stood and watched my friends fall to their death. Did they think to hide from me behind the sea, so small a barrier? I made a road out through the depths to them."

"Do you have one of the Phoenicians nearby?"

"Hiram, yes. Already known to you."

"Call him here for me to speak to him. I shall have a witness to my words."

Iskander leaves the tent and soon comes back. "I have sent for him. Sidon is his home. A man loyal to me, a man of letters and a sailor too. I saved his family from distress. You may ask him what you wish."

"Iskander, do not mention to him anything I have said or shown to you. This is a proud people and the secret is one they're sworn to keep. I must take a circuitous path to provide for you the proof you seek. If he will not speak to us, yet his inner weather shall tell all."

The Phoenician enters, swathed in white with a gray beard. Sun, wind, time and sea have joined to channel ridges in his face. We give him wine and urge his ease.

"Are you related to that famous Hiram," I ask, "the great Phoenician King that called King David 'brother' long ago?"

"It is possible. My family is very old. Such stories have been told."

"You are a sailor, Hiram? Have you been beyond the Gates of Heracles?"

"Of course. To the several islands offshore down the coast of Africa. But there are storms to the south if one goes far." Pleased with himself, Hiram takes a deep swallow of his wine.

"And have you been to the far distant land across the Atlantic Sea?"

Hiram chokes. He glances at Iskander to see if he has heard. Iskander is watching him attentively.

"I have not been very far."

"Have you been to the far distant land where the copper ore comes from?"

"Copper comes from many realms. Do you mean Tarshish?" He glares at me, disturbed, then at Iskander, then at me again, as though I've set a tiger loose inside his head.

"There is a North-man among my clan, Hiram. Have you heard their long calling horns?"

"North-men have entered the Black Sea?"

"Ha!" I laugh at Hiram's efforts to dissuade me from my course, but he will not. "His queen has sent him south to bring back stories of the Amazons to her, desiring more than those scant details they discover in the stories of the Greeks. This man has sailed numerous times to the western land, along that shorter northern route; he has told me all there is to know; and Iskander hears in turn from me."

Hiram shifts uneasily in his chair, eyes pacing the tent for an exit from distress.

"I understand your alarm, Hiram. I know the rules, who is to know and who may not. But Iskander is your king now. One day he himself may go across the western sea. He has promised me he will not tell the Greeks. Iskander is not a Greek! He is a Macedonian. You know how he had to fight to provide the Greeks some unity, to unite their warring city-states. They still resent his leadership! He and his father Philip were forced into battle with the Greeks at Charonea, forcing Greece to accept their plan for solidarity. He burned down ancient Thebes when their allegiance to him failed."

Hiram's eyes cloud over as he hears me out.

"Now he has subdued Persia, the ancient enemy of Greece. Still the Greeks rebel. Daily in Athens orators harangue against the 'Macedonian overlords.' They send him no ships though their fleet is huge. He is a lion on their Athenian back they would shake loose somehow. Hiram, tell the truth. Set Iskander free from the Greek tyranny. The truth that is withheld from them. You are not the first to tell him, after all — I am."

Hiram squirms. I give him no space. "Tell your King about your namesake, King Hiram of Tyre. Say where that earlier Hiram's ships were going so long ago, what he brought back to King David and to Solomon."

Hiram's quandary glistens in his eyes. Shall he tell the ancient secret, open all to Iskander now? Two stones, the king he loves and the secret so long kept, that grind to powder all his heart. The tears burn upwards through his throat.

"Hiram, your words shall be held discreet," Iskander softly says. "I only want verification of all this for my understanding of geography. My plans depend on it. Already, watching you, I sense wind where there was only sky before. And rain."

What inner seas let overflow Hiram forces back with his big hand. "Great King, it does exist. A great expanse of land far to the west. The Phoenicians have been going there for many centuries. And the North-men before us! King Hiram of Tyre had a great fleet of ships that he built at Aqaba for Solomon, the navy of Tarshish sent to bring back silver, gold, and copper ore to build their temple in Jerusalem."

"That temple where you went with me? When they read their scrolls to us, told me my part in them?"

"Yes, though Solomon's temple was destroyed by the Babylonians. You entered a second one."

"Who goes to the Atlantic now?"

"Now Carthage rules the Western Sea. The Greeks are not allowed to pass outside the Gates of Heracles. They are not allowed to know."

Iskander's eyes meet mine. Already in his mind he journeys there. The lightning of his spirit flows to touch that wide new world so far away, too long hidden from his plans.

Iskander thanks Hiram, offers a gift of gold and reassurances of secrecy. Hiram rises to leave, still stunned at what he's verified.

"Hiram," I say, "Before you go, give me your hand, so to provide my own small gift to you," uncorking the blue bottle, letting the red powder's stream flow down into his palm.

He puts it to his lips. "The tears of the sun! Yes, now I am sure you know!" He takes my hand into his own, holds it to his eyes for me to feel his tears. "Great Queen, who knows the secret of the Western Sea!"

On To Macedonia!

Iskander leans back into his chair. His eyes take on the color of the sky. "So then," words gathering fire to feed the act, "Let us go home to Macedonia! Soon! Now, today!"

We stare at him.

"We'll alert Carthage and Italy to send tribute to me as their King, as Sidon wisely did and Tyre to its great shame did not. Then on across the Atlantic, with Hiram at my side."

Hiram's face lightens at the prospect of going home, then darkens at mention of his being pilot on the Western Sea. "Great King! It will be so obvious to all what I have done, all I've said to you! The ancient oath I swore, all will know I've broken it!"

"Well then. I shall go along the northern route with Strax."

"Of course! Most wise," Hiram's smile grows wide.

"And I shall visit Thalestris at her Black Sea home en route!"

Not a question he puts to me — in his mind he has accomplished it! I pale. I had not counted on this twist.

"There is another way," I say, pressing down inside against the sudden urgency that overwhelms, "A way that shall provide you both your goals: India and the western land as well."

"Oh? How then?"

"Go east! Go on to India, Great King. Then on from there." I glance at Hiram. It's clear he does not like my saying this, no more than at the first. "There at the eastern edge of Ocean launch your ships, from India."

"East? Farther East?" Looking at me, at Hiram, back at me.

"Do you want to tell him, Hiram? That is the direction the ancient Phoenicians went, that time silver for Solomon was their goal!"

Hiram stares at me with eyes like swords, just as before.

"Hiram? Tell Iskander why the earlier King Hiram built the ships exactly where you say he did so long ago, at Aqaba on the Red Sea — and not up in the Middle Sea."

I wait.

"Why would he build ships there, when there's so much more timber in the Lebanon and also near Cadiz along the Middle Sea?"

Waiting again.

"Why would he choose to sail westward from Aqaba around the bulk of Africa with its fierce storms? Is that not inconvenient for anyone going west?"

Iskander knows well enough where the Red Sea is and how far westward around Africa they must have gone for an Atlantic voyage. He looks to Hiram, waiting to see what answer he may give. Hiram says nothing so I go on.

"King Hiram's ships had no easy access to the Middle Sea and needed none. That is why they weren't built there! They had no intention of sailing to the Western Sea! At least not when silver was their goal."

Iskander's curiosity compounds a storm, fire from his eyes to Hiram, to me, to Hiram again.

"Come, Hiram, are my words not true?" Smiling at him. "Phoenicians ply the Atlantic now; but in those days another route to the far-off land was used as well, through an ocean far more warm and peaceful than that western Atlantic one. Sweeping south through the Red Sea the ships sailed, then on east instead of west. East past Arabia, past India, east past the horizon's long thin line into the rising sun."

"East? They could sail east?" Iskander's mind is taking flight.

I smile. "East Iskander, yes. Huge ships built to retrieve the silver for King Solomon, that silver he possessed plentiful as river rocks. Tell him Hiram. Tell Iskander about the stepping stones across that far-eastern peaceful sea and those Phoenician colonies that were sown on them. That island named Samo after Samos, that Aegean gem. Islands named for the Scythian goddess Tabiti."

"Is it indeed so much you know?" Hiram squints.

I go to my quiver where I keep the ancient map. "Perhaps you may explain this to Iskander. A gift I've brought for him, that the Phoenicians gave to Strax, my brush-haired Northern friend." I set it into Iskander's hand.

"Strax! That is a name I know. You might have simply mentioned him!" Taking the scroll, unrolling it.

"Of course! Here is Africa. And near Africa is the great southern continent so cold, showing it as it was in early times before there was much ice on it. And far to the west of Africa the western land. Do you see the rivers, here? I have sailed these two and also this, but only part of it before we turned around."

"But Hiram," Iskander turns his world-sized eyes on him, "You said you had not traveled very far."

"Not very far," Hiram grins, "considering how far there is to go."

Hiram takes the map into his weathered hands. "Yes my King, it's true. We did go east those days so long ago. It is the western-most side of that same Western Continent we mentioned earlier, at its most thin part," uncurling the scroll to show the place, "this side where silver is most plentiful. We went east past India, yes. And so may you. You need not forgo your march on India for the sake of sailing to the Western Land. I will sail there with you."

Thalestris Returns
Strax

All Themiscyra held its breath while Thalestris was away. Great was the exaltation when she returned.

"His mind wrings substance from a thing," she said to us. "I told Iskander the riddles one by one; if he had been Bellerophon he would have won the battle of the mind and never sent an arrow through his lover's heart. The white house was an egg, he knew; the black babies were a melon's seeds; and the horse can eat because the rope's not tied to anything.

"His life, no less than Bellerophon's, is an enigma of conflict where he must prevail or drown. He wants so much to know he is a god. Is it not enough to be a man?

"My strategy was to strip away his need to be more than himself. To open his fist to let the darkness fly away. For him to know the difference between gods and kings. He is still captive in the labyrinth, though now at least he knows there is a way from it. He must be the one to recognize his chains. From his parting words to me I found hope he would."

Iskander's Gifts

"I am sad that you shall go," Iskander said. "I keep this wisdom you have shown to me; you take away my heart. Tell our child, if one is born, of that great dream of conquest Philip had which I fulfilled. How you won a Great King's heart; cleansed him of a father's blood untimely spilled then led him to the silence of his mind and set the compass of his heart.

"Say I have gone to India to fill a cup, to claim that eastern ocean's immensity as mine for that eternal moment it runs down through my hands. Say to our child, 'When India shall let him go your father Alexander will return to us to claim you for his heir, riding north on a great black horse with a fine black plume. Holding title to the many realms!'

"Then you shall conquer me again. Until then I'll wonder, what dreaming did I dream to have her come to me? Come night, and let me dream of it again! Come sleep, and wring from me one silver dreaming yet, for the stars to be so envious of the sparks we strike. Come dream, form yet one more glorious summer's soft green light where she shall bid me follow her to lie in flowers on a hill; to stir up the elements inside of us that funnel ever widening past this streaming lightning flash of sky, for me to put my head upon her breast as love plucks all the colors that I am away. Come sleep, for I am ready to be hastening to dreams of her again."

Thalestris Bids Iskander Farewell

"See, Iskander, your open hand where a fist had been. The dance that once had feet has wings. Your bright fire I keep with me, the child we'll have, that spark spun from our storm of light."

"Do you have a name?"

"Achilles, if a boy, after that hero you esteem so."

"A little boy among the Amazons?"

"I'll give him to the centaurs to bring up! And name her Svea, if a girl."

"Svea. What does it mean?"

"Summer. But not that brief summer-time that barely outshines spring, no; but that great summer when time shall be no more, to blot the darkness out. Broad bright wings to set the shadows free."

"So, Svea then. Let her spirit flow across the Earth, bright to ease the storm her father brought."

My three hundred surround me, ready to come west again. I turn to Iskander with my last words to him.

"What lasting prize may the acclaim of men hold out to you, Great King? The whole world is such a little place to gain, with its opinions so like the clouds, soon gone. Eternity lifts fame's pebble to its hands then lets it fall again, of such thin worth.

"I have heard the thunder shout your victories to all the worlds that flow across the avalanche of sky. I have seen your name embroidered on the wind, and watched the storm clouds kneel to you upon the swollen shouting air. The portals to be passed are behind you now nor do their guardians bar your way; and you command the five wild things. Your hand is open, ready to receive the world, a possession too vast to close upon. Fare well."

Your Story Now To Tell

The Ship Captain's letter concludes.

I have turned the ship around. How could I not?
Intention charts my course; integrity has become my prize.
And in their words these live.

They drew me aside in Carthage as they left the ship.
"Take this gift from us," Mara thrust a heavy package to my
arms. "We have gold enough. See!" Breaking the seal of a
leather bag for me to look inside. How wide my eyes became!
"Yes," she said. "Earth's bright tears, lightning-sown
and tempest-plucked. Gold of the Pharaohs. Of Solomon,
Sargon, Nebuchadnezzar, Ashurbanipal. From Babylon,
Nineveh, Israel, Egypt, Assyria, amassed from the realms
those nations crushed and seized from them when they were
crushed in turn. Selected for Iskander's child to keep, sparks
of that great fire he was to fuel her thoughts of him."
"And this is for Zhirus, please," Svea set her sack of
heavy toys between my feet, "He admired them so. I have all
these others I like as well."
Messengers were sent to call their friends. They bade
me protect their memory in the harbor of my heart. I wept.
"Do you know the story," Mara asked, "of the clan that
escaped a great invasion force because the invaders heard the
goal they sought was no longer present there? Such a clan is
the nation of the Amazons with young Svea gone, flown from
the invaders' grasp. It is a story those invading lords should
know. And the story is in your hands to tell."

And I have scribed a letter to accomplish that.

The Ship Captain's Letter to Antigonus

To the General Antigonus or his officers in both Ephesus and Cyzicus, Greeting.

I am the Captain of a ship harbored in Phoenicia. I am told you make a search for Iskander's heirs. One of my passengers may have been one of them, as I myself have become convinced.

The name of Iskander's child is Svea, eight years of age, from among the Amazons south of the Black Sea. She came aboard my ship, her identity then unknown to me, and was transported by me to Carthage. Her stated intention was to proceed westward through the Gates of Heracles, then north on the Atlas Sea, there to remain.

She was accompanied by a man called Strax, to whose far-northern home they claim to go. His is a name not unknown, he says, to your officers in Cyzicus should you inquire. Strax stood among King Philip's troops in the Battle at Cyzicus and was afterward appointed by Philip's officers to serve as their agent among the Amazon women, making monthly written reports to Cyzicus as part of the Amazons' agreement not to war on the side of King Darius. And as Darius is no more, nor Iskander now, he has quit his post.

As they disembarked at their destination in Carthage Strax instructed me in the matter and advised me to communicate to you, that you need not follow up your threat to invade the Amazons by the Black Sea where the girl was born. That there would be great loss of life from it, and no reason at all for doing it.

I write to you for the sake of those who might perish by the sword and spear and the arrow's flight, who now may remain alive. As justice and propriety decree I do.

Chapter Twelve

The Plan Unfolds

The Emir and the Sultan

The Emir invited the Sultan for dinner to finalize their plan. There was grilled lamb, dolmas, dates, figs, buttery bread and good red wine.

The Emir tossed bits of meat to his dog Kalb. "It doesn't matter that the girl left Themiscyra with some part of the gold," he waved a dismissing hand. "Whatever the three could take away would have been such a small amount, there's sure to be much more. Nine horses the Strax party had? Poo. Thalestris had three hundred warriors with her. Plus the two hundred horses Iskander provided her. Consider, even if each woman carried only one sack of it! We'll go discover where the rest is hid."

"So, how do we accomplish finding it once we are there?" The Sultan raised his cup.

"It's been buried in the ground or hidden among rocks, yes? For centuries it's been rained on and flooded and the soil's been dislodged. Rocks displaced as the Earth has quaked. Some surely spilled out into the open and was found. Though the rest awaits unseen, just beneath the surface . . ."

"Unseen indeed. What is your plan for urging it to view?" the Sultan's impatience began to show on his smooth brow.

"Kalb." The Emir pointed at the dog.

"The dog? That's your plan?"

"Wait, you'll see." The Emir lodged a finger toward the open door. "Kalb, go outside." And the dog went out.

The Emir pulled a gold coin from a pocket, held it up for the Sultan to view. "Tell me where in the room we'll have it hid."

"Where to hide the coin? Well, over there beneath the books."

The Emir hid the coin where he'd been shown. "Now you'll see, yes? Kalb! Come!" And the dog reappeared. "Kalb, find gold!"

Kalb went round the room sniffing eagerly and began pawing at the pile of books with the gold in it.

"See?"

But the Sultan had his hands across his face. Not wanting to see more.

"What?" said the Emir.

"It's not the gold the dog smells! It's the lamb on your hands he's attracted by, that you passed onto the coin."

The Emir thinned his eyes to ponder it.

"Any other marvelous plans you have in mind?"

"Well . . . You ought not give up on the dog you know."

"Why not?"

"It's not always lamb I'm eating when I'm training him."

Sharif and the Sultan

Some days later.

The Sultan and Sharif met again. "My sincere thanks for the fine story you've provided me," the Sultan told Sharif. "And I wonder now if I possess context enough for the rest of what you wished to say, the part related to the treasure map."

"You do. And allow me to advise, the Black Sea's coast is not the only venue for a treasure hunt."

"I shall pray that's so."

"Do you recall where Thalestris and Iskander hid the treasure map for her to take home with her?"

"In her quiver of arrows."

"It was that very quiver in which the old manuscript was encased when it was presented to my uncle for his translation work. Uncle had a hunch as he read and unwound the leather from inside the quiver and — There it was."

"Oh my."

"Uncle puzzled it through: Was this that exact quiver in which Thalestris had sequestered it, kept securely on the wall and snatched up at the last minute by Strax as the three made their departure? Or perhaps chosen by Svea to take away with her, more of a 'grown-up's' quiver than her little one? A quiver left behind on the ship when they disembarked in Carthage. That the captain simply employed to store the scroll of his letter in."

"Which explains what you say, that your uncle realized the danger he was in. He decided not to transcribe those parts about the quiver."

"Yes. Uncle copied Iskander's treasure map for his own use and put it back. Aware of what might occur if its presence became known and he'd had a look at it."

Treasure Sites

"The quiver remained in the captain's family a while perhaps, with the scroll he'd written conveniently stored in it. Going on to new owners and finally coming to the hand of the governor who desired to have the old manuscript's contents revealed --- with no knowledge of the hidden treasure map.

"The ship captain wrote in ancient Phoenician, not so difficult; though he also copied verbatim into his letter sections of the Greek Strax wrote, which local scholars declined to negotiate, being unlike anything they'd seen before."

"Hence the need for Uncle."

"Yes. As for the treasure map, it would have been reproduced by the Amazons and not the sole copy they possessed. Nor ought it come as a surprise that the Amazons secured those sites, sending women out to each of them with a plan they had. All the sites disclosed by Iskander's map had buildings planted on them when Uncle arrived to look. Charitable enterprises, each of them and — shall you wish to guess?"

"Controlled by women?"

"Yes. Each one held in a trust. With five women serving as trustees to oversee each institution's work, be it orphanage, hospital, a haven for women or the like, with an extended list of women awaiting service as trustees when called upon. Each enterprise seemed well enough supplied, hardly penurious, so Uncle decided the treasure had been sourced."

"Perhaps by some trap door in the ground."

"Though Uncle finally came on an area recently ravaged by war in which buildings lay in ruins on three

---

known sites, where he inquired if the properties might be for sale. The governor of the area, financially distressed, was happy to negotiate. Prices were discussed."

"And?"

"That's where you might wish to be involved. Uncle requires funds to secure these properties."

"He has reason to believe there's still something there?"

"Uncle couldn't just go in and dig. He needed to be discrete. Nor could he risk someone seeing him with treasure he'd unearthed. Uncle told the governor he'd consider taking a lease out on the sites and begin to build while meanwhile raising capital to complete the purchase. There was gold in the family, Uncle said, and he must await its arrival, at which time he'd sell enough to at least pay the lease price for a year, and hopefully soon the purchase price in full."

"And the governor liked the scheme?"

"He did. And that solved the problem of any gold Uncle found, as it might seem to be his own family's gold that had arrived."

"Brilliant."

"Though there remained the small detail of some first lease payment to the governor before Uncle could do anything."

"Ah. Where we come in."

"As you may decide. Though one unexpected factor you should know about."

"What?"

"The governor's wife."

The Challenge

The wife knew about the charity work. Knew about the women and the trusts. It even seemed she might be one of them, the modern day Amazons. 'Ought it not return to the purpose it once had?' she asked."

"Oh oh."

"Uncle replied, 'Absolutely so!' That his intention was to put new buildings up then turn the first one over to her or her assigns once he'd recouped expenses and secured an appropriate profit with business he'd do there on behalf of his family."

"Us."

"Yes. Uncle said that when the next two were built he'd do the same with them. That his ultimate aims were charitable as well, no less than her own. That the hardships of humanity filled his heart, and he had a concern for the downtrodden and a deep love for artists, those who paint or write or pluck the string."

"And she liked it?"

"Well enough. Though Uncle's sense of honesty led him on into an even deeper maze of possibility as he pondered this: 'Am I acting in integrity here? Defrauding anyone? Iskander has arranged this in trust for his daughter, has he not? Am I able to be true to that? At least as well as these women are?'"

"Commendable."

"And this: 'What happens when the other trustees hear of me and what I do?'"

"Ah. A dilemma with a thorn!"

"What would happen if he were to meet with them, he wondered? Those trustees would surely draw him through a labyrinth to spin him round and shake him off. 'This property exists in trust,' they'd say, 'And not for you.'

"Though not so easily deterred. Uncle had a labyrinth of his own prepared for them. A unique guardianship he believed he held related to the manuscripts he'd seen."

"Excellent!"

"He realized in all likelihood the ship captain's letter had never been seen by the Amazons, the only existing copy was the one he'd been working on. The stories of the thirteen days they would know well enough, though to the events on the ship they would be blind. So of those women Uncle would inquire . . .

'You say this property exists in trust. By whom bequeathed? And for whose benefit?'

"What might they respond? Would they prevaricate? Spin fables up? Uncle would note their perjuries, if such there be, and gently bring the women circling round to center as he tells them what he knows. He knows the story too, it will be evident.

'Iskander put the trust in place,' all will finally agree.

"Uncle would continue, *'For whose benefit?'* Will they with subterfuge go to work again, attempting to obscure? With that answer it succeeds or fails: He must have them admit the rest of it: for whom the trust is kept.

'For Iskander's daughter Svea's sake.'

"That's what he wants to hear. Though they'll not want to say."

"What then?"

"Uncle may need to wing a story out. Zhirus and the fish he caught. The battle Svea won on their way to the Middle Sea. The 'Daughter of the Storm,' and the near tragedy the Captain's quandary caused. For the women to hear with growing interest those parts of the Captain's letter as yet unknown to them, interspersed with stories of the thirteen days they would know well. And by the known part's light discern the rest as viable.

"The trustees know enough of it, being descendants of the Amazons sent out long ago, with stories handed down for centuries. They'd know for whom they're serving as trustees. Svea. It's Svea at the center of the labyrinth and Uncle will resolutely guide them there, to have them know he knows. At that center of shared knowledge unity has a chance to coalesce. With recognition of Svea as *beneficiary of the trust* his task is done."

"But how?"

"Watch how it ends!

'We all agree Svea went with Strax and Mara,' Uncle would say, *'bound to Carthage on her way to the far north.'* And they'd nod yes.

'And you've had word that she arrived with Strax at his far northern home, I suppose, where his mother Susa was awaiting them?' Uncle asks and waits for a response.

Have they received such a report? Likely not. They'll have had no clue as to Svea's success on her northward flight. Not even that she reached Carthage till Uncle disclosed that fact!

'No word from her?' Uncle utters his surprise and frowns. *'Now there a marvel is! You are her trustees and you don't know if she arrived?'*

'And we suppose you do?' They'd say.

'I have reason to think she did, oh yes, and that she has kin that live there still. And if you wish I'll make a voyage to them, for her high-born dynasty to come to you to give you thanks for all you've kept so well in trust for them.'

Uncle regards them as they wince at that.

'I have a copy of Iskander's treasure map to be providing them. And the original is hid somewhere I know, though in a place where none shall look. Yes! I have managed that with you in mind; for which it seems you might be thanking me.'

"He'd explain how he found the map and hid it again. With proof as required he'd name some of the other places too.

'So this makes me a trustee along with you! By right of my knowledge of the story and of Iskander's map, knowledge of young Svea and knowing where she went, all of which I've managed to safeguard on your behalf! And I bring you this: If not total assurance at least a fairly good sign that she arrived safe in her new northern home.'
'Show us that then, this good sign you say you have of her northern journey's end,' they pout, indignant, obstinate, 'and we'll consider this venture you have planned.'
'For me to be trustee of it! You'll welcome me as a trustee no less than you, sharing your charitable intents and resource, perpetually and as family, as you did Strax so long ago when you had need of him. For if not declared fellow trustee and family by you,' he shrugs, 'I've no room inside your hearts and shall have no safety here, an eagle with no way to fly, for it has no wings. My efforts shall have only led to my demise; thereby assuring quick publication of the manuscript I've left with relatives and the treasure map along with it, for all that northern world to know. For it will be taken there with an offer to guide them here.'

"That's me, of course. I would perform that chore."
"He's voiced the password Iskander set!"
"He has those trustees firmly in his labyrinth. Though a password only goes so far."

'Well then, let it hinge on that,' the women say to call his bluff, 'What proof shall you provide that we'd accept, that she arrived?'

"What proof will Uncle have for them?"
"He'd show them passages of history from books. And a map he has of those snow-crusted northern climes. Pointing to the place called 'Svealand.'"

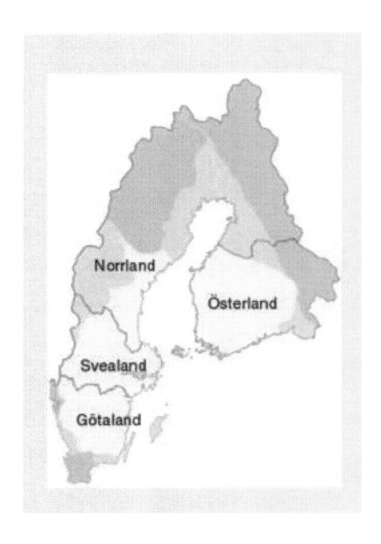

Svealand was the original Sweden (Svea rike / Sverige), to which it gave its name.

--- Wikipedia.

http://en.wikipedia.org/wiki/Svealand

ඥ

There was war between Geats and Svear, bitter battles carried across the broad sea.

— *Beowulf.* Lines 2472-3. Compiled in the 6th century A.D.

The Gutar always kept the victory and their right. Later the Gutar several times sent messengers to the country of the Svear, but nobody could obtain peace until Avair Strabain from Alva. He was the first to make peace with the Svea king.

— *The Guta Saga.* Compiled in the 13th century A.D.

Moder Svea (Mother Svea) in Sweden. Alfred Myström. (1891)

Fin

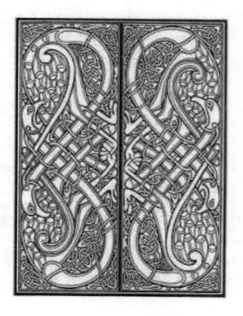

Recommended Reading

King Alexander's Gold: The Treasury of Ancient Tyre by James Saint Cloud. This story set in ancient Tyre during Crusader times (1124 A.D.) is a companion volume to *Treasure Map*, with continuation of the possibility of the "King Alexander Trust." Take a look if you enjoy Biblical exposition from a non-conformist's point of view. (Some of the material in *Treasure Map* is repeated.)

Last of the Amazons by Steven Pressfield. Tells the story of the Amazons attack on Athens before the Trojan War.

The Amazons: Lives and Legends of Warrior Women across the Ancient World by Adrienne Mayor. Princeton University Press, 2014. A definitive and lengthy volume of research related to the Amazons.

James Saint Cloud is a native of North Carolina and a graduate of the University of North Carolina at Chapel Hill. He is a pioneer in the field of wellness education in northern California and has served as a convalescent hospital administrator. James served in prison ministry in San Quentin State Prison for nine years through auspices of the Garden Chapel at the Q.

Please communicate with the author!

James Saint Cloud

Email: Rumistories@ yahoo.com

Or write care of the publisher.

ಔ

Made in the USA
San Bernardino, CA
16 February 2020

64548446R00155